GW00870059

Death Beckons

Mortis Series: Book One

J.C. DIEM

Copyright © 2013 J.C. DIEM

All rights reserved. Published by Seize The Night Agency.

No part of this publication may be reproduced or
transmitted in any form or by any means, electronic or
mechanical, including photocopying, recording, storage in
an information retrieval system, or otherwise, without the
prior written permission of the author.

ISBN-13: 978-1490978574
ISBN-10: 1490978577

This is a work of fiction. Names, characters, places,
incidents and dialogues are products of the author's
imagination or are used fictitiously. Any resemblance to
actual people, living or dead, events or locales is entirely
coincidental.

DEDICATION

To Carolyn, thank you for editing so many of my books, but especially for the effort you put into this one.

Amber Averay, fellow author and good friend, without your ongoing support I might have given up on the whole publishing gig. Thanks for all your help.

Last, but not least, to the girls from work: Anna, Jackie, Vesna, Mel, Pam and Chelsey. Your humour helped keep me sane…but only just.

Notes:

Unfortunately, there are no mausoleums in the Toowong Cemetery. There are, however, ghost tours on offer for the brave.

Chapter One

Finally closing up shop after a painfully long thirteen hour shift, I was struck by the absence of human activity when I stepped out into the chilly autumn night. The shoe shop to the left and handbag shop to the right were already closed. In fact, all of the stores seemed to be closed. Up and down the street, security shutters were in place and shop lights were off. It was fairly normal for at least a few shops to be late to close on Fridays, thanks to last minute shoppers.

Not only were there no customers, there were also no pedestrians. Where were all the people heading to the pubs and nightclubs? It was just past nine pm and I'd never seen the street so quiet before. "Weird," I said softly.

An unholy screeching noise issued from the security shutter as I pulled it down. It sounded a bit like the screams of a small animal being cut open during a ritual slaughter. And wasn't that a cheery thought to have when I was all by myself in a dimly lit street?

I snapped the sturdy padlock into place, then transferred my keys to my pocket. My black faux leather handbag that had seen better days was nestled snugly against my ribs. As always, I clutched it in a death grip in case of a mugging attempt. I'd fight like a madwoman to maintain possession of the few dollars I had in my purse.

Passing a rival clothing store, I sneered at the clumsy clothing display in the window. The store manager wouldn't know what style was if it danced up and poked her in the eye.

When I passed the store, I came to the opening of an alley that I both feared and dreaded. Unluckily for me, it was the only access point to the closest bathroom. Being the store manager and only staff member of my shop, I had one toilet break per day. That had been nine hours ago and I was busting to go. It was doubtful I'd last the fifteen minute walk home without having an accident.

Cautiously poking my head around the corner, I wished that there was enough light to see all the way to the end of the passageway. I could faintly make out the white door fifty or so feet away, but the rest of the alley might as well have been the throat of a gigantic monster.

The shop owners and managers in the area all had a key to the single, rarely cleaned bathroom. I sometimes had to wait in line for my turn to use the facilities on a Friday night. But not this time. Tonight, the area was eerily deserted.

I'd been working in this store for over a year now and I'd never liked this alley with its single light at the entrance. It was a popular place for drug addicts to shoot up in, for muggers to drag their victims into and, my personal favourite, for drunks to vomit in. I'd stepped in slimy, slippery alcohol tainted pools of upchuck more than once and never relished the experience.

Verifying that the alley was empty, I hurried into the shadows. When I was halfway to my goal, something scuttled toward me in the semi-dark. *Please be a cat,* I thought. The animal paused long enough to stand on its hind legs and squeak up at me angrily. I knew immediately that it wasn't a cat. *RAT!* My lips drew back from my teeth and I shrank away, huddling against the brick wall.

Having cowed me with a single squeak, the disease ridden river rat, continued on with its nocturnal journey. Shaking with fright and casting frequent glances over my shoulder to make sure the disgusting rodent wasn't following me, I also continued on down the alley.

A few months ago, I'd witnessed a short, but vicious war between one of the feral cats and a pack of river rats on my way home. I wasn't sure if I was amazed, or horrified when the rats won. Since then, I'd suffered nightmares about being overwhelmed by a flood of the furry monsters. I somehow stayed alive while they ate my flesh right down to the bone. Finally, I was nothing but a bloodstained skeleton being held together with stringy bits of sinew, screaming noiselessly because they'd eaten my tongue right out of my head.

My key-ring rattled from shudders of remembered horror when I fished it out of my pocket. Unlocking the door, I flicked on the harsh fluorescent light and immediately locked the door again once I was inside.

Once white, the walls were now an unhealthy shade of grey. Garish decorations of drawings and wording, made by permanent markers of all colours, covered the walls. The spelling could use some work, but some of the messages were almost profound: *Life sux, so suck life,* was one that spoke to me deeply. Taking a lengthy crap must put some people in an introspective mood. I had no contributions to add to the collection. Deep thought wasn't something I felt compelled to indulge in very often.

Hanging my handbag on the hook on the back of the door, I searched for any freshly made rat holes in the brick walls. There were none and I relaxed minutely. I'd been checking for rat holes compulsively at home, at work and in this very toilet for weeks. In the event that I ever saw one, I'd be out of there in a flash.

A cramp hit me, telling me that I was out of time. I shuffled over to the porcelain throne and shoved my jeans down as fast as possible. Bent in the awkward crouch every woman uses when dealing with a toilet they didn't want their flesh to touch, I peed for what felt like half an hour.

Relief washed through me as I flushed. I'd heard it was bad for your health to hold in your pee for so long, but what choice did I have? I worked alone and it was frowned upon by those higher above me to close the shop even for a few minutes to take a break.

Washing up at the rust-stained sink, I examined myself in the mirror. My hair, currently dark brown with blonde highlights, fell to almost halfway down my back. The puff of wind and my fright at the encounter with the rat had mussed it, but a swift finger-combing put it to rights again.

My summer tan was beginning to fade now that it was halfway through autumn and my face was turning pale. My eyes were grey and unremarkable in a face that could best be described as mildly pretty. As always, I'd dressed in clothes from my shop. The almost sheer red blouse was billowy on my slight frame. Thankfully, it came with a matching camisole, so it added at least some warmth for my walk home. I'd chosen jeans that were classic cut rather than the current skin tight fashion. I just didn't like how boyish my legs looked in them and liked to at least pretend I had some shape.

Promoting our own products was a requirement. None of the chain store's employees were allowed to wear their own clothing. Luckily, I was slender and average in height at five feet, four inches tall. I could pick and choose from most of the items I sold.

Being svelte wasn't a conscious decision that I'd made. Food was more of a luxury than a necessity on what I earned. Given a choice of paying my bills or eating, food always came in second place.

Running my fingers through my hair a final time, I deemed it to be suitable. It was doubtful I'd run into a tall, dark, handsome stranger who would sweep me off my feet during the short walk ahead. That only happened in fairy stories and let's face it, I was no princess.

Relocking the door before I left, I was a few steps away from the bathroom when the feeble light suddenly dimmed. Jerking to a stop, I squinted against the darkness. A man loomed near the mouth of the alley. I say 'loomed' because he was freakishly tall, with shoulders wide enough to almost touch the walls. There was no possibility that I would be able to slip past him. For a couple of seconds, I entertained the wild hope that I was invisible back here in the shadows. Then I felt his eyes on me and shuddered in an instinctive reaction to a sudden sense of imminent danger.

"I wonder if you might help me," the man said a nanosecond before I could voice the scream that had built up in the back of my throat. His accent was heavy, foreign and I was almost positive that it had an aged tremor. I choked out a strangled gasp instead of screaming at the top of my lungs as I'd been intending. Clearing my throat, I pretended I hadn't almost embarrassed myself horribly with a high pitched, girly shriek.

As I cautiously drew closer, light reflected from his shiny scalp. The poor guy was totally bald. His face was half hidden in shadow, but I could dimly make out a network of wrinkles. My fright must have played tricks with my mind because he wasn't the giant I'd imagined after all. He was just an elderly, shrunken old man.

For reasons I couldn't possibly guess at, he was wearing a cloak. I eyed the long, black material that fluttered around him from neck to feet and decided my eyes weren't playing tricks on me this time. Apparently, no one had thought to hand him a copy of the far more casual dress code we Australians went by. Jeans and t-shirts were more our style in autumn. We tended to go for shorts and t-shirts when it was warmer. Few of us wore anything as formal as a long black cloak. Not if we had any self-respect anyway.

"Are you lost?" I asked, hoping he didn't have dementia. I could kiss my plans of putting my feet up and turning into a couch potato goodbye if he had lost his marbles. I'd have to call the police and then they'd want to question me about where I'd found the old guy. It could take half the night to sort out where he'd come from and get him back to where he belonged.

"Lost?" He cocked his head to the side, eyeing me in a weirdly sly manner. He drew his cloak around him and grinned. It was the grin that made me begin to suspect that all was not right with the old guy. It wasn't friendly at all.

Ignoring his age for the moment, I took in his general appearance. Beneath the cloak, he wore a black suit and stark white shirt. Pristine white cuffs poked out the bottom of his sleeves. On closer examination, I noticed they had lace edges. His skin was almost as white at his shirt. I'd been born with more of a tan than this man possessed.

"No, I am not lost," he said. After a thoughtful pause, he continued. "Yet, I am hoping you can be of assistance."

Why me, I groaned to myself. *Why did I have to stumble across the confused old geezer?* If my urge to pee hadn't been so bad, I would have been long gone before he'd hobbled into the alley. "Look, I don't know what kind of help you're after, but I'm pretty sure I can't give it to you," I told him with false regret.

He cocked his head to the other side, reminding me of a cockatoo I'd had as a kid. It would eye me like that, as if I was a strange and tasty bug that it wouldn't mind taking a bite out of. "Ah, but I believe you are exactly the person to help me with my dilemma." He moved closer, crowding me back toward the far end of the alley. Now he seemed taller again, wider and much, much more menacing than any man his age had the right to be.

It was the cloak that made him seem sinister despite his age. It was like something out of an old black and white movie. One with monsters in it. In those types of movies, women who wandered the streets alone always ended up in trouble. Serious trouble. The kind of trouble that usually ended in their painful deaths.

That thought persuaded me to call for help after all. For me rather than for him. There was something not right about the old guy and I was getting a serious case of the heebie-jeebies.

"I'm not actually available to help you right now," I said to buy some time. "But I know someone who will be happy to sort you out." *Yeah, the cops. They'll drag your skinny butt back to the old people's home in no time.*

I took my attention off him for a second to search for my phone in my handbag. When I looked up again, he was standing right in front of me. Somehow, he'd closed the distance between us without making a sound. My heart gave a lurch, then started beating far too fast as fear flooded through me. My encounter with the rat suddenly didn't seem to be quite so scary anymore.

"That will not be necessary, my dear." He raised his arms and his cloak fell around me with suffocating darkness. I drew in a breath to vent a scream, but blacked out instead.

Chapter Two

When I woke, it was to utter darkness. Snuggling into my cold concrete mattress, I was comforted by the thought that my chance meeting with the crazy old man had just been a nightmare. *Wait a minute, cold concrete mattress?* Something was very wrong here.

Snapping all the way awake, I felt around in the pitch dark. Instead of a mattress, sheets and light blanket, I encountered only hard concrete and grains of dirt. Hysteria instantly reared its ugly head. Just before I could start actually gibbering in terror, light bloomed and chased the dark away. Squinting against the brightness, my heart sank when I saw a familiar black cloak and shiny bald head. *Oh, God, the nightmare continues.*

"Ah, good," the strongly accented voice said quietly, "you are awake." Faint echoes rebounded around the room: *awake, awake, awake.* I couldn't see the walls. The light wasn't strong enough to reach that far, but it felt like we were in a smallish space. One part of my mind was focussed on this, the rest was still caught somewhere between nightmare and reality.

With the light growing gradually brighter, I could see the geezer far better than I wanted to. I had to alter my assessment of him, he wasn't just old, he was ancient. His wrinkles had wrinkles. His eyes were black pools that bored through me and deep into my very soul. He was holding a lantern, kerosene by the smell of it. Putting the lantern down, he clasped his cloak around him as if he was cold, then squatted on his haunches a few feet away.

"Where are we?" It might not have been the brightest question in the world, but figuring out my location took priority. Getting away from the weirdo was second on my list. At least my clothes were still intact. If he was the world's oldest pervert, he hadn't disrobed me yet. Or tied me up. Or dressed me in his dead mother's nightgown. *Stop it before you freak yourself out completely.* It was a bit late for that, I'd passed the freaked out stage a while back.

"We are in a charming mausoleum in a nearby cemetery," he replied and smiled, exposing teeth that were a nasty shade of yellow-brown. Either he'd never owned a toothbrush, or he'd spent a few decades smoking several packs of strong cigarettes a day. His teeth were longer and sharper than average, especially the incisors. *He should shop for his dentures somewhere else,* I thought in pity. *Whoever made those has serious mental problems.*

His words sank in and my mind went blank for a moment. Then hysteria made a reappearance. "We're *where*?" My voice was almost high enough to become a squeak. *I bet the rats could understand me,* flitted crazily through my mind. *I could become their rodent queen and I'd never have to worry about them eating me again.* "What do you mean we're in the cemetery?" Come to think of it, how had he gotten me there? The man was decrepit. I'd have a hard time believing he had carried me anywhere without help. Did that mean he had an accomplice lurking somewhere nearby? I sincerely hoped not. One weirdo was enough to deal with in one night.

"It is ironic, no?" He gestured with one hand, holding the cloak closed with the other. "For you to experience your new birth in a place of death?"

He appeared to be amused by his skewed sense of irony, but I was far from it. *It's time to leave this asylum before they book me a permanent room.* Something weird was going on here and I didn't want any part of it. Any further part, that was.

Scrambling to my feet, I took a quick look around the place where my supposed new birth would take place. The light had brightened enough for me to see to the far edges of the room now. Cramped, damp and chilly, it housed four stone sarcophagi. Two were on each side of me and two more were at the back. Heavy iron crosses were stationed at the tip of each sarcophagus. Names and dates were engraved on the ends of the stone coffins, but I was too panicked to try to read them. One of the caskets at the back was cracked down the middle and a two inch fissure gaped darkly. *Great,* I thought in disgust. *I'm breathing in mummy dust.*

"Who *are* you?" I'd need a name so I could report him to the cops once I made my escape.

"My name is Silvius, little one." He bowed gracefully without taking his eyes off me. "And what are you called?"

"I'm Natalie Pierce." I winced as soon as I said it, wishing I hadn't given him my real name. Now he might be able to track me down once I escaped from his clutches.

"Charmed," Silvius simpered and flourished his cloak. Whoever he was, he had old fashioned manners.

"Look, no offence," I said to him, attempting to control my alarm. If I gave into it, I'd stop being able to think at all. "But I'd really like to just go home and take a shower. You'll have to find someone else to re-birth." I took a step toward the heavy looking wooden door and Silvius was suddenly standing right in front of me. I must have hit my head when he jumped me in the alley because people just didn't move that fast.

"I have made my choice, my dear, and you are it." He grinned again and I was riveted by the sight of his teeth. Was it my imagination, or were they even longer now? One thing was for sure, he could definitely benefit from some tooth whitening gel.

"What exactly do you want from me, gramps?" I said crankily. Maybe if I could figure that out, I could get the hell out of there and regain my sanity. My flesh was trying to creep off my body being this close to him. In the back of my head, I was gibbering, but I wasn't sure why. He was creepy, but he was also damned old. He'd managed to somehow kidnap me, but what damage could he really do to me? I had this short argument with my subconscious, but it ignored me and continued to gibber. It apparently knew something I didn't and it was scared out of its wits.

"My servant was lost in an unfortunate…accident quite recently." Tenting his hands together, Silvius stared at me over the top of long, unclean nails. "I require a new servant to guide me through this strange new land."

Ok, he really was nuts. "You're in Australia, not Uranus." I felt no urge to chuckle as I named my favourite planet. My humour had taken a brief leave of absence. "Stay away from snakes and spiders and you'll be fine. Anyway, I already have a job." It wasn't the best job in the world, but it was mine and I was suddenly appreciating it for the first time in years. "Thanks for the offer, but I don't want to be your servant."

"I'm afraid it is not a request, Natalie Pierce." His brows drew down and my eyes started playing tricks on me again. Lounging on the wall nearby, his shadow appeared to turn its head and laugh at me soundlessly. "I'm afraid it is a requirement," he added ominously.

"How much will you pay me per hour?" I asked, stalling for time and judging the distance to the door. *I have to get out of here right now. This lunatic might actually be dangerous.* Silvius hadn't really hurt me yet, but the hurting would begin soon. My instincts were telling me to flee for my life and I was willing to obey them.

Taken aback by the question, Silvius frowned again. "Turning you will be your only payment," he stated as if it should have been obvious to me.

"Turning me?" I sidled toward the door, not really concentrating on our conversation in my desperation to be gone. "Turning me into what?" *A pumpkin? Is it midnight already?* The panic was fighting its way to the surface, drawing closer and closer.

Silvius stared at me for a long, creepy moment. "Into a creature like me," he replied at last. When he smiled this time, I recoiled then made a run for the door. Utter lunacy had stared back at me from his black, soulless eyes. I wasn't sticking around to let him turn me into anything.

My hand just managed to grasp the rusty, old-fashioned doorknob when I was suddenly yanked backwards. An arm clamped around my chest, cutting off my air. My head was yanked to the side and a cold, clammy hand stroked my cheek before tangling in my hair. *Christ, his circulation must be non-existent,* I thought in panic. I knew old people had problems with their veins clogging up or whatever, but his skin was practically icy.

"Relax, my dear," Silvius said into my ear, "or this will hurt far more than is necessary." His voice was deeper, almost guttural and somehow monstrously hungry. I caught sight of his shadow again. It pointed, threw its head back and laughed in noiseless, dark hilarity. *I think I might actually be losing my mind.* It was impossible for shadows to move on their own, therefore I had to be going crazy.

Struggling against his grip, I was both amazed and dismayed at how strong the old man was. Most ancient people had bones like straw. I should have been able to snap his arm like a twig and stomp him into mush. Instead, I was being held captive like a scared little girl.

His head lowered towards my neck and my fear spiked. "What are you doing?" My voice sounded high and squeaky again. "You're not a cannibal, are you?" *You, you, you* echoed around the mausoleum.

Silvius cocked his head to the side and peered at me. I could see one pupil-less orb. No, it was more like his pupil had become larger than normal and his iris had disappeared. For a moment, I felt like I was standing on the edge of an abyss, about to fall. The fall would last for an eternity, but I'd lose my sanity in an instant. "I do not eat flesh," he replied distastefully.

"Good! Great! Because I doubt I'd be very tasty," I babbled. "I eat a lot of junk food, you know. Fatty, unhealthy junk food. And sugar. My arteries are probably clogged up with disgusting cholesterol." My relief that I wasn't about to be chopped into small pieces and devoured was short lived. Pain suddenly lanced through my neck and flooded through my body, rendering me speechless. *What the hell? He's biting me!* I heard a pained keening noise and was startled to realize it was coming from me.

When the pain finally stopped, my legs were too rubbery to hold me. I felt weirdly empty, as if I'd been drained of life. Silvius lowered me to the floor, then lay me on my side. Something warm and wet dribbled across my throat. *That's my blood,* I thought hazily and couldn't dredge up the energy to care. *Dying isn't so bad. I don't know why people make such a fuss about it.*

From the corner of my eye, I saw Silvius bite into his wrist. Black fluid welled sluggishly from the ragged wound. Whatever it was that ran through his veins, it didn't look much like blood anymore. He moved toward me, gaze intent on my face. Rolling me onto my back, he held his torn wrist over my mouth.

Drops splattered on my lips and I squeezed them shut. Even in my dazed state, the thought of the black ooze entering my mouth was utterly repugnant. Gripping my jaw, Silvius forced my mouth open. Helpless and unable to fight him, a glob of cold liquid hit my tongue. It was cold only for a second, then it was burning its way down my throat like acid.

Gagging, I managed to knock his hand away and rolled onto my side again, dry heaving. "God, that's gross!" I rasped. "Seriously, that tastes like arse!" My throat was on fire. It felt as though I'd eaten a thousand of the strongest curry dishes ever invented, one straight after the other.

Sinking down to his haunches, Silvius examined his torn wrist, ignoring my assessment of how bad his blood tasted. My overactive imagination had to be at play again because I could swear his wound was already healing. "Now, your new beginning awaits," he intoned gravely. On that ominous note, the real pain began.

My back arched as a cramp hit my stomach. I folded over and wrapped my arms around my middle. Garbled noises came from my mouth and I wasn't able to stop them. It sounded like someone was slaughtering a flock of turkeys with a blunt axe.

Burning pain flashed outwards from my heart. It spread up to my head and all the way to my feet. My heartbeat became erratic, beating too hard then stopping altogether only to triple in speed once more. An instant migraine hit me and I gagged at the agony, barely holding onto my last meal. The five minute lunch break I'd taken to eat a tuna sandwich seemed to have happened a lifetime ago.

More cramps hit me and I humped across the concrete, trying to escape from my own body in vain. I wished I had a gun or a knife just so I could end the torment. It occurred to me that I must look like I was in the throes of a grand mal fit. If the crazy old guy was filming this, I hoped it didn't end up on the internet.

All through my torment, Silvius squatted nearby, watching me intently. He was as emotionless as a snake watching its prey writhe to death from its poison. It hit me then. Pain this bad could only end one way. *I'm going to die.*

Chapter Three

After what felt like an eternity, I came to and discovered that the pain was gone. I almost sobbed in relief right then and there. First, I had to make sure the old geezer hadn't been snacking on me despite his claims that he didn't eat flesh. After a quick inventory, I was relieved to find that my body parts were all still accounted for. My clothes were also still intact, but they were filthy from rolling around in agony.

It was difficult to tell how much time had passed. I vaguely remembered Silvius biting me twice more and forcing his diseased blood into my mouth both times. The taste hadn't gotten any better with repetition. At least the burning sensation in my mouth and throat were gone. I felt no pain at all. Strangely, I didn't feel much of anything, except cold. *No pain has to be a good sign, right?* Cautiously, I sat up and found I wasn't alone.

Sitting on his haunches, Silvius looked like he hadn't moved at all since the last time I'd glimpsed him during my pained convulsions. "And so, after three nights, you have survived your ordeal and are now reborn," he said. His tone and expression were self-satisfied as if he had achieved something great and wonderful. I, of course, had no idea what he was talking about.

Three nights? It didn't seem possible that so much time had passed, but it felt true anyway. "What did you do to me?" I felt my neck where he'd bitten me, but the skin was unbroken. Maybe he'd drugged me with something and I'd imagined the whole unnerving experience. In a way, I'd prefer it if it was just a hallucination. Otherwise, it might have been real and how was I supposed to deal with that?

"I have given you the gift of unlife." As an explanation, it sucked.

I stood shakily and he stood as well, far too smoothly for an elderly man. Squinting at Silvius in the dim light, I could have sworn he looked younger, maybe seventy instead of a hundred. His skin was tighter, less wrinkled and papery. Whatever drugs he'd given me had done an excellent job of screwing with my perception.

"Unlife, huh?" I said to humour him. "That's great. Well, I've had a really shitty time and now I'm leaving." Nothing was going to keep me in that room any longer. If I had to take the old man down, I would. He wasn't about to get the jump on me again. I was wrong about that, I discovered as soon as I'd thought it. Too fast to track, he was suddenly in front of me.

"I'm afraid you are now bound to me." Silvius didn't sound afraid. He sounded smug. I really hated smugness. It never boded well for those who the smugness was aimed at. "For all eternity," he added and grinned. That had an ominous ring to it that I didn't like.

"What the hell are you talking about, you deranged old weirdo?" I didn't normally disrespect old people like that, but he was frankly asking for it by now. He'd kidnapped me, drugged me and had held me captive for three days. Or so he said. There was no way for me to tell what he'd been up to during that time. Putting me in humiliating poses and recording them for all I knew. *As soon as I'm out of here I'm searching the web for photos and videos.* I didn't know if I could destroy anything I might find, but I'd try.

Silvius gave me a dire frown and his brows drew down over his dead, empty eyes. "Be wary how you speak to your maker, girl."

Putting my hands on my hips, my lips thinned in annoyance. I'd had enough of this crap. My fright had slowly ebbed away and this was all beginning to seem like a ridiculously bad joke.

"You did not 'make' me." I held both hands up and made the required quotation symbols in the air then my hands returned to my hips. "My parents made me and I'm a thousand per cent sure you aren't my father." Both of my parents had died in a car accident when I was nineteen so I couldn't call them up and ask them to verify the truth of this.

Silvius took a step closer, grinning slyly. "I am your father now, my child. I shall teach you the old ways and in turn, you shall do my every bidding." He followed up the statement with a leer like a terrible actor in a C grade movie.

"Mmm hmm." Judging the distance to the door, I poised to bolt. "Well then. Bye."

I was a step away from the door when he
strange question. "Have you not noticed that yc
longer beats?"

Did anyone ever actually notice their heart be __ng? I'd
certainly never put much thought into it before. But the
thought held me captive now. When I'd woken only a few
minutes ago, I'd known that something was different. I
was cold, clammy and felt a sense of loss as though
something vital was missing. I'd seen doctors and nurses
on TV taking people's pulses often enough so I knew what
to do. Placing my fingers on my wrist, I searched for the
tell-tale beating of my heart. Nothing. Nada. Zilch. *You're
just not finding the right spot,* I told myself desperately.

Putting my fingers on my neck, I felt around and came
up empty. Eventually, I noticed that I'd been holding my
breath for an unnatural length of time. In fact, I hadn't
drawn a breath since I'd woken up. "I'm not breathing."
Numb with shock, I stood there with my mouth open, but
with no air going in or out.

"As I said," Silvius gloated, "we are now bound. It has
been seventy years since I last made a servant." Sizing me
up, he added some information that made no sense to me.
"Usually, they aren't as…coherent as you seem to be for at
least a few weeks." He seemed puzzled, as if he'd expected
far different behaviour from me than what I'd been
displaying so far.

Still stuck on the fact that I wasn't breathing, I hadn't
quite grasped what was going on yet. Then it finally
dawned on me. "You've turned me into a zombie. Oh my
G-G-G," I stuttered trying to say God. The word just
wouldn't come out.

Silvius smirked at my broken attempt at speech. "We are forbidden to speak the Lord's name, child."

"Zombies can't say G-G-G?" I gave up when it became obvious that something in my head was broken. I'd never read anywhere that zombies stuttered. They usually just moaned, drooled and went after humans like starving dogs.

Annoyance settled onto Silvius' pasty face. "You are not a zombie," he ground out through his yellow teeth.

"What am I then?" Zombie was the only explanation I could think of. A sickening thought struck me. Was I going to get a sudden insatiable craving for human brains?

"You are a vampire," he informed me.

It was so absurd that I laughed. I checked his expression, found it to be stony and humourless and that set me off into fresh gales. "A vampire?" I said when I had myself under control again. "That's a good one." I tried to wipe away a tear, but my eyes were strangely dry.

"You believe in zombies, but not vampires?" Silvius' eyebrows rose again then furrowed in puzzlement. "Maybe something went wrong when I turned her," he muttered almost beneath his breath. "She is not a normal servant."

"Hey, I've read books about voodoo magic," I said defensively, hardly believing we were having this conversation at all. "Zombies could be real."

"You are not a zombie." His black stare pinned me in place. "You are a vampire, just as I am." His lips peeled back to reveal his teeth again. As I watched, the incisors lengthened and sharpened into wicked points.

Holy shit, he really is a vampire! In instinctive reaction at the irrefutable proof that the strange old man really was a dreaded creature of myth, I screamed and cringed away. Silvius roared with laughter and the noise boomed around the crypt, echoing louder and louder until my ears were ringing. His shadow doubled over, holding its stomach and slapping its thigh as it laughed just as hard, if soundlessly. Silvius wasn't the only one who was crazy, his shadow was, too.

Backing up against one of the stone sarcophagi, I reached out and snapped off the cross that adorned it. Silvius' shadow looked up, saw what was in my hand and went into a panic. It tried tapping its master on the shoulder to get his attention, but the vampire either didn't feel it, or ignored it. It was far too late for Silvius anyway, the cross was already in motion. It flew through the air like a miniature spear, deadly and far more accurate than I could have ever hoped.

The jagged end lanced directly into the creature's chest, sinking in for several inches. Silvius' laughter broke off and he stared at me with a stunned expression. His shadow wrung its hands, then raised them in the air in despair. The vampire dropped his eyes to his chest and saw the cross standing out from his flesh. It had been a fluky shot and had hit him right in the heart. Horror finally broke over his face as it dawned on him that he had a cross sticking out of his chest. "What have you done?" he asked in a choked whisper.

"Um, killed you?" I admit my tone was hopeful. The man was a vampire, for Christ's sake. Of course I had to stake him through the heart. Anyone else would have done the same thing. It was our duty as human beings to kill anything that threatened us. *But you're not human anymore,* my mind whispered traitorously. I might be able to think the Lord's name in my head, but I could no longer say it out loud.

"You have killed us both, you stupid girl," Silvius hissed while his shadow shook its fist at me. Bending over, the shadow began coughing noiselessly. Shrieks began to issue from the old man's mouth and black gobs of blood splattered on his clothes. My lips wrinkled back from my teeth at the thought that I had ingested that ichor. No wonder it had burned on the way down. My last hope that this had all just been a dream fled. No nightmare I'd ever had before had been this vivid, loud or stinky. I covered my nose with my sleeve, but the smell of old, diseased blood didn't diminish.

Clutching the cross, Silvius attempted to pull it out. It proved to be a bad move. As soon as his flesh touched the metal, it caught on fire. More shrill, high screams came from him, along with fresh gouts of blood. Now the small room smelled like a charnel house. My stomach turned and I gagged, but nothing came up. Maybe because I hadn't eaten anything for three days. *Yeah, but you've had something to drink, remember?* I bent over at the memory of acidic fluids flowing down my throat and into my stomach, burning the whole way down. I tried to vomit again, but had as little success this time as I'd had just a few seconds ago.

When my attempt at dry reaching subsided, I watched in fascinated horror as my maker bled and burned to death. His shadow writhed in sympathetic torment. Gouts became rivers as more and more black fluid escaped from his mouth and chest. Sinking to his knees, then slumping onto his side, Silvius beseeched me with both burning hands. The flames were blue and the smell of burning flesh was awful. Thankfully, his shadow fell with him. It futilely tried to stand, fell to its knees then finally lay exhausted on its face. It had seemed to go on forever, but the whole dramatic death scene had probably taken less than a minute. At last, the screams stopped and Silvius lay still.

Cringing against the far wall, I was afraid to approach him just in case he hadn't quite finished dying. This might just be a ruse to lure me closer so he could pounce on me. The strange blue fire flickered then died. It hadn't touched his clothes, just his flesh. I figured Silvius really was dead when his body began to break down and melt.

Soon, all that remained of the vampire was a noisome puddle and soiled clothing. Even his shadow had disappeared, much to my relief. Seeing that thing acting like it had a mind of its own was something I hoped I'd never have to see again.

Lying in the middle of the mess was the metal cross. It was made of plain iron and was about six inches long and four inches wide. Attached to the crosspiece was a smaller, far more elaborate cross. This one was tarnished silver, maybe two inches long and an inch and a half wide. It had exquisitely intricate filigree detail that almost looked like lace. Although it was beautiful, I wasn't about to touch it when it was covered in ooze.

Sinking to the filthy, cold floor, I sobbed out my fear and confusion. My sobs were dry and unsatisfying. Apparently, my tears had died right along with the rest of me. Lying on my side, I stared at the stain of my former creator numbly. In all my hopes and dreams for the future, waking up dead had never made its way onto the list. I'd gone from being an average twenty-eight year old clothing store manager to becoming an undead spawn from hell. I was glad my parents hadn't lived to see me fall so low.

What was I supposed to do now? I couldn't return to work like everything was normal. From what I'd read and seen in the movies, I should now be severely allergic to sunlight. Checking my watch, I saw that dawn should be only moments away. On that thought I was suddenly unbelievably tired. It was impossible to keep my eyes open any longer no matter how hard I tried.

I remembered Silvius saying that I had killed us both. If I was lucky, maybe I'd join him in death and wouldn't wake up in the morning. *Morning? Don't you mean night?* Thankfully, unconsciousness rose up, grabbed hold of me and dragged me down into nothingness.

Chapter Four

Waking slowly, I had to fight my way out of a horrible nightmare about a weird old man who had bitten me on the neck and had turned me into a vampire. Snuggling into my cold concrete mattress, I groped for my blanket, but it must have slipped off during the night.

Wait a minute, I thought. "Cold concrete mattress?" I said out loud. The words echoed strangely around my bedroom. Rolling over onto my back, I opened my eyes and saw the cobwebbed ceiling of the crypt above me. "Ah, crap."

With a roll of my head, I ascertained that everything that had transpired during the past few nights hadn't been the product of a fever dream as I'd hoped. The stain of the old man was still there. So were his clothes and the soiled cross.

Sitting on the floor across the room was the lantern. The flame had burned out, but I could see just fine. There were no windows to let moonlight in, yet the room held a soft glow. I had apparently acquired a form of night vision. "Just one of the perks of being unalive." I giggled at my own wit, then clamped a hand over my mouth before my giggles could become hysterical screams. There had been enough screams in the dank and chilly room already.

Taking stock, I saw that my clothes were beyond filthy. Even a hobo would hesitate before stealing them from my lifeless corpse. That thought brought crushing despair. "I'm a lifeless corpse," I wailed, then tried to cry again. My disappointment that I'd woken up dead again was acute. Silvius had been wrong when he'd said I'd killed us both. I'd only killed him when I'd speared the cross through his chest. Was I now doomed to an eternity of living death?

After a while, my tearless sobs seemed pointless, so I gave up my attempt at weeping. What I needed was a change of clothes. A shower would go a long way towards making me feel human again. Not that I ever really could be. I guessed that ship had sailed.

I'd lost my purse and phone at some point. My best guess was that I'd dropped them in the alley when I'd been attacked. In that case, they would most likely have been found by one of the workers in the area. If they didn't just keep the phone and money then toss the purse, they might have handed it over to the cops. I was on polite speaking terms with a few people in my apartment building. They would probably all jump to the conclusion that something bad had happened to me when the police came knocking to ask questions about my disappearance. I was fairly sure their wildest guesses wouldn't even come close to my reality.

Feeling in my pockets, I located my apartment keys. I always carried them in my pocket on the way home from work. If I was ever mugged and they managed to wrest my bag away from me, at least they wouldn't get my keys.

With some trepidation, I pulled open the heavy wooden door. Rusty hinges squealed in protest, but the door opened easily enough. It mustn't be as heavy as it looked.

Standing in the doorway, I peered uneasily at the grave markers that spread out from the crypt in every direction. I'd already figured I'd been taken to the Toowong Cemetery. It was the only graveyard close by.

I seemed to be in a very old section of the grounds. Most of the headstones were worn and difficult to read. Not that I felt the urge to wander around aimlessly reading about people who had died a long time ago. The mausoleum was in a shallow valley between two small hills. The entire area seemed to be hilly. Headstones marched up a slope to my right and out of sight. To the left was a sea of graves and a downslope that led to unwelcoming dimness. The odd mausoleum was dotted here and there. Each was as decrepit as the one I'd just emerged from.

The sun had only just set and faint light still glowed through the trees to the west. My eyes burned when I glanced at the last dying rays, but they didn't water. Tears were a thing of the past, just like my heartbeat. I'd never noticed my heartbeat before, except on the rare occasions when I exerted myself and I could hear it thudding in my ears. I suddenly missed it with startling intensity.

With the goal of a shower in mind, I at least had a reason to leave the dubious safety of the crypt where I had so recently died and had then been monstrously reborn. Since I'd never been to the cemetery before, I had no idea where the exit was. I could see myself wandering around the place all night, searching for a way out and getting hopelessly lost.

Birds that hadn't yet roosted for the night called to each other from the nearby trees. Crickets, invisible in the grass, rasped their annoyingly monotonous night song. Wind ruffled the branches and teased my hair. Further away was the sound of traffic. The living would be heading home from work to their families for dinner and to lead their ordinary little lives. I envied them their normalcy.

Staving off the self-pity that there was now nothing normal about my new life, I headed toward the closest sounds of traffic. With my newly enhanced vision, I was able to navigate around the graves without tripping and sprawling on my face. Now I knew why I'd avoided visiting my parent's graves back in New South Wales where I'd been born and raised; graveyards were creepy.

Crossing my arms in a futile attempt to generate warmth, I increased my pace. Dark shadows from the taller grave markers crowded around me. Anyone or anything could be hiding amongst them. Watching me. Stalking me. Searching for weaknesses it could exploit when it finally attacked.

I was thoroughly spooked before I remembered that I was already dead. What could possibly happen to me now? If a mugger attacked me, they couldn't kill me again. Not unless they punched a stake through my heart. Maybe that would be a blessing. My first instinct had been to kill Silvius when I realized he was a vampire. If I were to reveal my new nature to some poor slob on the street, would they find something sharp and pointy and put me out of my misery with it? How could I prove to them that I was a vampire, anyway? Touching my teeth with my tongue, they appeared to be as normal as ever. My incisors hadn't magically lengthened. I wondered if my blood was still red, or if it had already turned into black goo.

As I trudged downhill, the sounds of passing cars grew louder. Lights twinkled through the foliage, guiding me toward the road. A wrought iron fence appeared to my left. It took several minutes of walking downhill before I found a gate. It swung open easily and without the rusty squeal I was expecting.

Standing on the fringes of a busy road, I avoided looking directly at the too bright headlights. If this light sensitivity kept up, I'd have to start wearing sunglasses. A few hundred meters down the hill, I saw a familiar congested roundabout and a motorway that I knew led to the west.

I had my bearings now that I recognized the Toowong roundabout. Waiting for a break in traffic, I jogged across the road and headed for a dark side street. Keeping to a steady jog, I made my way homeward. My apartment was right in the centre of the Brisbane CBD area. By car, it would have been a fifteen or twenty minute drive from the cemetery, if traffic was light. It would take me more than an hour to walk the distance. One happy by-product of being the unliving was that I didn't seem to get puffed. I could probably run all night if I had to. Despite my general unhappiness at my circumstances, I couldn't help, but be impressed with my stamina.

Using the back streets and staying in the dark as much as possible, it only took half an hour to reach my apartment. I didn't want anyone to see me just in case my disappearance had made it to the news. I ducked out of sight whenever someone came close. Leaving a trail the cops could follow might lead them back to the crypt. I shuddered at the idea of the police stumbling across the remains of Silvius. Tests would be performed and I doubted his DNA would show up as being human.

My home was on the fourth floor of a plain, unpainted red brick building. Craning my head back, I saw that the windows in my apartment were dark. I figured no cops were inside waiting for me to magically appear and tell them all about my wacky adventures. I'd never been good at thinking on my feet, so coming up with a believable story would have been chancy.

Heading inside, I scurried up the seldom used stairs rather than using the elevator. It would be best if my neighbours believed I'd simply disappeared. I had no family, friends, pets, plants or dependents of any kind. There was no one to miss me or to mourn me. It was sad, but life would go on without me. In fact, I was pretty sure that it already had.

Quietly letting myself into my apartment, I shut and locked the door. I then crossed the small living room to close the curtains before flicking on the light. No one needed to know I was back. My visit would be as brief as possible.

Cheap, mismatched furniture graced my small, one bedroom apartment. I barely earned enough to pay the rent let alone to splash out on an expensive couch. There were no knickknacks clogging up the shelves of my six foot bookcase. Books were supposed to go into the bookcase, not dolls or bears or other cute things that were ultimately useless. Hundreds of books were crammed into the sturdy case. I'd read them all multiple times, but they were still in pristine condition. Books were my one true love.

Stripping off was my first goal and I shoved my filthy rags into the kitchen bin. Walking naked to the bathroom, I took a quick, but thorough shower. My hair was dirty, but not oily. It was another happy by-product of being a walking corpse. I wouldn't have to wash my hair as often. Not unless I rolled around in dirt again and that wasn't an exercise I was planning on repeating any time soon.

After drying off, I examined the new me in the floor length bedroom mirror. The myth that vampires didn't have reflections was obviously bogus because I could see myself just fine. I might be undead, but I was still made of flesh and blood.

At first, I couldn't see much difference. My skin was paler now, almost translucent. The last of my summer tan was gone. My irises had darkened to a stormy dark grey and the pupils were way larger than normal. My eyes had aged during my transformation and seemed decades older now. My face was still fairly ordinary, damn it. I hadn't gained an unholy beauty with death.

My figure was even more slender than normal now. The couple of extra kilos of unwanted blubber I'd been unable to rid myself of were gone. I admired my newly svelte form until I started shivering. Apparently, my body heat had gone the way of dinosaurs and was now extinct.

Sorting through my closet, I changed into underwear, jeans, a plain black t-shirt and a thick, dark blue sweater. A pair of fairly new black sneakers would do for shoes. All the better to blend into the night with, I figured. After a brief search, I pulled out a large backpack and stuffed it full of similar clothing.

Taking what little money I'd kept stashed in my drawers, I shoved the notes into my jeans pocket. I automatically checked the fridge on my way through the kitchen. Opening the bottle of milk, a sniff almost made me gag. It must have gone off some time during my absence. Nothing in the fridge or cupboards appealed to me. Not even coffee. I tried a sip of water and it did nothing to ease the increasing dryness of my throat. There was nothing here for me now and it was time for me to leave.

With one last look around, I left my apartment. It was hardest by far to leave my book collection, but a bagful of books would just slow me down if I had to make a run for it. Carrying my keys around seemed redundant, so I dropped them into a sewer grate after walking for a few blocks. I jogged through the streets of Brisbane with numb inattention and my feet led me right back to the crypt.

Pushing the creaky door open, I avoided the mess that used to be Silvius and stashed my backpack in a corner. Sleeping on the bare concrete floor didn't hold much appeal, but I couldn't think of anywhere else to go. No one would come searching for me here in the middle of the cemetery. From the lack of broken bottles and syringes, it wasn't a favoured hang out for street rats and druggos. Forlorn and forgotten, no one bothered to clean the crypt. It should be safe for me here until I could think of better accommodations.

I'd heard ghost tours were held fairly regularly in the cemetery, but I'd never been tempted to attend one. Now I was one of the creatures that haunted the vast area of the dead. At least the tours were run at night, so I would have time to hide if they came my way. It wouldn't be much of a ghost tour if it was run during daylight hours.

Wishing I'd thought to bring a spare blanket, I decided to go in search of one. I might be undead, but that didn't mean I had to lack for comfort. Pulling the door firmly shut behind me, I slunk away from my new abode.

Back in the darker side streets again, I went on the prowl. It was still early enough for health conscious people to be out walking. They moved in pairs, alone or with their dogs. Avoiding people as best I could, I casually peered over the fences of each house I passed, searching for a blanket I could borrow permanently.

Shortly into my search, I hit pay dirt. Spying a ratty old cane chair on the veranda of a small single story wooden house, I peered up and down the road. No one was in sight at the moment and the house was dark. If anyone was home, they'd gone to bed early. The fence was about five feet high with wicked wooden palings and flaking white paint. Hyper aware of how damaging stakes could be to my health, I carefully vaulted over the fence and landed in something squishy.

Crouching down below the fence line, I grimaced at the brown substance that was stuck to my right shoe. Apparently, I didn't need to breathe to still be able to smell. Scraping dog poo off on the grass as best I could, I peered back over the fence to make sure no one was coming. It was clear, so I ran in a crouch over to the house.

All was still and quiet inside. I couldn't detect any sounds of human activity. Weathered floorboards creaked as I approached the rickety old chair. My hand was on the blanket when the growling began. A blob that I'd assumed was a beat up old cushion lifted its head and bared its teeth at me.

The owner of the poo stared at me. Its growl gradually increased in volume and menace. Grey and decrepit, the mangy old mongrel wasn't about to give up its prized blanket without a fight. Our eyes met for the space of three seconds. Then mine narrowed in determination and the dog's growl deepened as if it sensed my intent.

Yanking the blanket out from beneath the animal, I turned and leaped over the veranda railing. The dog tumbled to the floorboards, let out an enraged howl and scrambled after me. Vaulting one handed back over the fence, I turned to flee and came chest to chest with a surprised dog walker. The mongrel's head appeared over the fence behind me as it continued the attack. Saliva flew from its mouth as it snapped at me in rage.

"It's just a blanket," I told the dog, "get over it." Ignoring my advice, the dog lunged at me, feet scrabbling for purchase. Lucky for me, it was too damn old to scale the fence and tear my throat out.

"Are you ok?" the dog walker asked. Being caught stealing a grungy blanket from an old dog hadn't been in my plans, but caught I was. Now I had to talk my way out of it.

I turned my full attention to the guy and was instantly riveted by his smell. Sweat stained the collar and armpits of his white t-shirt, but it wasn't the rank, sour stench I usually associated with exercise. It was salty and somehow very appealing.

He was average looking, with short sandy hair and a slight paunch. A tiny tan dog danced at his feet, turning in circles and letting out little yips of excitement. The dog walker smiled at me quizzically with soft brown eyes. They widened when our gazes locked. Then his pupils dilated, his smile became dreamy and he swayed toward me. *Jesus, I think I just hypnotized him.*

Staring at his neck, I swayed towards him as well. His mouth aimed for mine, but I tilted my face away so his lips grazed my jaw instead. Sudden longing hit me. I wanted this man like I'd never wanted anyone or anything else in my life before. I had to have him. Now.

My hands were in his hair, pulling him toward me. His hands came around my waist, holding me tight. At our feet, the tiny tan dog yipped crazily, dancing in distressed circles. My mouth was an inch away from the dog walker's neck before I realized what I was about to do.

I was going to eat him.

Chapter Five

With a cry of horror, I shoved the dog walker away. We'd shuffled in a half circle while I'd briefly contemplated eating him. He hit the fence, flipped over it and landed with a thump and a groan. Seizing the moment, the mongrel went on the attack. High screams and vicious barks echoed throughout the neighbourhood.

Snatching up the dog blanket from the ground, I made my escape. Three blocks away, I slowed to a walk and realized I'd also snatched up the little dog. My close encounter with its owner had awakened something in me that couldn't, that wouldn't be denied; an unholy hunger for blood.

Hunkering in an alley, I held the dog up, critically judging its size and how large a meal it would offer me. Shivering in fright, whimpering in terror, it wasn't much bigger than the rat that had passed me in the alley a few nights ago. Soft brown eyes, just like its owner's, stared at me. A small pink tongue came out and licked me on the nose. My dead heart tried to lurch in my motionless chest. I couldn't do it. As hungry as I was, I couldn't eat the poor thing. I'd have to find my meal somewhere else.

Backtracking, I spied the dog walker milling around in a dazed circle. From the way he was rubbing his butt cheek and bleeding from the arms, I figured the mongrel had taken a few bites out of him. I had a sudden moment of intense envy for the dog's taste of blood before squashing it. The dog in question was still barking and growling, reaching as far as it was able to over the fence.

"Misty? Here, Misty," the distraught man called.

In my arms, Misty gave a shrill bark and wriggled madly. Setting her down, I melted into the shadows as the small tan dog and her owner were reunited. He scooped the mutt up and hugged her to his chest. Her small pink tongue was in a frenzy, licking the man's chin, cheeks and even his mouth. They disappeared with many disturbed glances back over their shoulders. Forcing out a sigh, I rubbed my empty stomach. *There goes my meal.* On the plus side, at least I now had a blanket.

Crossing the road to stay out of the mongrel's range, I ducked into another dark alley to search for something to eat. Rats nosed through garbage that had spilled from a knocked over wheelie bin. My lips wrinkled back at the thought of biting into one of them. Just the thought of touching them made me want to barf. Clutching my hard won prize, I gave up on the thought of a meal and trudged back to my crypt in disgrace.

Spreading the blanket out as far from the remains of Silvius as possible, I sat down and waited for the sun to rise and for the unconsciousness that would invariably follow. My second night as the undead was spent huddled on a filthy, flea infested dog blanket, wondering what I'd done to deserve a crappy fate like this.

As dawn neared, I could feel sweet oblivion only moments away. Using my backpack as a pillow, I lay down on the blanket and sank gratefully into nothingness.

Awakening just after dark, I lay on the chilly concrete floor and wondered if I should even bother getting up. What would I get up for? I had no plans, no goals, no reason to continue on with this terrible unlife. So far, I sucked at being a vampire. Eating humans just seemed so wrong. Munching on animals was just as bad.

Growing hungrier by the second, I pondered on my dilemma. What exactly was so wrong with taking a snack from a human? I had never heard of an actual case where someone had died from blood loss via vampire bite. Logically, this meant we didn't need to drain people dry when we fed. The thought of tearing the dog walker to pieces had sent me running. If I didn't have to actually kill to feed, then why shouldn't I be able to take a pint of blood? They'd be able to regenerate it easily enough. I was pretty sure the Red Cross took that much from their blood donors.

An empty pit had opened in my stomach and was growing larger by the minute. It had a helping hand in convincing me that it would be ok to hunt as long as I didn't get carried away. I had the unnerving feeling that if I didn't feed soon, the pit would grow until it consumed me. *I'll just have to pick a likely target.* I had a vague thought of choosing someone who deserved a fright and a bit of pain. Rising, I dusted dog hair off my clothes and decided I didn't need to change my outfit yet. Another handy thing about being undead was that I didn't sweat. The pros just kept on coming.

One place in Brisbane that would be a decent hunting ground for someone like me was the Valley. Fortitude Valley could be a rough place if you were unwary. As each second passed, I cared less about being careful and more about feeding. I was becoming obsessed with filling the hole in my middle.

Keeping to a fast jog, I took the darker streets and made it to the Valley in an hour. There was a variety of pubs and nightclubs in the area that drew a crowd most nights. It was Tuesday night, but the footpaths were still crowded with people of all nationalities. Some were heading to the watering holes of their choice. Others were heading to or from dinner at the plethora of restaurants and cafes. I blended in easily enough despite being a female on my own. Keeping my head down and walking normally instead of slinking around like the creature of the night that I was seemed to help.

It was just after eight, too early for the real degenerates to be out and about just yet. Finding a suitably dangerous looking alley, I settled in to wait.

It was surprisingly easy to blend into the shadows and wait for my prey. It seemed that I had finally acquired the art of patience. First, I studied my hunting spot and tried to come up with a workable plan. I'd chosen an alley with a dead end so there could be no escape for my meal. The carcases of discarded beer bottles and used syringes littered the ground. A dumpster hulking off to one side overflowing with trash. It reeked so badly that my eyes would have watered if they'd still been capable of producing liquid. New to the idea of being a hunter, I couldn't think up a real plan of attack. If someone deserving of their fate happened to wander close enough, I'd grab them and see what happened.

After a couple of hours, my patience was rewarded. Four young men in their early twenties stumbled into the mouth of the alley. Their unwashed hair, torn jeans and worn shirts screamed 'dole bludgers' to me. There were plenty of jobless people like this in the city. They depended on government welfare to get by and it didn't pay very well. With my new night vision, I made out their dazed expressions from twenty feet away. They were already stoned, but took out fresh joints anyway.

I'd expected hard core druggos or muggers. Instead, my prey was a few weed smokers too poor to afford entry into the clubs. They'd hang around the nightclubs begging for smokes or money, hassling the pretty girls and getting high. I was supposed to maul losers like this for a meal? Frustrated and hungry, I kicked a can. It whistled through the air and hit one of the young men on the back of the head. Staggering forward a couple of steps, he turned to investigate the source of the attack and his friends turned with him.

"What was that?" one of the guys said in a slurred voice.

"I think someone threw something at me," his injured friend replied, rubbing the back of his head. It was lucky the can had been empty. It might have fractured his skull if it had been full. Who knew I could kick like that?

Pulling a switchblade from his grimy pocket, a third guy flicked his joint to the ground. "No one throws shit at my mates." With a small metallic snick, a four inch blade appeared.

All four guys started towards me and I suddenly wished I'd thought through my rudimentary attack plan some more. I hadn't expected to face so many victims at once, even if they were a bunch of losers. Reassuring myself that they couldn't kill me because I was already dead, I let them come to me.

They stopped a few feet away and peered at me in the darkness. The fourth guy pulled a lighter and it flicked to life. I flinched at the brightness, but only for a moment. The hole in my stomach was demanding I fill it and the thought of food consumed me. Eating these guys didn't seem like such a bad idea. In fact, it seemed like a great idea.

"You're pretty," said one of the men in a daze and noises of agreement came from the others.

Momentarily distracted from my hunger, I self-consciously ran a hand through my no doubt messy hair. "Really? You think so?"

"Yeah," one of the others replied.

"Gorgeous," breathed another.

When I'd looked into the mirror, I'd at first been surprised that I had a reflection at all, then I'd been disappointed to see I hadn't changed much. Obviously, I now had some kind of vampire mojo that made me attractive to men. For a second, I wondered why Silvius hadn't been the least bit attractive. Repulsive would have been closer to the mark. Then the hunger roared through me and cognitive thinking was gone.

Guided by weird new instincts, I grabbed the nearest guy, yanked him forward and bit into his neck. My usually blunt teeth effortlessly sheared through skin and found a vein. Sweet, salty blood flooded into my mouth. Hands tightened on my waist and the guy made a sound of intense pleasure that I couldn't ever remember causing in a man before.

After a few seconds, he was torn from my grasp. Blood trickled down my chin. I wiped it off with the back of my hand then licked my hand clean. One of the other men stepped forward and grabbed me by the shoulders. "Do me. God, do me next."

Accepting the invitation, I munched down on him and intoxicating warmth swept through me as I drank. All four men demanded I drink from them and I happily complied. When the hole in my stomach was full, I pushed the last guy away. He wore a huge, stoned smile just like the others. His legs wobbled and I sat him next to his friends. Lined up side by side, sitting on the filthy ground, they looked a bit like tired children who were pretending they didn't need to take a nap.

The whole feast had only lasted for a few minutes, but I was lucky no one had stumbled across us. I'd only taken a few mouthfuls from each of the guys, so they should recover quickly enough. *So much for mauling them.* They'd been surprisingly willing to feed my hunger. Maybe that was why they hadn't suffered the excruciating pain I'd felt when Silvius had bitten me. I hadn't been the least bit willing to be his victim. I had a lot to learn about my strange new status of undeath. Wiping my mouth on my sleeve, I touched my fangs with my tongue in wonder. They were already beginning to retract. Automatic fangs that popped out when you needed them. What next?

Jogging back towards my new home, I felt powerful and almost alive again. My cheeks felt like they had a rosy glow and my skin was room temperature rather than clammy.

Halfway home, I stopped when I saw the moon shining down from above the buildings. "Oh, wow, look at that. It's so pretty." It was perfectly round and utterly mesmerizing. My smile was huge, happy and slightly stoned.

Chapter Six

Staggering back inside the crypt, I pushed the door shut and leaned back against it with my eyes closed. I'd sprinted most of the stoned feeling away, but a slight amount of weed remained in my system.

"What have we here?" a voice said and my eyes snapped open.

A stranger stood at the far end of the crypt. He was about six feet tall, leanly built and had short black hair that was expensively cut. Wearing a pricy pair of black slacks, leather shoes and a black cashmere sweater, he was overdressed for the cemetery. My mouth dropped open when I took in his face. With high cheekbones, full lips and burning black eyes, he looked like a model for a cologne ad.

"Who are you?" I asked, then followed up with a more pointed question. "What are you doing in my crypt?" *Maybe he's from a ghost tour and got separated from the crowd.*

Dark eyebrows rose as he swept his gaze from my face down to my feet then back up again. The sardonic twist to his mouth indicated he wasn't particularly impressed with what he saw. "I am Lucentio," he replied. I detected a European accent and frowned. The last European man I'd met had killed me. What horrors would this one have in store?

Examining him further, I took in more details that I'd missed on my first inspection. Lucentio's skin was pale. Unnaturally pale. His eyes were so dark they didn't appear to have irises. Most importantly, his chest didn't rise and fall. My theory that he was from a ghost tour evaporated.

"Great." I threw up my hands in disgust as I came to the only conclusion possible. "Another vampire. You should have brought all your vampire friends and we could have had a full moon, undead cemetery party." My sarcasm was thick enough to walk on.

"I do not have friends," Lucentio responded. Glancing at the empty clothing nearly covering the nasty smear on the ground, he pointed at them gracefully. "Who was this?"

"That was Silvius. My, uh, maker." I winced as the intruder's sharp gaze bored into me. Killing your maker probably wasn't a good thing. I was betting it went against vampire etiquette. "I'm sure that if he was still alive, he'd be very pleased to meet you," I finished lamely.

Switching his stare from me to the mark on the ground, the intruder hunkered down for a closer look. "I doubt that. We were already well acquainted and we were not what you could call close." Studying the empty clothing intently, Lucentio asked the worst possible question. "What happened to him? How did he die, exactly?" His gaze skittered away from the cross lying in the middle of the mess.

Walking over to the nearest stone coffin, I leaned back against it. "This is probably going to sound bad," I said reluctantly. Touching the tarnished silver cross in the centre of the much larger iron one, I tried to pry it free, but it was stuck fast.

Luc, as I'd automatically nicknamed him, glanced up and went absolutely still. After a few seconds, he rose slowly and took a step back. I didn't know much about fighting, but from the way he was balanced on the balls of his feet, he looked like he was readying himself to attack.

"Look, in my defence, I did just find out he was a vampire and that he'd made me into his servant," I said a bit desperately. "What was I supposed to do? Become his unholy slave for all time?"

Rocking back on his heels, Luc pondered the question. "Yes," was his eventual answer.

"For the love of G-G-G. Shit!" I wiped a hand over my face in exasperation at my inability to say the Lord's name and gripped the cross tightly. It bent slightly and I eased up on the pressure. The metal must be worn from age to bend so easily. "Just because some decrepit old man took a bite out of me, I'm expected to serve as his slave for the rest of my unnatural life?"

My question was followed by another short pause. "Yes," my strange visitor said again. He now seemed wary and on the verge of fleeing rather than attacking. I'd always had a particular way with men. Luc wouldn't be the first man to flee from me and he definitely wouldn't be the last. "Would you mind," he ventured, "telling me the circumstances of how you were turned?"

Since the question was polite and I had nothing better to do anyway, I filled him in on my capture and subsequent re-birth. "And then I finally figured out he was a vampire," I finished up.

"So, you decided to kill him?" Luc asked.

"It was more of an impulse than an actual decision," I explained. "He was laughing like a crazy man and before I knew it, I'd snapped off the cross and was throwing it at him." Without really meaning to, I snapped off the second cross and held it in a throwing position, aimed at my unexpected visitor.

Luc cringed away, holding his hands over his heart protectively. "A further demonstration will not be necessary," he said hurriedly.

"Oops. Sorry." I very carefully put the cross down on the sarcophagus. *Way to make an impression, Nat.* My usual lack of charm was in full force once more.

Straightening, Luc warily eyed the snapped off cross. "Does that not hurt?"

I stared at him blankly. "Does what not hurt?"

"When you touch the holy object?" he indicated the cross with a nod.

"Nope. Should it?" I asked. It dawned on me then that Silvius had burst into flames when he'd touched the cross. Of course vampires couldn't touch crosses without dying horribly. *So how come I can touch them?* Unfortunately, I was about to find out why.

"The prophecy has come true," Luc whispered and his face filled with despair. I'd seen that expression on men before. Usually it was when they were trying to break up with me and I was having difficulty grasping the concept.

"Prophecy? What prophecy?"

"What is your name?" he asked me instead of answering my question.

"Nat."

"Gnat? You are named after an insect?" His surprise was comical, but laughter was the last thing I was capable of right at that moment.

"Nat-a-lie," I enunciated carefully. "Natalie Pierce."

"Well, Natalie," Luc said grimly, "I regret to inform you that your birth might very well herald a dark age for vampirekind."

"What? Why?" I heard the whine in my tone and tried to notch it back a little. "What could I possibly have to do with a dark age? I didn't even believe in vampires until I woke up as one."

"The ancient Prophet speaks of you, Natalie Pierce. You bear one of the signs of Mortis." The words were spoken portentously with the weight of thousands of years of superstitious dread behind them.

I nodded thoughtfully as my feet automatically shifted towards the door. "Mortis, huh? I'm not familiar with that word." Although it did ring a bell somewhere deep down. Maybe I'd heard it in a movie, or read it in a book. "What exactly does it mean?"

"It is Latin for death," was his heavy answer.

I went still for several seconds, then I was rapidly moving for the door. *I do not need this right now. Meeting one crazy vampire in one lifetime is more than enough to deal with, thank you very much.*

Luc caught me with a hand on my shoulder before the door was even halfway open. "No one can run from their destiny, Natalie. Not even a creature such as you."

Clearly, he was faster than me and that meant I wouldn't be able to outrun him. Conceding defeat, I glumly trudged back to the dog blanket, trying to come to terms with the fact that I was now a creature. Taking a seat, I stared across the crypt at my new best friend as he moved back to his original position. Luc hunkered down into a crouch and stared back at me. He might be faster than me, but I was apparently the legendary Mortis. We were at a stalemate.

"So," I said with false brightness, "tell me about the prophecy. I'm dying to hear all about it." Technically, I was already dead, but I didn't want to quibble.

Lacing his hands together, Luc grimaced at the dirty floor, leaned back against the sarcophagus and slid to the ground. I'd heard that sitting on cold concrete could give you piles. Could vampires even get haemorrhoids? Why was I grossing myself out like this?

"Over two thousand years ago, the Prophet had a vision that sent him into a coma for three months. When he woke, he spoke in a language that no one could understand." Luc studied me broodingly in the dimness before continuing. "Occasionally, he would revert to his native language and his servants would jot down his ramblings."

When the silence dragged out for more than a few seconds, I circled a hand in the air for him to continue. "And?"

"It is said that Mortis will defy the natural order by being able to touch holy objects." He gestured at the cross I was idly playing with. I couldn't even remember picking the thing up again. I dropped it and it hit the floor with a metallic clang. "'When she rises, the damned shall fall.'"

I still wasn't sold on the idea that I could really be this Mortis creature. "All right, so I can touch crosses," I conceded. "Surely others have been able to do that." I wondered briefly why I couldn't say God out loud if I could still touch crosses. No doubt Luc would say it was part of the prophecy.

Luc shook his head grimly in the negative. "None of our kind has ever been able to touch holy objects and survive. We have the disturbing tendency of bursting into flames."

"Yeah, I caught some of that action already. The flames were pretty," I said absently. "They were bright blue, like a gas fire."

My unwelcome and unwanted companion shuddered and clasped his hands more tightly together. "None of us has ever been able to survive the death of our maker at our hands. That was not spoken of in the prophecy, but it is surely another sign."

We both examined the remains that used to be Silvius. "So, that's it then?" I asked glumly. "I'm definitely Mortis, huh?" He nodded back just as glumly. "What does that mean, exactly? Who am I supposed to bring death to?"

For a long moment, Luc didn't speak. His answer, when it came, was completely unsurprising. "Us."

Of course it was. If any creature on earth could be considered damned, it would have to be vampires.

Chapter Seven

I didn't particularly want to hear any more details, but figured it would be prudent to find out what further horrors destiny had planned for me. "Can you tell me more about the prophecy?"

Luc shrugged and examined his immaculate fingernails. I wondered if all foreign vampires were as well groomed as he was. Then I remembered the unkempt fingernails that had once graced my dead maker's hands before he'd melted down to slush and decided not.

"It is more of a legend than fact." Luc's accent thickened with the distress he was unsuccessfully attempting to hide. It must have been a kick in the nuts to be the one to walk into the crypt of vampirekind's worst nightmare. "Stories of you are passed down from maker to servant. I remember my maker scaring me with the tale when I was young." His lips twitched in something like a smile, but his eyes remained mournful.

I studied him closely, searching for signs of great age. He didn't look much older than me, around thirty maybe. I didn't interrupt and let him continue.

"When our kind began to disappear several months ago, the whispers became louder. Most believed that Mortis had risen and that our end was near. Some of the elders retreated to their fortified estates. Others wanted to form hunting parties and find Mortis before she could annihilate us all." He flicked a quick look at me.

"Let me guess which plan you were in favour of," I said dryly.

"Do not fear, Natalie," Luc said with a hint of humour. "If the legends are correct, you are not so easy to kill."

I perked up at that. Finally, something about being chock full of evil was working in my favour. "Why are you here, anyway? In Australia?" As far as I knew, we didn't have any vampire legends. I couldn't imagine why creatures of the night would want to come here anyway. There weren't that many people living in Australia compared to just about everywhere else in the world. Someone would notice if we suddenly started going missing in droves.

Turning his attention back to the smear on the ground, he pointed at it. "I came to kill your maker."

"Oh." I paused, searching for something to say. "I guess I saved you the trouble then." Surely that would win me some points?

"I had hoped to destroy him before he made another servant," Luc muttered. "But I was too late."

"Why were you hunting him?" Probably because the old guy, not to mention his shadow, had been so damned abnormal.

"Silvius had broken several vampire laws. I was sent to bring him to justice."

"So, you're a vampire cop?" I laughed at the idea, but it trailed off when he didn't share my humour.

"Yes," he replied. "Someone has to enforce the laws that keep us safe."

It occurred to me again that I knew nothing about being a vampire. "Maybe you'd better tell me about these rules," I said uneasily. Knowing myself well, I'd probably already broken half of them. Not that I went out of my way to break the rules. It was just that if they seemed stupid, I saw no reason to abide by them. Take waiting for the traffic lights to change to green in the middle of the night when there were no other cars in sight. Call me a criminal, but a couple of times I've checked twice for oncoming cars, then drove straight through.

Weary and disturbed, Luc didn't appear to be in the mood to give me the rundown, but he shrugged and laid it out for me anyway. "We are not to bring attention to ourselves, or to reveal our true nature to humans. It is not permissible to kill humans when we feed. Their wits must be befuddled so that we remain a mere hint of a memory. We may only have one servant at a time and may only make a servant if our maker dies. We are not to kill our own kind unless we are defending our own lives."

Nodding thoughtfully, I was relieved to discover that I hadn't broken any of the rules so far. Apart from killing our own kind. That was probably a pretty big no no, but I wasn't going to dwell on it. It was done and couldn't be undone. I hadn't needed to befuddle the wits of the four stoners I'd fed from. No one would believe them if they told the truth about my brief encounter with them anyway.

Reading my expression, Luc's gaze sharpened. "How long ago were you turned?"

"Uh," I counted back to what seemed like a thousand nights ago. "This is my fifth night as," I lowered my voice so no one lurking nearby could possibly overhear the complete absurdity of it, "a vampire."

Despair washed over my dark companion's face again. "Then I am already too late. By now you must have killed several humans. The authorities will already be on your trail."

I'd picked up the cross again and had been idly playing with it. I pointed it at him and ignored his flinch. "I'm going to stop you right there before you go jumping to too many conclusions. I haven't killed anyone yet. In fact, I just had my first snack tonight." I went dreamy at the memory of the sweet, salty meal and smiled.

Luc's mouth dropped open as he stared at me incredulously. "You have only fed for the first time tonight?"

"Yeah, just before I came back…home." I glanced around the crypt unhappily.

"Tell me about your hunt. How did you resist killing them?"

Shifting uneasily, I fiddled with the cross. "Keep in mind I have no idea what I'm doing here," I warned him then described my bright idea of hiding in a dark alley and waiting for my prey to come to me.

"So," he summed up when I was done, "you fed from four men and didn't kill any of them?" If I had to describe his expression, I'd go for 'stunned amazement'.

"What is your obsession with me killing people?" Crankily, I crossed my arms, hugging the cross to my chest.

Black eyes were riveted to the sight of the cross resting where my un-beating heart lay so still in my chest. "Perhaps I should explain what usually happens when a vampire is made."

"Please do." I was curt, almost to the point of being rude. Ok, there was nothing 'almost' about it.

"When our mortal bodies die, hunger awakens within our undead flesh. Feeding that hunger is all that consumes our minds. For the first few nights, we must feed until our hunger is sated. It can take several weeks for reason to return completely." After a short pause, he continued. "You do not act like a newly born vampire." I had the sense that he'd left out some vital information during that explanation, but I was too busy feeling special to question him. I tried to look modest, but failed when I smirked. "You do not act like any vampire I have ever known," he concluded. I wasn't sure Luc was being complimentary with that statement.

"Hey, I was starting to get pretty hungry," I defended myself. "I tried to hunt last night, but it didn't go so well." If I'd still had live blood in my veins I would have blushed in embarrassment at my complete failure to secure a meal.

"What happened?" He seemed overly interested in my answer. The answer I didn't want to give.

"I felt, um, sorry for the guy," I mumbled. Telling him that I'd felt even sorrier for his dog and couldn't eat it would make me feel even more stupid. I decided I'd keep that bit of information to myself.

"You have retained your compassion," Luc mused. "I had not anticipated that. I must think on what this all means." Standing fluidly, he gestured towards the door. "We should discuss our situation in more…comfortable surrounds." He gave a slight sneer at my lack of amenities and I couldn't blame him. My new home was a pit. Just about anywhere would be more comfortable than our current surrounds. Still, I was suspicious that he would want me to accompany him anywhere. I was Mortis and he was a vampire cop. Shouldn't he be trying to stake me?

"Natalie, I promise I will not try to harm you," Luc said with great sincerity, reading my expression accurately. Behind his promise was an unspoken 'yet'.

Forcing out another sigh, which was hard to do now that I didn't breathe, I stood. "Fine, I'll go with you, but I'm bringing the cross just in case you get any funny ideas." His lips quirked up for a moment in an almost smile again. He waited for me to retrieve my backpack, then pulled open the door for me.

Holding the cross in one hand, I shouldered the backpack and left the dank, cobwebbed crypt. I doubted I'd need the dog blanket again. For a moment, I felt nostalgic for the dirty, ragged thing. I'd had to fight to gain possession of it and now I was leaving it behind. Why did that sound like a metaphor for my entire previous life?

Chapter Eight

Luc glided through the graveyard smoothly. His muscles bunched and moved beneath his clothing. My enhanced vision had no trouble making out the details in the gloom. I followed closely behind him, occasionally tripping over low grave markers. Maybe if I kept my eyes on the ground rather than on his butt I'd trip less often. I tried to order my traitorous orbs to swivel downward, but they continued to defy me.

Another kind of hunger was growing within me now. It was a vastly different hunger to the blood thirst, but was no less powerful. Watching the graceful vampire move swiftly through the shadows was having a strange effect on me. A picture of him naked popped into my mind with amazing clarity. Luc glanced back and did a double take when he caught me smiling in appreciation of his butt. He increased his speed until he was almost jogging.

Reaching a black rental car, he gallantly opened the passenger door for me. I tripped while attempting to climb inside and he caught me by the elbow. *Jeez, Nat, try to be a little less suave,* I chided myself sarcastically. Seeing me in safely, Luc swiftly closed the door and jogged around the car. Automatically buckling the seatbelt, I stashed my backpack at my feet.

Luc opened the driver's door, but didn't get in. "Natalie, could you please move the cross?" He ducked down to look at me through the open door. Dark eyes watched the cross warily.

A haze was beginning to descend inside my head, making it hard to think. Realizing I held the cross in my right hand, I changed it over so it would be as far away from my companion as possible. "Sorry." I watched him slide inside and my hunger increased. "What's happening to me?" I asked as the car surged forward. My speech had a strange, drawn out quality as if I was speaking in slow motion.

Luc took his eyes off the road long enough to assess my condition. "Now that you have sated your blood hunger, you must now sate your flesh hunger." His reply sounded worried and unhappy. *Ah, that's the information he left out before. I now have flesh hunger. Whatever the hell that is.*

Whatever it was, it didn't sound good to me at all. "Silvius said he wasn't a cannibal. Surely I won't become one?" Snacking on blood had turned out to be pretty ok, but the idea of tearing an arm or leg off and biting into raw meat made my stomach want to churn.

"That is not the kind of feeding you crave," Luc replied and put his foot down on the accelerator.

Brisbane flashed past the windows too fast for me to focus on any particular detail. Harsh streetlights and headlights from cars made me wince away. I closed my eyes and held tightly to the cross. The metal didn't warm in my clammy grasp. Hollowness filled me at the thought that I might never be truly warm again. The warmth I'd gained from my meal had already dissipated although I still felt full.

Opening my eyes when the car lurched to a halt, I saw we had reached the valet parking entrance to a swanky hotel. Luc appeared beside me and opened the door. His grip on my elbow was firm almost to the point of being painful as he guided me inside after handing his keys to the attendant.

I didn't protest as I was rushed into an elevator. My gaze flicked to the faces and forms of the men that we passed. Cataloguing their appearance, all were dismissed as inadequate. None appealed to my strange new hunger. When the mirrored doors of the elevator closed, I slumped against the wall. Luc stood beside me, worry pouring from him in waves. He kept glancing at me sideways, checking on my condition. My eyes didn't have to be open to sense his movements. When the elevator doors opened again, he kept a tight grip on my arm and hurried me to a door halfway down the hall.

Pausing to put the 'Do Not Disturb' sign in place, he locked the door and dropped my arm. I was shivering like a junkie in full withdrawal. "Is t-this n-normal?" I managed, teeth chattering.

Luc nodded cautiously and sidled away from me, avoiding the cross that I held tightly in my left hand. "It has come on far more quickly than usual, but it is a natural part of becoming one of our kind." Natural? That just didn't sound like the correct word to me. There was nothing natural about becoming a vampire. "You must feed before your hunger consumes you." He read the query in my expression and answered my unspoken question. "If you do not feed, you will lose control and many humans will lose their lives," he explained.

"By f-feed…," I let the question hang, dreading the answer yet knowing what it would be.

"Sex," he said succinctly and began stripping off. Throwing his sweater onto a chair, he toed off his shoes. "You have the choice, of course, of intercourse with a human. But," he warned, "they will probably not survive the encounter and you will remain unsatisfied."

Stripping off he might be, but he didn't look happy about it. Wearing black boxer shorts and nothing else, he approached me gingerly. I dropped my eyes to his body and he was exactly as I'd pictured him; lean and muscled with only a light dusting of hair on his chest. Hunger roared through me and I doubled over in something close to pain.

I reached out and Luc's hand caught mine. "I can help you, Natalie," he sounded even less enthusiastic than he'd looked, "but you must drop the cross."

My left hand was clenched around the cross so hard that I felt every detail of the filigree carving on the smaller silver piece on my palm. Opening my hand, the cross didn't automatically drop to the floor as I expected. Shaking my hand, it finally dislodged itself and landed on the carpet with a dull thud. Then my clothes were disappearing one by one as my companion stripped me off. Like magic, I was naked.

Luc was a full eight inches taller than me and I craned my head back to see his face. Our eyes locked, his unwilling, mine hungry. My hands were on his shoulders, in his hair, drawing his mouth down to mine. Our lips touched and my hunger was unleashed.

Surrendering to the inevitable, Luc's hands cupped my butt and lifted me. His ribs groaned as I wrapped my legs around him. He stumbled to the bed and crushed me to the mattress. Our hands and mouths explored each other in a frenzy of need.

"Now, quick," I begged, completely unable to stop myself. I'd try to take him by force if he didn't co-operate. With the way I felt, he wouldn't stand a chance against me.

I got my wish seconds later as Luc ripped off his boxer shorts and plunged into me. It was quick, hard, rough and exactly what I needed. Muffling my moans, I bit Luc's shoulder when I climaxed. My legs tightened and I heard something crack in his spine. He gasped out a word in his natural language that I mentally translated as "fuck". Then he shuddered and rolled off me.

Basking in the afterglow, I rolled onto my side, about to compliment Luc on his supreme performance. His arm covered much of his face, but I could still read his expression. Utter misery painted him from head to toe. It occurred to me that our naked session hadn't exactly been a mutual decision. He hadn't wanted to have sex with me at all. I had just used the man for my own enjoyment. *Oh my God, I practically raped him!*

With a strangled cry, I threw myself off the bed and darted into the bathroom. Locking the door, I sank down to the cold tiled floor and sobbed dry tears into my knees.

After what he deemed had been a suitable length of time for me to pull myself together, Luc knocked on the door. "Natalie, are you all right?" His tone was weary and just made me sob harder. He'd had to sacrifice his dignity and his very body to sate my unholy hunger and he was asking if I was all right. No, I wasn't all right. I had reached the ultimate conclusion that death sucked.

"Go away!" I shouted and resumed sobbing.

"It wasn't entirely unpleasant," Luc said unhelpfully. "Apart from when you broke my vertebrae, it was actually quite nice."

"It wasn't nice," I snarled back. "It was h-h-horrible."

A short silence came from the other side of the door. "I don't believe it was horrible for you." Luc's tone held a touch of amusement.

I was standing before I'd consciously decided to move and snatched open the door. Luc backed away from my expression. I must have appeared as dangerously on the edge as I felt. "I'm going to have a shower and we are never going to talk about what happened in this room again, Luc," I said in a low, ominous tone.

"Lucentio," he corrected me. "Your hunger will rise again," he pointed out while staring at my breasts. The bite mark in his shoulder was fading, but I could clearly see the imprint of my teeth. Luckily, my fangs hadn't descended, so I hadn't torn his flesh.

Hiding behind the door, I repeated myself so he'd get the point. "Never. Again." Slamming the door in his face, I locked it, stood beneath the shower and sobbed some more.

Chapter Nine

When I finally emerged from the shower, my skin had a faint pinkish cast from the almost totally hot water I'd been soaking in. Normally, I'd have been parboiled to the point of blisters and fainting after a few seconds beneath that kind of temperature. The heat was now as unsatisfying as my tearless sobs were.

Drying off, I wrapped one of the thick, fluffy white hotel towels around myself. My hair was a tangled mess and I finger combed it, then blow dried it. Only after my hair was back to its normal neatness did I bother to look at my face. I did a double take and leaned in for a closer examination just to make sure I wasn't seeing things. Sometime over the last couple of days, my face had undergone some changes. Just a few subtle alterations had turned me from being ordinary into being actually quite attractive.

My eyes were larger and my cheekbones and jaw were more defined. Now I could see what the stoners had seen;

I was more than mildly pretty now. It was about time being undead did something for me. I had my suspicions why this miraculous occurrence had happened, but would need to check with Luc to find out for sure.

I cracked the door open to see my companion lounging on the couch in front of the TV. He had thoughtfully sat my backpack next to the bathroom door. Thankful that I wouldn't have to parade around wearing only a towel, I snatched up the bag and quickly dressed. Feeling less exposed and vulnerable when fully clothed, I stepped out into the main room.

Now that my mind wasn't clouded by my unnatural need for sex, I could examine the suite in more detail. The room was decorated in shades of cream and brown. Rumpled white sheets and a tan bedspread gave evidence of our naked romp. Beige carpet covered the floor. The furnishings in the tiny living area consisted of a cream couch and matching armchair. They were arranged around a large black coffee table. A huge TV was mounted on the wall. A few reproductions of famous paintings adorned the other walls. It was easily the most luxurious hotel room I'd ever been in and must be costing Luc a fortune.

Luc, now also dressed, sent a glance at me over his shoulder and nodded at the armchair in invitation. A wide picture window to the left of the TV would have given a spectacular view of the Brisbane River far below if the curtains hadn't been pulled tightly shut. I thought uneasily of how the sun would rise soon and hoped the curtains would be enough to keep the sunlight out. I didn't relish the idea of being barbequed at dawn.

Rounding the couch, I sank into the deep cream cushions of the armchair. "Why have my face and body changed?" I asked before Luc could bring up the unspeakable event that had occurred so recently on the bed.

Crossing his legs, he examined me critically. "All vampires develop their own abilities to make hunting more effective. Some learn stealth and cunning. Some have enhanced beauty."

I thought back to my deceased maker and how he'd caught me. "What was Silvius' trick?" He'd lulled me into a false sense of security at first by pretending to be aged and feeble. By the time I realized he wasn't all he seemed to be, it had been too late. His tall and scary shadow should have warned me. As a typical human, I'd brushed it off as a trick of my eye.

"Your maker was over three thousand years old," Luc explained. "He had gained the ability to cloud human minds from a distance. He could make them see what he wanted them to."

Momentarily intrigued with the idea of being able to make people think I was a famous movie star, I tried to figure out Luc's hunting trick. It was a no brainer really. "I guess you only hunt females." He inclined his head in agreement. "One glance from you is probably enough to have a harem chasing you around." If I wasn't mistaken, he smirked just a little as he shrugged modestly.

"With your increased beauty, you will be able to draw hapless men to you like flies after honey."

Or like flies after dog poo, I thought glumly. They were equally attracted to both. "What rules did Silvius break, anyway?"

Shifting so his arm ran along the back of the sofa, Luc made a graceful gesture with his hand. "He formed a rebel group and organized them into hunting our kind."

"Why?" Since this was my new life now, I'd at least try to grasp what the hell was going on. If I was the great and much unanticipated Mortis, then it was time to start paying attention. Unfortunately, just like back in high school, my mind wanted to wander from a topic that really didn't interest me. There was a reason I barely passed my exams. I just hadn't cared enough about the topics to learn from my teachers.

A slight shrug and grimace was his initial reply. Seeing that I wasn't going to settle for that, he gave in. "I believe he joined the faction that sided with," Luc hesitated, then nodded in my direction, "Mortis."

"I have a faction?" I asked, slightly disturbed by the idea. How could I have a faction when I'd only found out what I was a short time ago?

"Yes. A certain few believe you will annihilate the vast bulk of vampires, keeping only a small number as your servants. They think you will then create a new army of our kind, elevating your loyal followers to generals. They believe they will rule the world and enslave humans for food." His lips quirked in derision for his sadly deluded colleagues.

I pondered the idea for a while, then shook my head. "Nah. That sounds like too much hard work to me. I couldn't be bothered enslaving the whole world. Maybe just New Zealand," I said as an afterthought. Hey, a person had to eat and the Kiwis were fairly close to Australia.

"There is only one course of action that we can take," Luc said seriously. "We must consult with the Prophet directly."

"I thought you said he doesn't speak in any known language."

Luc ran a hand through his hair in what I took to be baffled frustration, tousling it and sending a flare of fresh hunger through me. I fought it down and smothered it before it could rise. One bout of sex with the unwilling vampire cop was enough, thank you.

"We must try," he said with strained urgency. "We must also leave here soon."

It was nice in the hotel room. I hadn't been this comfortable in days. "How come?" I'd be happy to sleep on the sofa if I had to. As long as the curtains were drawn and a few boards were nailed over the window for good measure.

"Silvius wasn't the only one who fled to Australia from me. When the others learn of his demise, they might band together and retaliate."

"Don't tell me you're the only one they sent after these guys?" I let my dismay at the idea show.

"Yes," Luc nodded. "I was all they could spare."

"Who are 'they', anyway?"

"The Councillors of the Court," he replied. "They rule the European vampire nation. All decisions are made by them and justice is delivered swiftly."

"Where does this Court operate from?"

"France."

"Really?" I pictured a bunch of snobby French vampires and instantly felt uncultured and unworthy. Then I remembered we were off to see the prophet, not the Court and was relieved. I wouldn't have to pretend I had any form of class in front of a bunch of upper crust types. "Is the Prophet in France, too?"

"No," Luc gave a short shake of his head. "He is in Romania."

I rolled my eyes at the answer. *Of course he is.* Romania was the home of the original vampire stories, as far as I knew. Rubbing my hands together for warmth, I froze when I felt welts on my left palm. After a long stare at my hand, I showed it to Luc. "I don't suppose you can explain this?" A perfect impression of the delicately filigreed silver cross was carved into my palm. Every exquisite detail was imprinted on my hand perfectly. I knew I'd been holding it tightly, but this was ridiculous.

Awe and fear warred for dominance on the vampire cop's face. "It is one of the holy marks," he whispered.

Before he could explain himself further, my eyelids grew heavy. I knew what that meant. "Looks like dawn is com-" before I could finish the thought, my world went dark.

Chapter Ten

"-ing," I said groggily and sat up. I was in the hotel bed and I was stark naked. The curtains were still drawn against any lingering rays of sun, but the room was only in semi-darkness, thanks to my enhanced eyesight.

Turning my head slowly to the left, I found Luc in bed beside me. The sheets were pooled around his waist, leaving his nicely muscled stomach and chest exposed.

"I thought it would be more expedient if we were both naked when you woke," he explained. One eyebrow rose and he gave me a slow smile that made something deep inside me quiver.

Rolling off the bed, I grabbed a pillow and used it to cover my nakedness. "No. Uh, uh. No way. We're not doing that again, Luc." I didn't care what was quivering inside me, I wasn't doing the horizontal mambo with him again. Retreating from the bed, I searched for my clothes and found them folded neatly on the back of the sofa.

Standing, Luc displayed his readiness to go ahead with the arduous job of sating my flesh hunger again. "My name is Lucentio and I wish you would remember that." He clearly had no idea how lazy Australians were. We always shortened names. Naturally I wasn't going to use a cumbersome name like Lucentio. "Why delay the inevitable?" Luc continued. He seemed more willing to have sex with me today, but I still wasn't going to put either of us through it again.

"Forget it, *Luc*." I said his nickname with emphasis as I snatched up my clothes and hustled toward the bathroom. He followed me, naked and ready. "Go find someone else to sate your hunger on. I'm off limits." And so was he. Slamming the door, I leaned back against it, sensing him standing right on the other side.

"I do not have the insatiable craving for flesh that I once did," he said softly. "I am able to control myself. You however," he lectured primly, "are newly born. We shall see how well you can control your flesh hunger." There was that vampire smugness again. They all must have it to some degree. The ones who had been around long enough to gain control of their hungers anyway.

"We shall see how well you can control your flesh hunger," I mimicked in a childishly high tone. I hated being lectured, which was one of the reasons I didn't bother with University. The other was that my grades hadn't been up to par.

Apparently, Luc was correct and I couldn't control my new hunger all that well. I was burning up from the inside without feeling any actual heat. Stumbling into the shower, I took care of matters myself. Self-gratification wasn't anywhere near as good as the real thing, but it seemed to do the trick. The hunger abated and I was able to think again. *I have to get a grip on this thing.* It was a pity I had no idea how to go about it.

Luc's eyes widened when I emerged, clean and fresh and didn't leap on him to tear his clothes off and salivate over his body. "So," I said as I took a seat on the armchair again, "what's the plan?"

"We will have to make the journey to Romania in several stages. First, we will fly to Singapore, which will take about eight hours. We will then fly to France the next night, which will take fourteen hours or so. Then it is just a short, six and a half hour flight to Romania."

"That's a lot of time up in the air." He was talking about a total of over twenty-eight hours just in flight time, not including hiding from the sun during the day. Faced with the sudden prospect of leaving the country of my birth, death and strange re-birth, I felt panicked. "There is one small problem, I don't have a passport," I said with some relief. Maybe this would put the trip off for a few days.

"You won't need one," Luc responded with quiet confidence. "We should hurry, our flight leaves in two hours." Doubtful, but left with no other option, I followed him from the room.

Standing at the airport half an hour later, I fidgeted with my backpack uneasily. The heavy iron and silver cross was wedged firmly inside, hidden from view, but handy if I needed it. Standing at my side, Luc put a calming hand on my shoulder. An instant picture of my legs wrapped around his waist filled my mind.

Shaking it off, I noticed that we stood in a small space of our own in the line. People either sent nervous glances at us, or stared in outright fascination. Luc ignored them all with studied indifference.

We'd arrived at what seemed to be peak hour. Roughly two hundred people were packed within the guide rails. Those not in our sphere of influence wore expressions of annoyance, or were dull-eyed from the tedium of shuffling forward every minute or so. I tried not to focus on how tasty they all smelled. The pressure on my shoulder increased when I swayed towards a man standing in line ahead of us.

"You should have fed before we left," my companion scolded me quietly.

"I wasn't hungry then," I gritted back. That was then and this was now. Blood hunger raised its head, took a sniff and decided it wanted a snack.

"Not here," Luc warned and gave me a slight shake.

It was enough to snap me out of my daydream of pulling the overweight, balding man in front of me backwards and taking a bite out of him. The space around us had miraculously increased. There was now a five foot wide circle surrounding us. No one seemed to notice. I figured it was vampire mojo at play. Luc's or mine, I couldn't tell.

Finally, it was our turn at the check-in desk. "I am Lucentio Black and this is Natalie Pierce," Luc said. I slanted him a look at the surname he'd given. It didn't sound very French to me. His accent didn't sound particularly French either. I was pretty sure he was Italian, but I didn't want to embarrass myself by asking. "I believe you should have records of the seats I purchased via the telephone."

Snorting a laugh at how archaic he sounded, I pretended I had a tickle in my throat and forced out an unconvincing cough.

"Identification?" the bored man behind the counter asked. Luc handed over two passports. I was torn between anxiety and curiosity. One of the passports was supposed to be mine. Opening the first passport, the clerk took a long look at Luc and verified he was the man in the photo. Opening the second passport, he frowned at the blank page and looked at me. Our eyes met and he was caught in my snare. A dreamy smile appeared on his face and stayed in place. "So pretty," he crooned.

"Tell him to give us our boarding passes," Luc murmured. I dutifully followed his directions and took the proffered items.

Receiving a few stares at our lack of baggage to be checked, we followed the steady stream of people to the x-ray machines and did the usual stripping off of our shoes and placing metal objects into plastic trays. My cross received a puzzled frown, but it was passed through as being acceptable. It was only dangerous to my kind.

In a daze of hunger, I allowed Luc to propel me towards our gate. I caught the eyes of several men during the journey, but my tall, dark guardian broke the contact each time. I sensed my prey would follow me blindly even to their deaths if he hadn't. Keeping my attention on the floor, I thought of the long flight ahead and of how very hungry I was going to be by the time we landed.

Miserable at the idea of the pit growing in my stomach again, I didn't take much notice of where I was being led. This probably didn't bode well for my future survival, but I was too hungry to care. Luc pushed open a door and I wrinkled my nose at the sudden stench of stale urine and fresh faeces. Spotting a line of urinals bolted to the wall, I opened my mouth to protest about being dragged into the men's room. Luc put a finger over my lips and indicated he heard someone coming.

Shuffling both of us to the side, Luc waited for the door to open, then grabbed the man that entered. Putting a hand over the unfortunate victim's mouth, he dragged him into the cubicle at the far end of the row. Luc sent me an impatient look over his shoulder. "Hurry, our flight leaves soon."

Sidling into the cubicle, I pulled the door shut and turned the flimsy lock. The vampire cop easily held the man quiet with a hand over his mouth and the other around his throat. We stood in a tight circle with our bodies pressed up against each other. How was a girl supposed to get into the mood to eat in a situation like this? *You don't have to be in the mood to eat, numb nuts.* No, I just had to be hungry. And hungry I was.

In his fifties, red faced, sweating and blubbering in terror, my snack wasn't very appealing despite my increasing appetite. Shaking my head, I tried to back away, but had nowhere to go. "I can't, Luc. Sorry, but he's just too pitiful."

Luc rolled his eyes impatiently. "You have to stop feeling sorry for them. You don't mean the man any harm. All you require is a little sustenance and then he can go free."

Perking up at that last part, the man started nodding frantically. He fumbled for his wallet in his back pocket and handed it over. Taking it doubtfully, I met his eyes and he was caught. Pale green and bloodshot from fear, they went blank and his entire body relaxed. Luc took his hands away and the man swayed toward me.

"I'll give you anything you want," my meal said. "Anything at all." He tried to reach for me, but Luc held his arms straight against his body.

Even taller than my companion, my snack's neck was too high for me to take a bite from. I went up to my tippy toes and he bent down for me, smacking his head into the cubicle door. In his hypnotized state he didn't even seem to feel the blow. My teeth sheared into his vein and he made a sound of pleasure as I fed.

Luc pulled me away too soon, but I let him. The pit in my stomach was half full again and I was in a comfortable state of contentment. With our interaction complete, Luc sat the snack down on the toilet and eased the door open. Taking a pristine white handkerchief from his pocket, he wiped a corner of my mouth. A tiny smear of red bloomed on the fabric. "You are going to persist in your annoying habit of butchering my name, aren't you?"

I nodded then shrugged. "It's the Australian way," I explained. "We all do it. I think it's in our blood." *Mmm, blood,* I thought dreamily.

With a huffy sigh, Luc checked that all was clear. I dropped my meal's wallet on his lap before leaving the bathroom. His Aussie cash wouldn't be of much use to me in Romania.

Luc sent me worried glances as we hurried towards our gate. Our flight must have been called minutes ago because we were at the tail end of the line. A few stragglers were left ahead of us.

I managed to regain some focus by the time we took our seats. It was a pleasant surprise to be seated in first class.

After the twentieth cautious glance from Luc, I turned to face him. "What?"

"Now that you have fed your blood hunger," he said quietly, "I am waiting for your flesh hunger to rise."

"Going to take another one for the team, huh?" It was uncharacteristically cynical of me, but I figured I'd earned a bit of cynicism over the past few days after what I'd been through. "Don't worry about it. I took care of it in the...," I trailed off when I realized what I was about to divulge. "Never mind." I'd suffered enough embarrassment without spilling the beans about my solo shower gratification.

"I have to mind," he argued. "You are new and cannot control yourself yet. It is my job to make sure you don't expose us."

Grumpily turning away, I looked out the dark window as the plane prepared to take off. Luc's pale reflection stared at me over my shoulder. "I don't feel hungry in that way," I mumbled and ignored the twinge of heat inside that made me a liar.

"When your hunger does rise, let me know." Settling back against his seat, Luc folded his hands neatly across his stomach and proceeded to ignore me.

"Sure, we'll just cram inside the toilet and have a quickie," I muttered to myself sarcastically, then turned as far away from him as I could. The idea of a quickie in the bathroom actually didn't sound that bad. *Don't even think about it,* I scolded myself. I might be a vampire and subject to hideous hungers, but I still had my dignity, or so I told myself.

This wasn't my first time on a plane, but I'd never been out of Australia before. I was now about to travel to

Europe, via Singapore. Soon, we'd be thirty-odd thousand feet in the air. If something horrible happened and the plane went down, what would happen to us? Since we were already undead, would we die again when our bodies were smashed to pieces? What exactly did it take to kill us anyway? Apart from a cross speared through your heart, that was. I'd stumbled across that particular killing method all on my own.

Disturbed by the direction my thoughts had taken, I turned to find my companion waiting with a raised eyebrow. He could either read my mind, or I telegraphed what I was thinking harder than I thought I was. "What sort of things can kill us?" I asked very quietly, practically mouthing the words.

"Fire. Holy objects. Holy water. Being pierced through the heart. Beheading. Sunlight. Consuming the blood of our kin." The list was short and about what I'd expected. Except for that last one. I'd never heard of that before.

"So, if we fell from thirty thousand feet, we'd survive?"

Thinking about it, he shrugged. "You might. I would probably not. The impact would most likely shatter my body beyond repair." I pictured Luc as a runny, splattered, bloody pancake and held in a shudder.

"What would happen to me?"

Taking my left hand, he gingerly examined the cross mark without touching it. He met my eyes briefly. "I do not know."

On impulse, I took his hand in mine. He went rigid, then relaxed when he didn't burst into flames. "I should have known it wouldn't hurt me. After all, this is not the first time you have put your hands on my naked skin." His tone was suggestive and he slid his gaze across to my face slyly.

I yanked my hand free. "We're not talking about that. It never happened."

"My spine took half an hour to heal," he said conversationally. "You're very strong."

I remembered snapping the metal crosses off the sarcophagi easily and vaulting over fences in search of a dog blanket. I'd never been particularly athletic before and it was still a novelty to me. For a moment, I almost felt special. Then reality set in again. I was Mortis, doom of the vampire race. It was unfair that I would be the total destruction of beings I'd never truly believed existed. Why couldn't I have been an ordinary vampire? *Because if you were, you'd currently be bowing and scraping for Silvius. Would you prefer that?* It was a toss-up; being a slave to a creepy old man for eternity, or being the curse of the undead.

It was a long flight and I eventually grew bored enough to engage my vampire companion in conversation. "Ok," I turned to him to ask, "so, if we're real, then other myths and legends must be, too."

Slanting a look at me, Luc crossed his arms and shook his head as the flight attendant appeared to ask if we wanted anything. I waited for her to walk away before continuing. "What myths and legends do you have in mind?"

"How about werewolves?"

"No." His response was immediate and final.

"Oh." I thought for sure they had to be real if we were. If werewolves didn't exist, then who were our natural enemies? *Duh, that would be me.* "What about zombies?" I was almost disappointed when he shook his head.

"Witches? Wizards? Unicorns? Fairies? Giants? Leprechauns? Hobbits? Ghosts?" Each one was followed by a shake of his head. I was exasperated by now. "What about aliens?"

This time, Luc hesitated. Most of the other passengers were sleeping. Snores and a few quiet murmurs surrounded us. We'd turned our lights off so we wouldn't draw attention to ourselves more than we already did due to our weird vampire charisma. We were easily able to see each other in the dim cabin light.

"There is a legend," he began, leaning in toward me, "that says we are descended from a being that was not originally from our planet."

"Are you talking about little green men with creepily big heads and gigantic black eyes?" Despite myself, I leaned in closer to hear his answer, fighting down an urge to giggle at the idea of a spaceman being the creator of vampires.

"Whatever it was, it was here long before mankind crawled out of their caves. It is said that the creature, our Father," he made a slight face at the title, "made a bargain with a human who then became the first of our kind. Our Father sealed their bargain by feeding the First his blood."

"What was the bargain?"

Luc's reply was his usual shrug. "He offered the First immortality."

I mulled this over with a frown. "I wonder what our dear old Dad got out of their deal?" I mused.

"That is something no one knows," Luc said broodingly.

My new friend didn't seem inclined towards further conversation, so I spent the rest of the trip watching movies. My hearing was so sensitive that I could hear what others in my general vicinity were watching through their headsets.

Bright lights caught my attention as we neared Singapore. I stared at the dazzling sight until we were too low to see them anymore. Upon touchdown, Luc hurried us to the head of the line and we were the first off the plane.

Minutes after we finally bamboozled our way through customs, we were in a taxi and were heading for a hotel. Our driver sent frequent glances at us in his rear view mirror. Ok, he sent frequent looks at *me* in his mirror. I'd been careful not to catch his eye and accidentally hypnotize him. The last thing we needed was a zombie for a driver.

Our hotel for the day was far less luxurious than the one we'd stayed at briefly in Brisbane. The two women manning the reception desk were valiantly trying to pretend they weren't half asleep. Since it was nearing sunrise, I couldn't blame them for their tiredness. I was also feeling the tell-tale signs that meant I would go down for the day shortly.

Noticing me suddenly beginning to blink owlishly, Luc quickly paid for our room and took the key card. He guided me to the elevator with a steadying hand on my elbow. "Just another couple of minutes, Natalie," he soothed, but that was two minutes too long for me and my circuits shut down.

Snapping awake far quicker than usual, I found myself sitting in a cramped, uncomfortable chair with my head resting against the wall. Slightly confused and wondering why I wasn't lying in a bed, the seat suddenly shook from side to side and my eyes sprang open. A quick examination of my surroundings told me that I wasn't in a normal chair at all. I was buckled into a seat on a plane and had no recollection of how I'd gotten there.

"Ladies and gentlemen, we are experiencing some heavy turbulence at the moment." a woman announced over the speaker system. "We ask that you remain in your seats until the seatbelt sign is switched off," She gave the message in both French and English to cover both bases.

Calmly sitting beside me with his headphones on, Luc raised an eyebrow inquiringly when I glared at him. "Is there a problem?" he asked quietly.

"How the hell did you get me to the airport, through security and onto the plane?"

"I told anyone who enquired about your health that you were narcoleptic," he replied with a shrug.

"Narcoleptic?" It came out higher pitched than I'd intended and a few heads turned in my direction. "That's the best story you could come up with?"

"It worked, didn't it?" Clearly annoyed that I wasn't impressed by his cleverness, Luc turned his attention back to whatever program he'd been watching while I'd been unconscious.

We spent the next twelve hours ignoring each other. From time to time, I left my window seat in the pretence that I needed to visit the facilities. In reality, I did it to annoy Luc. The elderly man in the aisle seat didn't mind getting up to let me out. He needed to visit the bathroom even more often than I pretended I needed to.

Part way into the sixth or possibly seventh inflight movie in a row, I turned to the window and squinted at the slight hint of greyness. Hadn't it been pitch black just a moment ago? What would happen to us after we landed and it was full daylight? Incineration was my first and only guess. I had enough time to turn my head with the intention of asking Luc what his next clever plan was when darkness struck.

Chapter Eleven

When I woke next, it was to find myself lying face-down in someone's lap. Sitting up, I tried to scramble away, but didn't get very far before my back hit a firm object. After a few seconds of confusion, I realized I was in a car. Black curtains had been drawn on all the windows, preventing any moonlight from illuminating the back seat. Three other vampires were in the car with me. I recognized one of them and sagged in relief.

"If you're in the mood," the strange vampire beside me smirked with a heavy accent, "you can lie back down again and finish the job." He gestured at his crotch where an unimpressive bulge had appeared.

Luc sent a withering glare over his shoulder. "Behave yourself, Geordie."

Geordie sent a sarcastic salute at the vampire cop and sat back to sulk. He was young, maybe fifteen in mortal years. God only knew how old he was in actual years. He sulked exactly like a normal teenager would have, with his bottom lip stuck out and his arms crossed. His hair was a messy dirty blond and his eyes a dark, stormy blue. His pupils were gigantic. The blue was just a faint touch of colour around the edges. I wondered how old a vamp had to be before their irises completely disappeared.

An older man was behind the wheel. He might have been fifty or so when he'd been turned. His black hair was coarse and what I could see of his face was grizzled. He barked something foreign at Luc and peered at me briefly in the rear view mirror. I translated the words in my head to be along the lines of 'We'll be there soon'.

Turning, Luc sent me a reassuring smile that wasn't quite genuine. I could sense his worry and immediately tensed. If he was worried, then I should be in a state of panic. "Igor says we'll be there soon." I marvelled at how eerily his words echoed my translation of what the driver had said. It had to be a coincidence.

Both Geordie and Igor wore the kind of clothing I associated with farm work. Dark brown pants had been teamed up with matching jackets and plain white t-shirts. In my jeans and dark green sweater, I didn't really fit in. Neither did Luc in his stylish black clothes. Both of us were overdressed.

Pushing aside the dense curtain, I saw farmland, scrub and not much else. I wasn't sure if vampires could suffer from jetlag, but I felt like I'd been out of it for longer than usual.

"Where are we heading?" I asked the car in general. I thought we were supposed to be heading for Romania. Shouldn't we be on another plane? Maybe we were already in Romania and I'd spent the bulk of the journey in an unconscious state. It was a slight comfort to know I couldn't drool anymore. I couldn't humiliate myself in that way at least.

"We are going to the Court," Geordie replied in his now obviously French accent.

I caught Luc's warning glance not to blurt out anything stupid. I'd always wanted to travel and France was definitely on my list of places I wanted to see. Now of course I'd only be seeing it at night. That was if I survived my encounter with the rulers of vampirekind. It looked like I'd have to pretend to have a vestige of class after all. *You have about as much class as a dog with mange.* I couldn't argue with my subconscious when it was unquestionably right.

Igor turned down a driveway that extended far into what seemed to be a large estate. Several men and women moved around the grounds, mowing the grass, clipping hedges and tidying up in general. From their unnaturally pale skin, it wasn't hard to figure out that they were like us. Besides, I was pretty sure humans didn't tend gardens in the dark.

Discovering I'd been killed only to rise as a vampire's servant had been a short-lived shock that I'd quickly gotten over. Not the vampire bit, that would take a few centuries to get used to. The idea of being anyone's servant for all time had been the source of the shock. After killing my maker, I'd become my own person again. These poor bastards would be servants for all eternity. I mulled over the idea that they might be happy for me to destroy them all. Who the hell wanted to mow grass for several thousand years?

My musings were interrupted as we pulled up in front of a magnificent manor house. It was four stories high, with

J.C. DIEM

the main building made of sandstone. Two wings of some kind of darker stone spread out to either side. I gaped up at the building while Luc retrieved our bags from the back. Two men dressed in old fashioned livery of red jackets and pants, white wigs, white gloves and knee high black boots, bowed to Luc and ignored the rest of us. The servant was British and spoke with an upper-crust English accent. "The Councillors await you in the ballroom, Lord Lucentio. A servant will escort you to them after you have freshened up."

'Lord' Lucentio handed me the bags, then crooked his finger, clearly expecting me to tag along behind him like an obedient dog. Geordie smirked at me, then pouted when Igor smacked him in the back of the head. The grizzled chauffeur then clicked his fingers for the boy to follow him. They slouched off down a gravelled path that led toward the back of the mansion with Geordie rubbing his head. Left with little choice, I tagged along after Luc, carrying our bags like a lowly porter.

Inside the mansion, soft lighting from crystal chandeliers in the high ceilings spilled down to illuminate what I could only describe as sheer opulence. Dusky pink wallpaper with rose patterns covered the walls. Thick maroon carpet graced the floors. Antique, highly polished furniture in some kind of dark wood adorned the place. Priceless paintings, or so I assumed since I wasn't an art critic, hung on the walls. Luc caught me by my elbow when I tripped over my own feet from gawking at the splendour. His warning glare was enough for me to rein in my curiosity.

We were led up a sweeping staircase to the fourth floor and down a hallway to a bedroom suite. Thanking the servant, Luc closed the door and hustled me through the bedroom and into the bathroom. I caught a glimpse of a magnificent king-size bed and large fireplace before the door closed.

Luc paced the maroon tiled floor while I slumped against the door and dropped our luggage to the floor. He seemed to be agitated, which didn't fill me with confidence for our situation. "So," I ventured, "care to update me on how we ended up here?"

Ceasing his pacing, Luc leaned against the maroon sink and ran a hand through his hair. The whole room was done in tones of red, including the towels hanging neatly on racks. I believed the colour was as close to fresh blood as the decorators could manage. Privately, I thought it was tacky, but I wasn't about to voice my opinion out loud.

"We were met by guards sent from the Court upon landing."

"Am I the only one who has to sleep during the day?" I complained.

"Older vampires can resist the need to sleep for a time if needed." So, I just had to wait for a few hundred years before I wouldn't fall unconscious on my face at sunrise. *Good to know.* "They were dressed in military uniforms, which allowed us to be taken aside to avoid customs," he explained. It was a clever tactic and if I hadn't been kidnapped by these pretend soldiers, I would have felt more impressed. Instead, I felt annoyed and almost violated at being manhandled in my sleep, again. "We were bundled into the back of an enclosed truck during the daylight hours."

"So, someone just carried me around like a sack of unconscious potatoes?" At Luc's shrug, my mouth sagged open. "How were you planning to get me through customs in that state?"

"The same way I got you onto the flight in the first place. I have done this before, Natalie." His tone implied he'd done it many times and that I shouldn't be concerned. *Screw that.* I was completely vulnerable when the sun came up. How was I supposed to trust a man, a *vampire*, who I'd only just met? *You must trust him to some extent, you jumped his bones for Christ's sake!* I didn't want to think about that, so chose to ignore it.

"What exactly is going on? Why were we brought here?" I sensed our situation was dire, but that was mainly going by Luc's reactions.

"I am not sure," Luc replied uneasily. "The guards were waiting at the airport, but I do not believe they were specifically waiting for me. I could hardly tell them I had pressing business elsewhere and had little choice but to pretend I was heading for the mansion. Igor was sent to retrieve us. Moments before you woke, he informed me that the Councillors seem to be recalling the members of the Court."

If my blood had still been able to run through my veins, it would have run cold. "Do they know who I am?" I should have phrased the question did they know *what* I was.

"Not yet. Hopefully they will not discover your true identity." Resuming his pacing, Luc thought furiously. "Igor advised me that there have been portents of your birth." At my quizzical look, he explained. "The moon turned blood red the night you awakened as one of us. Several animals and one child in this area were born with two heads over the past few days. I'm betting the occurrence wasn't restricted just to France. Milk went instantly sour when poured. There are more signs, but you don't need to hear them all."

Great, now I was giving off portents of doom. *What do vampires need milk for?* It seemed unimportant so I didn't ask. At least I knew why my milk had gone off so quickly now. I'd never have guessed that I'd been responsible for it.

"How are you going to explain my presence?" I hoped he had a plan because I was fresh out of ideas.

"Igor assumed you are my newly made servant and I did not correct him. The word will spread quickly." He gave me a small, bitter smile. "I'm afraid you might be a curiosity for a short while, but no one will attach any real importance to you."

I was supposed to be Luc's servant? I stared at him in disbelief. "Do you really think anyone will fall for me being your servant?"

"They will if you behave appropriately and don't call attention to yourself." We shared a grimace at the likelihood of that happening. "Just do as I say and act humble," he instructed.

Humble? I'd heard of the word of course, but it was difficult to apply the concept to myself. In exasperation, Luc gave me a series of quick instructions. "Do not meet anyone's eyes. Stay two steps behind me at all times. Obey my every word instantly. When I do this," he pointed at the ground, "drop to your knees and touch your head to the floor."

"You've got to be kidding," I whined, then jumped at a knock on the outer door. We'd been practically whispering, but I was still worried we might have been overheard. My hearing had become more sensitive since I'd become the living dead. I assumed this meant all vampires could hear things human ears couldn't.

Striding over to me, Luc placed his hands on my shoulders. His expression was utterly serious. "Do you want to survive, Natalie?" I nodded, eyes so wide they must have been bulging out of my face. "Then never, under any circumstances, show this to anyone." He lifted my hand to reveal the cross on my palm. "There are nine Councillors who run the Court, but the one who is really in charge is known as the Comtesse. Our lives can be crushed at her merest whim."

"What is a Comtesse exactly?" I was guessing it was some kind of French nobility.

"In English the word would be 'Countess'." It was nice to be right for once. I hadn't met this Comtesse yet and I already didn't like her. "Quickly," Luc continued, "we must attend the Councillors before they become suspicious."

Staying the required two steps behind my pretend maker, I followed him through the bedroom and out into the hallway. Another liveried servant bowed, then led us down to the second floor. Almost trotting to keep up, I resisted the urge to gawp like a country bumpkin again as we entered an immense ballroom.

Dark red drapes covered the windows. They swept from just below the ceiling to almost brush the floor. The floor was polished wood, stained the same dark shade as the antique furniture. I wondered how many of these creatures had been alive when the four or five hundred year old furniture had first been made. Most? All? For all I knew, some of these people might be thousands of years old.

Silvius had been. He'd been alive a thousand years before Jesus had even been born. A feeling of unreality swept through me. It was difficult to believe this was really happening to me, that I was really standing somewhere in France amongst a crowd of my fellow undead.

I'd felt overdressed in the car, but now I felt way underdressed in the room full of vampires. The men all wore black tuxedos with blood red cummerbunds. Their gazes measured me, some lingering, some dismissing me instantly. The women wore dresses in a range of styles and colours and all were breathtaking. Pale breasts all but overflowed from their low cut gowns. Gold chains and sparkling gems abounded. Low, contemptuous laughter rippled through the room and I assumed it was aimed at poor raggedy little me. At least two hundred vampires were in the room, but there was still plenty of space for more.

A stage had been erected at the far end of the room so that the nine seated vampires could look down upon their minions. After one quick scan, I summed them up as being ancient, deadly and extremely pompous. Several fidgeted, unwittingly displaying their nervousness. Six were male and the other three were female. They wore elaborate clothing that made the rest of the creatures in the room look like they were wearing rags.

As ordered, I kept my eyes on the ground after that single brief look around. My curiosity was overshadowed by my sense of self preservation. Luc swept down the centre of the room and I was unwillingly drawn along behind him. We stopped a few feet away from the stage and Luc pointed at the ground with his left hand. Gritting my teeth, I dropped to my knees and touched my head to the floor. Being a Lord, he simply went to one knee and bowed his head. *Never again,* I fumed silently. This kind of subservience might be acceptable, or even expected in Europe. In Australia, you'd get a swift boot up the arse if you pulled this kind of pretentiousness on your servants.

"Lord Lucentio," a female voice tittered. "How fortunate that you have returned to us." Her accent was hard to understand. English did not come naturally to her and I wondered why she bothered. Was it for my benefit? That was laughable simply because I was so insignificant. Besides, how could she possibly know I didn't understand French? *Because Luc had been sent to Australia to kill Silvius and he came back with me in tow. Being Australian, I most likely don't speak French.* It seemed like a logical conclusion to me.

"I am glad to be of service, my Lady." Inclining his head again, Luc must have sensed my bile rise because he shot me a warning look.

Stiff clothing rustled as she rose, followed by dainty footsteps. Pointy gold shoes came to a stop in front of me. "What is this? Have you made yourself a servant, Lucentio? After so many centuries of resistance, have you finally chosen a new bed mate?" At Luc's silence, she impatiently kicked my hand. "Stand up, servant, let me look at you." I bit my bottom lip to contain an expletive when my hand went numb from the blow. I was not enjoying the experience of being treated like a dog.

Luc rose to his feet. As he did, he tucked a hand beneath my elbow and smoothly pulled me up to stand beside him. As ordered, I made sure I didn't meet the head vampire's eyes. Even in four inch heels, the Comtesse was barely the same height as me. Her dress was the same shade of gold as her shoes. The neckline was higher than most and only the tops of her breasts peeked out through the lace. Her waist had been cinched in so tightly that it was a good thing she didn't need to breathe. The tiny waist emphasized her voluptuously rounded hips. Her hair rose in an elaborate white up-do, giving her several more inches of height. I felt her derision as she inspected me from head to toe.

Making an impatient gesture at me, she followed up with a command. "Let us see what the great appeal is. Surely you must be remarkable to have captured Lord Lucentio's eye. Take your clothes off, servant."

Cutting a look sideways, I caught Luc's stiff nod to comply. *She's got to be kidding.* She wasn't. I felt her cold stare burning into me and knew that to defy her would end in my undoing. Silvius had been crazy, but even he hadn't given off the aura of evil that this dainty creature did. She would think nothing of ending my existence. This I sensed even without meeting her sharp gaze. *Ah fuck it.* I might pale in comparison to most of the beauties in the room, but at least I wasn't completely hideous. Thanks to my transformation from alive to unalive, my face and figure had improved. If the old hag wanted to see me naked so desperately, then so be it.

Keeping my gaze lowered like the good servant I was pretending to be, I felt Luc's tenseness as I stripped off as ordered. Standing in my bare skin, I held back a shiver and did my best to ignore the avid stares. *Thank God I had a bikini wax recently.*

"She is attractive enough, I suppose," said the Comtesse after a lengthy inspection. "If you like skeletons in your bed." At her snide comment, titters ran through the crowd. I heard a hint of disappointment in her tone that I hadn't made a fuss about being naked in front of a couple hundred people. Maybe she was in a bad mood and was looking for someone to take it out on. I was going to make a fuss all right, but not here and not now. To do so would mean my instant death and possibly Luc's as well.

At another hand twitch from Luc, I dressed myself and waited for further instructions. I had a tight hold of the anger that wanted to burst out of me and throttle either Luc, or the Comtesse. Possibly both.

Satisfied that my humiliation had sunk in, the Comtesse spoke a few words in French and the crowd began to mingle. I kept the required two steps behind my pretend maker, willing my face to remain blank. From the corner of my eye, I took in the true ruler of vampirekind.

Her skin was even paler than mine and was almost ghostly white. A light dusting of old fashioned white face powder sat on her skin. It didn't sink in like it would have if her body had been warmer than room temperature. I'd thought her hair was white, but it was actually a very light blonde. Her black eyes were set wide apart, reminding me of a praying mantis. Her lips, painted bright red, were thin and showed a hint of fang. It was impossible to tell how old she was in mortal years. I grudgingly supposed she was beautiful in an exotic way. Considering the ill will I currently felt towards her, even conceding that was a chore.

Taking Luc's arm possessively, she drew him aside for a private conversation. They kept their voices down, but I overheard snatches of 'Mortis, 'doom of us all', 'must be stopped', 'consult the Prophet' and more along that vein. The Comtesse might be smiling, but beneath her amusement was a quiet desperation. I became aware that every vampire in the room shared her fear. I was their bogyman and they'd just made me strip down like a cheap hooker. In all honestly, I didn't think this looked good for their survival as a species.

Chapter Twelve

An interminable hour or so later, Luc made his excuses and we were graciously allowed to retire. A servant escorted us back to our suite, just in case we'd forgotten the way. Either that, or it was to make sure we weren't going to steal anything.

Luc closed and locked our door, then shot a wary glance my way. I stood at the end of the bed with my arms crossed, staring into space. "Are you angry?" His question was spoken softly and with great caution.

I turned my head slowly in his direction and cocked it to the side as I pondered his question. "Angry? Me? Why should I be?" As if I'd just remembered, I smacked myself in the forehead. "Oh, that's right, you just made me strip naked in a room full of strangers!"

Normally when I was this enraged, my chest would be heaving and veins would be standing out on my forehead. The only visible sign of my extreme anger this time was in my clenched hands and slight trembling. I'd kept a tight rein on my emotions for too long and they were about to spill out.

"Give me one reason why I shouldn't scrag all of their arses and release Mort-" before I could finish the word, Luc was across the room with his hand over my mouth. Wrestling me into the bathroom, he closed the door.

"You must be very careful not to speak that name," he whispered with his hand still over my mouth.

When he cautiously released me and stepped back, I paced the few steps away that the bathroom would allow then paced back again. "They," I pointed down to the second floor beneath us, "are a pack of arseholes." I said it in a whisper-shout that probably hadn't carried much further than halfway down the outside hallway.

Leaning wearily against the door, Luc didn't try to deny it. His expression was sad and almost forlorn. "Those 'arseholes' are the closest creatures I have to a family."

Taken aback, I felt my anger draining away. I knew what it was like not to have any family. I'd been alone for nine years now. Sometimes, it felt like I'd always been alone. Something the Comtesse said came back to me. "What did the praying mantis mean about your centuries of resistance?"

Staring over my head, Luc crossed his arms. "I do not want to talk about that."

"Ok. How about we talk about me being forced to strip naked so two hundred perverts could point and laugh at me?" Now my anger was back, pulsing in my head, making my hungers rise. "Do you have any idea how humiliating that was?"

Luc shot me a wise, knowing and somehow ashamed look. "Unfortunately, I know very well. There are worse things, Natalie Pierce, than being forced to merely shed your clothing for strangers."

Another knock came at the outer door. Luc hid his dread well and went to answer it. I followed reluctantly and was relieved when my pretend maker motioned me to stay behind this time. He closed the door and followed the liveried man down the hall. Like a good pretend servant, I remained in the room as ordered.

Tense, nervous and bored, I took a shower and borrowed the blow drier I found in the cupboards beneath the maroon sink. At least the ancient creatures were capable of using electricity and modern tools. Wearing a fluffy red towel, I searched through my backpack and pulled out fresh clothes. It might be spring in France, but it was still pretty cold. I couldn't seem to rid myself of a constant chill. Judging by the low but well-tended fire, I wasn't the only one lacking essential body heat.

There wasn't much to see in the suite, just the bed, a couple of bedside tables, a large dresser and a sturdy wardrobe. A quick search in the bedside table revealed a lone book that had been pushed to the back and then forgotten. I pulled it out, lay down on my stomach on the bed and began to read without bothering to check the title.

Several hours later, familiar footsteps approached. The door opened and I deigned to flick a glance up at Luc. He closed and locked the door, then began pacing up and down. I continued to read, engrossed in a story of fiery love, lust and betrayal. The novel had been written well over a hundred years ago. The language was hard to decipher at times, but it was better than sitting around twiddling my thumbs.

Luc stopped pacing and bent to read the title. "I did not know you spoke French."

"I don't," I replied and turned the page.

"Then how can you possibly be reading that book?"

I focussed on the foreign words and dropped the book as if it was on fire. Had I spontaneously taught myself how to read a foreign language? "I, ah, hmm." I couldn't come up with an explanation.

Luc rattled off a string of words at me. "What did I just say?" he demanded.

Trying to remember it all, I wrinkled my brow. "Something along the lines of 'this should not be possible, the Prophet never mentioned such a thing, if the Comtesse finds out she will flay the skin from us both'." The words sank in and I was on my feet in a flash, stuffing my dirty clothes into my backpack.

"What are you doing?" Luc asked.

"I'm leaving." I thought it was pretty obvious, but maybe that was just me.

"Dawn is almost upon us. We won't be going anywhere until nightfall," he pointed out.

At that warning I felt instantly and tremendously tired. Lurching toward the bed, I dropped onto it face-first and knew no more.

Waking to the sensation of strong arms around me and a chest at my back, I stretched and luxuriated in the sensation. I rarely had one night stands, but I'd obviously gotten lucky last night. It was funny, I'd had the longest and weirdest dream of my life. I dreamt that I'd been attacked by a crazy old vampire and had been turned into something called Mortis. I'd had fantastic sex with a guy called Lucentio and had flown to France. Then I'd had to strip naked in front of a bunch of vampire perverts and had somehow learned how to interpret French.

"Good evening, Natalie," an accented voice whispered into my ear and I knew it had all been real.

"Ah, crap," I moaned and pulled the pillow over my face. If I'd been able to, I would have suffocated myself to death.

Luc's hands tightened around me, then one rose to cup my breast. This time he'd only stripped off my shoes and sweater instead of stripping me completely naked. His lips tickled the back of my neck when he spoke. "Since you are pretending to be my servant, perhaps you could provide me with your...services." He ground his pelvis into my backside suggestively.

Rolling away, I put the pillow between us. Luc smiled knowingly, probably well aware of the flesh hunger that was currently raging through me. "Sure," I replied brightly, "just as soon as you explain your centuries of resistance, et cetera."

Luc's smile disappeared and a small frown took its place. "We should get going," he said heavily.

"Going where?" I asked, then scrambled out of bed and started searching for my shoes.

"To the very place we wished to go," was his enigmatic reply. Unlike me, Luc was completely naked. Pale white, he was as perfectly formed as a Greek statue. I remembered breaking his spine from intense pleasure and wished I could do it again. Turning away before he could detect my lust, I laced up my shoes and pulled my sweater over my head.

After a moment or two, I remembered what our original plan had been before we'd been waylaid by the Councillor's guards. "So, we're off to Romania, huh?"

"Yes. The Councillors, and by that I mean the Comtesse, wish for me to check to see if the Prophet has any new information for us. We leave immediately."

"Why doesn't she just pick up a phone and call the guy?"

Luc gave me a rueful smile. "She doesn't trust telephones."

"C-C-C. Cripes," I substituted for 'Christ' and ignored Luc's fleeting grin at my stutter. "She really needs to get with the times." Personally, I was glad to be leaving the place. All in all, we'd gotten off very lightly considering I had been prophesized to kill most of the vampires in the building.

With our bags in hand, I kept two steps behind Luc as we were guided by a red suited servant to the ground floor and then outside. It was drizzling and after taking a few steps, a fine mist clung to my face like cobwebs. The same black car awaited us with Igor as the driver again. Geordie sat in the back with his arms crossed, clearly sulking. I climbed in beside him and gave him a curt nod.

Brightening, he slid closer and put an arm around my shoulders. "It is a long drive to the airport, *chérie*," he said in a low voice. "Perhaps we could keep each other company." His wink was sly and far too old for his young face.

"Hey, Luc," I said to the back of my pretend maker's head, "Geordie wants to have sex with me in the back seat. What do you think?"

"I think," he replied without turning around, "that Geordie should keep his distance from my servant."

Sliding away again, Geordie eyed me speculatively. "So, the rumours are true. He finally made a servant after swearing he would not."

Barking something over his shoulder, Igor put his foot down on the accelerator and the car surged forward. My ears heard an unintelligible language that wasn't French and might have been Russian. My brain translated it just fine: "Keep your mouth shut, servant. Do not speak of things you have no knowledge of."

I smirked at Geordie as he subsided back into his sulk. My curiosity about Luc increased. What did I really know about him? He was a vampire version of a cop. He was possibly Italian. He'd flown to Australia to take down my maker and any others from the faction that supposedly supported me. Instead of trying to kill me on the spot after finding out who and what I was, he'd flown me halfway across the world. Instead of ratting me out to the Comtesse and Councillors, he'd pretended I was his servant. Everybody seemed to be amazed that he had chosen someone after apparently going centuries without his own personal slave. I wanted to know more about him, but I didn't want to ask while we had company.

At the small airport, Igor dropped us off, then took off without ceremony. The black car disappeared and we were on our own. I presumed this was the same airport we had arrived in, but I had no recollection of it. We headed straight to the check-in desk. We had a female clerk this time so my powers would be fairly useless. Luc pulled his vampire mojo and got her to hand over the boarding passes without question. It really was handy being able to bamboozle humans.

Hungry for blood, I was too preoccupied and worried to do anything about it at the moment. On the plane, I sat several rows behind Luc. I tried not to feel like an abandoned child who expected a grownup to scoop her up and rescue her. I might have been twenty-eight in human years, but as the undead I was still brand new.

An elderly woman with blue hair that had been recently permed sat beside me. She wore an expensively tailored linen suit in the same shade as her hair. She'd drenched herself in lavender perfume and the smell was overpowering. Maybe that was just my vampire senses at work, but I doubted it. All around me I could hear the quiet whispers of my fellow passengers as plainly as if their conversations were happening right next to me. Most were in foreign languages, but my strange and quirky mind translated them all.

An announcement came over the speakers to say that our flight was delayed due to a mechanical problem. Groans issued around the plane. After half an hour of listening in to the private conversations around me, I was bored. People spoke about the lamest things. I tried to remember if I'd been that boring and realized I probably had been. All the things that had once worried me had faded into insignificance; being unable to pay the rent, rats chewing a way into my bedroom, not finding shoes in my size, never having enough food in the cupboards, rats eating me while I slept, getting mugged on the way home from work, losing my job, rats feasting on my tongue as I tried to scream for help. The list went on and on, mostly focussed on how much I feared and hated rats.

Now there were only three things that I worried about; blood, sex and survival. Most prominent right now was survival. I'd always thought the earth was a big place and that if I ever wanted to disappear it would be easy. I'd just have to choose a destination, sell enough of my belongings to buy a plane ticket and fly off into the sunset. Now I wondered if I would be able to hide from the Comtesse, the other Councillors and the Court when they finally discovered who I was. As for flying off into the sunset, I might as well douse myself in petrol and light a match. It would have the same effect.

After two and a half hours of waiting, we were finally cleared to take off. Sitting up as high as I could without actually standing, I peered over the seat in front of me and spied Luc's arm on the armrest a few rows ahead. As if sensing my scrutiny, his head turned and his face came into view. One eyebrow went up in silent query. I nodded to indicate I was fine and sank back down out of sight again. It was pathetic, but I felt reassured after seeing my brooding companion checking on me.

Why was Luc helping me? What was in it for him? *Maybe he wants to see the destruction of his race.* I didn't know why that thought popped into my head. I didn't know him well enough to make that kind of guess. Maybe I was projecting my own wishful thinking into the equation. What I'd seen of vampires so far hadn't been flattering. It seemed the more powerful they were, the bigger arsehole they turned into. I had the feeling that Silvius had been very powerful indeed. *Yeah, well look at him now,* I scoffed inwardly. The great and powerful Silvius had been reduced to a stinky puddle by a brand new vampire. Sure, it hadn't been planned. I'd killed him in sheer self-defence, not to mention by accident. I wondered what I could do if I really put my mind to it.

A snore came from my right, then I was engulfed in a cloud of lavender as the old lady's head came to rest on my shoulder. Grimacing at the flowery smell, I peered around her to see the passenger in the aisle seat was also asleep. His mouth was open and drool ran down his chin. Moving slowly and carefully, I put a hand beneath the old lady's blue head and gently shoved her upright. When she began to slide toward me again, I pushed her further to the right. When her head was resting on the drooler's shoulder, I sat back and stared out through the dark window. Trapped in the window seat, I was almost glad to be undead during the six and a half hour flight. Without any form of circulation, at least I didn't get cramped. I also didn't need to climb out to go to the toilet.

My thoughts were going around in circles and were getting me nowhere. I needed a diversion. Pulling out the French romance book, I switched on the overhead light and began to read. Reading without the light might have been suspicious and I didn't want to stand out if I could help it.

Now that I knew I was reading a foreign language, it took me longer to translate the words. I was just as captivated by the story as I'd been when I'd had no idea I was magically reading French. Who knew cheesy romance novels could be so entertaining? Especially one that had been written before my grandparents had been born.

Eventually, the captain pronounced that we were about to land. I wondered how far away dawn was. I had a feeling it was closer than I'd like thanks to our lengthy delay before taking off.

Luc appeared as soon as the plane coasted to a stop and we were cleared to disembark. The old lady squawked when he reached across and dragged me out of my seat. My legs scraped across the drooler and the old lady rather rudely. I shot them an apologetic look when I was plonked back on my feet.

"Have some patience, young man!" My mind translated the old lady's words half a second after she said them. Luc ignored her and yanked my backpack from the locker above and shoved it into my arms.

Startled stares followed us as he bullied his way through the line, pulling me after him. "Jeez, what's the rush?" I complained. I'd barely had time to shoulder my backpack before he'd started dragging me along like a naughty kid.

Flicking a glance at his watch, Luc pointed to the windows. "Dawn is near and we must be under cover before it arrives." The windows were still dark, but I could now sense what he could. The earth was rolling closer and closer toward the sun.

Motivated not to fall unconscious and draw unwanted attention to us, I hustled along beside him as we exited the plane. It was my turn to use my mojo on the customs officer after close to an hour of waiting for our turn. Six feet tall with wide, manly shoulders, she sported an extremely short buzz cut hairdo. I could see her scalp through her dark hair. After one look at Luc, she dismissed him instantly. The smile she gave me was unprofessionally warm. *Ok, she is clearly into girls.* Luc sent me a sardonic grin and I unleashed my new charm on the officer. She let us go through with a huge smile, missing my fake passport completely and stamping the counter instead.

Without baggage to claim, there was no need to hang around the airport. We headed straight to the rental car desks. Luc chose a desk with a female clerk and managed to procure a small, foreign car without providing any identification. Taking the keys, he grabbed my hand and we fast walked toward the exit.

I was beginning to feel lethargic now as sleep came knocking. "I'm not going to make it," I slurred as Luc pushed the door open. Whatever magic had created our kind was too powerful for me to fight. It demanded that I sleep and I was helpless to disobey.

"I will take care of you, Natalie," Luc promised. My feet left the ground and wind began swishing past me as he scooped me up and broke into a run. I would have felt safer if his promise hadn't sounded quite so grim.

Chapter Thirteen

Sleeping in the back seat of a car the size of a can of tuna wasn't comfortable, I discovered when I woke. Luc was still asleep, squashed beneath me with his knees bent almost to his chest and his neck bent at an awkward angle. I was half on him, half on the floor. Touching Luc's pale and clammy face, I revised my idea that we slept when the sun was up. He was absolutely and without question dead. For that matter, so was I. I just looked less dead because I was moving.

Squirming forward to the front passenger seat, I looked curiously out through the windscreen. We appeared to be in an underground parking lot. *Genius. At least one of us was capable of thinking.* At least one of us had still been awake enough to get us to safety. Luc might have built up some resistance to the need to become unanimated, but I was probably still centuries away from that.

He had backed into a parking spot as far from the entrance as he could get. There was no chance the sun's rays could find us this far back. No other cars were near us at the moment, but he'd taken a huge risk by parking here.

Luc's eyes opened and he was instantly alert. He sat up and checked his watch. "How long have you been awake?"

"A minute or two," I replied with a shrug.

Too big to climb through into the driver's seat, Luc got out, straightened his clothes, then climbed back in the conventional way.

I voiced the disturbing question I'd been thinking of just before he woke. "What would happen if someone found us while we were down for the day?"

"The police would be called, we would be examined and taken to the closest morgue," Luc explained calmly. "If we were extremely unlucky, they would perform an autopsy immediately."

Shuddering at the idea, I brought my knees up to my chest. "Has that ever happened to you?"

He shook his head. "No. I usually find safer places to while away the daylight hours than this."

"Would the pain wake us, do you think?" At Luc's enquiring stare, I elaborated. "When they started the Y incision." I mimed cutting my chest open with a pretend scalpel.

"No. We do not feel pain when we are…asleep." We both pondered how helpless we were when the sun came up. Humans definitely had the upper hand there. Pain usually woke them up, unless they were dead drunk. I guessed we didn't feel pain when we were out of it because we were just plain dead.

With our disturbing discussion over, Luc started the car. Buckling myself in, I finger combed my hair as we exited the underground parking lot. It was automatic to tidy myself. Dead or alive, we women were all alike.

We drove in silence and I took little notice of the scenery. It was very different from Queensland, that much I took in. Even in the dark, it was too green. Where was the dry, brown grass? Where were the gum trees? It was the lack of flies that told me I was in a foreign country. Maybe it was too cold for them here. I was desperately trying to distract myself from my growing hunger and wasn't having much luck.

When I began to fidget, Luc increased his speed. "Which is it?" he asked cryptically, but I knew what he meant.

"It's a toss-up," I replied honestly. Both blood and flesh hungers were assailing me. I alternated between dreaming about the salty sweetness of blood and the sleek hardness of Luc's body. Given the choice, I'd take his body anytime. It was a pity he was off limits.

We were driving down a deserted, ill kept road with nothing resembling human habitation anywhere in sight by now. I was becoming desperate enough that I was going to jump my pretend maker in another minute, promise or no promise. Red and blue lights suddenly flashed us from behind as a cop car took chase after us. We must have run through a speed trap. Unfortunately for the cop who had set the trap, he'd chosen a very remote spot to stop unwary travellers in.

"Thank G-G-G. Shit, will I ever get used to that?" I asked in exasperation as Luc slammed on the brakes.

"It took me a year before I trained myself to no longer try." He grinned in amusement at my inability to remember I could no longer say 'God'.

The car skidded to a halt and I unbuckled myself with unseemly haste. Blood hunger was roaring through me, demanding immediate fulfilment. The cop exited his car warily and panicked when I started running towards him. Using his door as a shield, he yelled at me in Romanian to put my hands over my head and to lie down on the road.

Ignoring the order, I ran over and yanked his door out of the way. I pulled a bit too hard and it popped off its hinges with a metallic screech. A loud bang that sounded like a firecracker going off nearby seemed unimportant, so I ignored it. Grabbing hold of the panicked cop, I forced him to stare into my eyes. The fight drained out of him and he became pliant in my hands. My fangs descended, then I bit into his neck and warm blood flooded into my mouth.

After drinking my fill, I eased the cop into the car and sat him down. Wearing a foolish grin, he attempted to holster his weapon and dropped it to the floor instead. "Sleep," I told him. His eyes closed and he began to breathe evenly, still smiling faintly. I wished him happy dreams.

Luc stood a few feet away, shaking his head in disgust. Wind rustled through the trees that grew alongside the road and ruffled my hair. "You must not let your hunger grow out of control." Lifting the door easily, he rested it against the car. "Humans become suspicious when they can't explain this kind of destruction." It *would* be difficult to understand how the door came to be detached from the car.

"I'm still new at this," I reminded him and frowned at a strange whistling noise. "Do you hear that?"

"Hear what?"

"A kind of…whistling sound." It was coming from somewhere nearby. At another gust of wind, I realized it was coming from me. Bending down, I saw a small hole in my sweater. Lifting my clothes, I verified that I had a hole in my stomach. Numbly feeling behind me, I encountered a much larger hole in my back. Darker red than normal, my blood sluggishly oozed from the wounds. It hadn't turned black and noisome yet, but it was on its way to it. *I've been shot in the guts,* I thought dazedly. Feeling lightheaded, I took a step away from the car on wobbly legs. *So that's what the loud bang was.*

Luc was suddenly on his knees before me with his hands on my hips to steady me. In any other circumstances, it would have been erotic. Right now, I was trying not to dry heave onto his head. He peered through the hole, assessing the damage. "I've had much worse," he decided. "You'll be fine. The wound is already closing."

In disbelief, I bent to take another look. Sure enough, the hole was smaller. The blood had already stopped oozing down to stain the top of my jeans. It was strange, I hadn't felt a thing when the bullet had passed through me. Maybe my hunger had masked the pain. Climbing back into the car, I sat hunched forward on the seat.

"What are you doing?" Luc asked, taking his eyes off the road every now and then to watch me.

"I don't want to get ooze on the seats." My stomach tried to lurch at the explanation, but couldn't quite manage it. Whatever I had in my veins, it wasn't just blood anymore. I was pretty sure it was the thing that made us into what we were. *'Evil' is the word you're looking for.* Yeah, that felt about right.

Feeling my back a few minutes later, I determined that the wound had closed. My shirt and sweater were bloodstained and ruined, so I threw them out the window. I didn't want to wear them again, not even if I could get the ooze stain out of them.

Luc drove using his peripheral vision only and stared at me openly. Wearing my bra, I wasn't quite half naked, but felt embarrassed anyway. We might have had a quick bout of sex, but I still barely knew him. "Has your flesh hunger risen yet?" he asked in feigned innocence as I sorted through my backpack.

"Keep your eyes on the road, Luc," I ordered and pulled a t-shirt and sweater on. Still not warm enough, I turned on the heater. Compelled to ask, I turned to my companion. "What do you care about my flesh hunger anyway? You weren't exactly thrilled when you had to do the naked mambo with me."

Keeping his eyes strictly on the road, he was reluctant to answer. "I swore I would never lower myself to break in new vampires ever again," he replied softly.

It was stupid, but I was hurt that he thought so little of me. "Well," I promised, "you'll never have to lower yourself to sleep with me again."

"It was not so bad." Luc slid a sly glance at me and dropped his eyes to my chest briefly.

"Never. Again," I said with cold finality. *Screw him,* I thought bitterly, *I'll find someone else to take out my flesh hunger on.* I'd have sex with a disease ridden hobo before I'd get naked with 'Lord Lucentio' again.

"You are angry." It was a statement, not a question.

"Am I?" I asked in faux amazement. "I can't imagine why." After a few seconds of strained silence, I couldn't take it and exploded. "Do you know what it felt like to hear you say you had to lower yourself to have sex with me? It felt really, really shitty." I subsided into dry sobs, covering my tearless face with my hands.

Waiting until I had sobbed myself out, Luc started speaking. "I was made over seven hundred years ago. My master chose me because of my physical beauty." It was said as fact rather than with pride. "My only purpose was to serve as her sexual slave." I was finally getting the explanation I'd been pestering him for and it was more disturbing than I'd ever imagined.

"She would…loan me out when other vampires required their servants to be broken in." His expression was stony as he recounted his history. "For four hundred years, I was a whore for my maker. When she wasn't using me, she watched as I was ravaged by the newly risen." Just when I thought it couldn't get any worse, it did. "Sometimes, she didn't watch alone."

I grasped the implication immediately. "You mean the whole Court would stand around watching while these women screwed you?"

"Yes."

"Why did you put up with it?" I demanded.

"Because it was my master's wish," he replied simply.

I remembered something Silvius had said after I'd risen. He'd said we would be bound for all eternity. "Do servants have to do everything their masters tell them to?" The thought horrified me. He nodded in response. "How did you manage to stop her?"

"I didn't. Only when my master was killed was I freed from her whims."

"Who killed her?" I admit, the story was as fascinating as it was horrifying. It was even more gripping than the French bodice-ripper had been.

Luc hesitated then shrugged. "I do not know." Something told me he was lying, but I wasn't going to push it. There was one thing I did want to know.

"So, after centuries of abstinence, I'm the one you broke your fast with." He nodded again and now I was appalled. "I'm, uh, really sorry," I said in a small voice.

"Why are you sorry, Natalie?"

"Because it was crap! I was a bad lay and a guy deserves better after three hundred years or so of a dry spell."

"You weren't a bad lay," he said with a small smile.

"I broke your spine," I reminded him.

"Out of sheer pleasure," he reminded me in turn.

"Well, it isn't going to happen again," I reassured him unhappily. "You can go back to being abstinent again."

"What makes you think I want to?" he asked pleasantly, then turned the car onto a lumpy dirt road.

Chapter Fourteen

We drove for several hours along increasingly eroded dirt roads. Occasionally, rustic stone farm houses with thatch roofs would suddenly appear out of the darkness. Eventually, we started climbing. The small rental car laboured to make the steep climb up what appeared to be a large mountain.

Narrowing into a single lane, the road ran alongside sheer cliffs most of the time. If another car came toward us, someone would be forced off the road to their deaths. My hand was on the doorhandle, ready to make a jump for freedom just in case another car did come along and we were the unlucky ones.

Driving with apparent unconcern, Luc had retreated into silence. He seemed to know the road well, anticipating corners almost before they happened. A deer bounded out in front of us and was gone before I could let out a startled yelp.

As the road finally levelled off, I had my first glimpse of the prophet's domain. In a word, I'd describe it as spooky. An ancient, scarred castle sat crouched in a patch of cleared forest. Tall trees were slowly beginning to encroach back on the territory they had reluctantly given up centuries ago. Two of the four towers were broken, leaving jagged bricks and cracked mortar exposed to the sky. Two of the grey stone walls were covered in dank moss and dead vines. Windows gaped without glass. A gigantic pair of doors had long ago fallen due to rusted hinges. The empty entrance beckoned darkly, like the open maw of a monster. I did not want to enter that decrepit, slowly dying building. Luc would have to drag me by the hair if he expected me to go inside.

Angling the car away from the castle, we drove around the side of a large wooden building. Once dark red, the paint had faded to dusky pink. It badly needed a new coat, but it was in much better repair than the castle. Large windows with white trim were boarded shut. Twin doors, large enough to drive a tractor through, were chained shut. Overall, the castle and surrounds didn't exactly send out welcoming signals. The vibe I got from the place was 'stay away'. I would have been happy to comply.

Luc drove the car out of sight of the road, then parked. He climbed out calmly and I copied him with trepidation. I did not like this place at all. I wondered what humans would make of the castle. From the looks of it, it wasn't exactly a thriving tourist attraction.

From the smell of petrol and oil nearby, I surmised that cars were kept inside the wooden building. Someone must use this place then. Did I want to meet them? *Nope.*

"Lord Lucentio," a deep voice intoned from the shadows of the building, startling me badly. "It has been a long time since you have darkened our doorstep." I couldn't make out the creature's face even with my heightened vision. Maybe making himself invisible was his vampirish talent.

"Vincent," Luc said with cautious respect. He stepped forward and offered his hand. "I have come to see the Prophet."

Vincent stepped forward out of the shadows to shake Luc's hand briefly. I was glad I couldn't gasp in revulsion anymore. He was close to seven feet tall and was as emaciated as a POW survivor. His cheeks were deep hollows and his black eyes were mournful. A dark brown robe covered him from head to toe. Only his face and hands were visible. The realization that he wasn't really invisible and that his robe had merely hidden him from sight was a relief. Vampires had enough of an advantage over their prey without having that kind of power. My inspection of the hooded arrival ended at his hands. They were large and resembled albino spiders. Black fingernails about two inches long had been sharpened to wicked points. Silvius had been almost handsome compared to this guy.

"I am afraid the Prophet has lapsed into a coma again," Vincent said in tones of regret that sounded false to me. Luc slanted a glance at me, but I didn't need the warning. He could also tell that Vincent didn't really give a crap about the prophet's wellbeing. Great, we were in another situation I could never really understand due to ancient vampire politics.

"When did this happen?" Luc asked.

"A week and a half ago," was the reply. Luc and I exchanged a glance. That was right about the time I'd been turned. It was yet another portent of the doom my new birth had brought to vampirekind. Finally deigning to notice me, Vincent raised a hairless brow in faux surprise. "You have brought a guest?"

Luc motioned me forward and I reluctantly complied. "Vincent, this is Natalie."

I stuck my hand out and tried not to cringe when his nails scraped the back of my hand unpleasantly. It even felt like a spider. A cold, hairless spider. "Nice to meet you," *not,* "I really love what you've done with the place." I nodded toward the broken towers of the castle that could just be seen rising above the wooden building. I hid my shudder, but only just.

Vincent raised his non-existent eyebrows again and Luc gave a small shrug. "She's Australian and new," he said to explain my uncouth behaviour. *Hey, I've been on my best behaviour so far.* If they thought this was uncouth, they'd clearly never met a drunk Australian before. A typical tipsy Aussie could uncouth their pants off with one hand tied behind his back.

"Ah." As if my nationality explained everything, and it probably did, Vincent swept his arm toward the door. "Please, enter. Dawn will soon be upon us. I shall show you to your rooms."

Although every fibre of my being screamed at me not to follow the tall ghoul, I liked the idea of having a room to myself. Some space and time alone would be welcome. To my intense relief, our guide headed away from the castle.

Luc shot a look over his shoulder to make sure I hadn't taken the opportunity to sprint off into the distance. My smile was meant to be reassuring, but from his slight grimace, I mustn't have been very successful. I had already reconciled myself to the idea that, while I could run from these people, I probably couldn't hide. My options were limited, so trudge after them I would.

Vincent led the way to a small brick building that was in far better repair than either the castle, or the barn. A sign advertised that it was a public toilet and so did the smell. The place really was a tourist attraction then. We trooped inside the female toilet, which disturbed me greatly because I'd never seen a man in the girl's loo before. I was just starting to become alarmed when Vincent bent and lifted the lid from a manhole set in the floor. A large padlock that must keep the manhole secure from intruders was already unlocked. It was a relief to see the tunnel. I'd had vague thoughts that the emaciated old creature might tear us limb from limb, then flush the pieces down the toilet.

I crossed to the hole and peered inside. It was so deep that I couldn't see the bottom. A narrow, rusty ladder was the only way down. I resisted the urge to kick a pebble into the shaft. The noise as it bounced its way down would echo upwards, giving away my juvenile impulse.

"Ladies first," Luc invited. Faced with the idea of having Vincent following right behind me and possibly treading on my fingers, I took him up on his invitation. Shooting a fulminating look at Luc on general principal, I shouldered my backpack.

There was just enough room to fit inside the tunnel with the pack on my back. The ladder was even colder and clammier than I was. Grabbing the sides of the ladder tightly, I slid downwards. Wind rushed past me, blowing my hair back from my face. Spying light rapidly approaching beneath me, I tightened my grip and stopped my descent a couple of rungs from the ground. The speed of my controlled fall had been fun and my hands didn't even hurt. If I'd still been human, my palms would be raw meat and I probably would have fallen to my death halfway down.

As I stepped off the ladder, I was instantly surrounded by a curious gaggle of vampires. "Ooh, a newcomer," a female purred in a thick Romanian accent. Circling me, she was skeletally thin with straggly black hair, prominent teeth and a vulpine face. *Jesus, Vincent must have scraped the barrel when he turned this chick into a vampire.*

"She's pretty," a boy about Geordie's age sniggered and danced forward to yank my hair sharply. His hair was a shaggy brown mess and his eyes rolled wildly in a dirty face. I slapped his hand away in annoyance and wondered if he was mentally all there. Trapped beneath a mountain with someone like Vincent in charge, I wouldn't have been.

"I wouldn't mind a taste," an older male vampire said. He'd been losing his hair when human and was doomed to be half bald forever. If that wasn't bad enough, he also had an unfortunate squint and warts on his hands.

The vamps were dressed in home-made garments of coarse brown fabric. Clearly, these were lowly minions who were far down on the chain of importance. Much like I would have been if Silvius had still been alive. With him dead, I was my own master, even if I had to pretend to be Luc's servant half the time.

Vincent suddenly appeared in their midst, startling all of us. "Be gone," he roared and the servants fled with wails

127

of fright. They moved with shocking speed, so fast my eyes could barely follow them. *My God, how old are they? How long have they been down here?* "I apologize for the poor reception, my dear," Vincent said with a courtly bow.

"Don't worry about it," I mumbled and was glad when Luc stepped up beside me. He hovered at my shoulder protectively. I nodded at his look of concern to indicate I was fine. I was anything but fine, but I also didn't want Vincent to know that I was quietly freaking out.

Studying our dynamic, Vincent's eyes became crafty slits. It was impossible to guess what conclusions he had drawn from our interaction. I had zero interest in vampire politics and was only along for the ride, but he didn't know that.

"This way," our guide invited with a toothy smile and glided off down the hallway. We were in a tunnel at least a couple of hundred feet below the ground. The rock had been hand carved thousands of years ago, long before the invention of machinery. Every now and then, a bare light bulb shed a weak pool of light. Our shadows loomed large, then retreated behind us each time we passed beneath a bulb.

Watching Vincent, I was strongly reminded of my first encounter with Silvius. My flesh began to creep unpleasantly as I compared the two men. Both had been old in mortal years as well as vampire years. Both were bald and exuded evil like humans exuded sweat. They also had one other thing in common; their shadows moved independently.

Vincent looked back over his shoulder and smiled at me winningly. I wasn't going to be lulled into a false sense of security by an aged monster like this again. Not when his shadow was a large, humpbacked creature with a misshapen head and four inch claws that dragged on the ground. Checking Luc's and my own shadows, I was relieved to see that they were normal. Seeing my own shadow suddenly acting independently would be the worst thing I could imagine right now.

A heavy metal door awaited us at the end of the hallway. It swung open with a suitably spooky metallic groan at a light push from our guide. Vincent fished a key-ring from a pocket of his robe and sorted through the collection. Dozens of keys in all shapes and sizes jingled and swayed on a short chain. I wondered how extensive the tunnels were beneath the mountain and saw the answer for myself when Vincent ushered us inside.

Opening up into a thirty foot wide space, the hallway continued onwards far into the distance. More hallways and doors branched off at regular intervals. I had the sense of a great weight hovering above us. As a human, I'd been slightly claustrophobic. As a vampire, I ignored the fear. I had far worse problems to worry about than the unlikelihood of the mountain suddenly imploding and burying me in tons of rubble.

Locking the door behind us, Vincent made the keys disappear. Taking one of the branches, he strode along it for a few minutes, then entered yet another, smaller hallway. Luc hid his discomfort well, but I was sure he was enjoying Vincent's company about as little as I was.

We walked for a good five minutes before Vincent stopped at a rough wooden door. Producing his keys again, he granted us access, then gestured to the rooms inside. "I shall see you both when you rise." With a ghastly smile and another courtly bow, he was gone.

Luc waved me inside and I decided being forced to stay in a small suite with him was better than falling asleep in the hallway. Tiredness was setting in as I stepped inside. In a short time, I would once again fall dead asleep and searched frantically for a bed to collapse on.

We stood in a small living room complete with a couch, armchairs and a television. It resembled a cheap motel, but had the difference of being far underground. Three doorways branched off to the left, right and to the back. Choosing the door to the right, I spotted a bed and dived onto it. I didn't feel particularly safe beneath the mountain and needed some kind of insurance that I would wake up intact. One way to ensure that would be to go to sleep holding a weapon that would turn any other vampire into a messy stain on the ground.

I had just enough time to pull my cross out of the backpack and to clasp it tightly before my lights went out for the day.

Chapter Fifteen

Waking from a dreamless sleep once more, I stared at a cheap brown bedspread and couldn't remember where I was for a minute. Then the memory of Vincent and his weird servants came flooding back. Groaning, I closed my eyes and rolled over onto my back. I tried to rub my face with my right hand and something cold and metallic clunked me on the forehead.

Opening my eyes, I found the delicately wrought centrepiece of the cross embedded in my palm again. "Great," I muttered, "just what I needed." *Seriously, why do these things keep happening to me?* Nothing like this happened to any other vampires. *Yeah, because none of them are the dreaded Mortis.* Lucky bastards.

Prying the cross from my hand, I stuffed it down the back of my pants, then shifted it until my t-shirt covered my skin. The metal was too cold to wear pressed up against my naked flesh. I no longer possessed any body heat to warm it. I sat on the bed glumly, studying my now matching palms. This had to mean something and I suspected it wouldn't be good. *Just one more portent of doom, I'm sure.*

Luc knocked softly on the door and entered at my unwelcoming grunt. He could tell something was wrong at a glance. "What has happened?" Closing the door, he crossed the room and sat on the end of the bed.

"Oh, not much," I said, trying to remain calm, "just this." I held my hands up palm out and he was off the bed and pressed up against the door before I could blink. "Calm down, drama queen," I said crossly. "They can't hurt you."

"According to the prophesy, your hands can now destroy even the strongest of us." He was staring at my hands like they were covered in leprosy. To him, they might as well have been.

"I'm not planning on destroying anyone," I snapped as I slid off the bed and headed for the door. *Not yet, anyway. Give me another hour or two beneath this mountain and I might change my mind.* Luc cringed away when I reached for the doorknob and I did my best to ignore him. "Except for that bitch of a Comtesse," I continued on my way to the bathroom. "I'd like to make her strip off in a roomful of strangers." The last was muttered beneath my breath. Not that I had any breath these days.

When I emerged from my shower, Luc had composed himself and was sitting on the lumpy, cheap brown couch. His spooked look was gone and now he just appeared to be resigned. "We should eat before we seek admittance to the Prophet," he told me.

"I doubt many tourists stumble across this place after dark," I replied doubtfully.

"Vincent and his servants have…," he searched for a suitable word, "volunteers that they feed from."

Eyeing Luc mistrustfully, I felt behind me to make sure the cross hadn't fallen too far down the back of my pants. It was still firmly in place and required only a minor adjustment. "Volunteers, huh? I gotta see this." I sincerely doubted anyone would volunteer to be vampire food. *Oh, wouldn't they,* my mind whispered slyly. It showed me a picture of the four men I'd fed from the first time I'd gone hunting. They'd been pretty damn happy to be my snack for the night.

As Luc opened the door, we came face to face with the boy who'd yanked on my hair last night. He dropped the begrimed hand he'd been about to knock with. "I bet you're hungry." He grinned, revealing brown teeth that still held the red traces of his last meal. "Come this way." He spun away from the door and began trotting down the hall. He reminded me eerily of a slinking hyena as he snapped glances at us over his shoulder to make sure we were following him.

"I thought you said we could only have one servant each," I said to Luc to make conversation.

"There are exceptions." At my raised eyebrow, Luc explained further. "The guardian of the Prophet may have up to ten servants. Vincent, as caretaker of the Prophet's domain, can have up to ten as well. The Councillors may have up to twenty each."

"Jeez, it pays to be in power," I muttered. It made a grim sort of sense, though. Someone as powerful as the Comtesse wouldn't be satisfied with just one measly servant. She'd need lots of minions to boss around so she could feel all superior. It was a snide thought, but I was still annoyed about being ordered to strip naked by her. That humiliation wasn't going to fade anytime in the next century or two.

Since it didn't look like I had to pretend to be his servant at the moment, I walked at Luc's side. Each time the boy approached a light, his shadow became stark and hideous. It was bent, twisted and almost unrecognizable as belonging to a former human being. I could easily believe that our kind had come from aliens when I saw something this unnerving.

"Are you seeing this?" I whispered from the side of my mouth.

Sparing me a brief glance, Luc returned his scrutiny to the boy scuttling ahead. "Am I seeing what?"

"His shadow," I replied in as quiet a voice as I could.

"What's wrong with it?"

"What's right with it?" I countered. At Luc's blank look, I struggled to explain. "It's all warped, bent and kind of crozzled. Vincent is the same and so was Silvius."

"I don't understand what you mean." Luc slowed to allow more distance to build between us and our young guide.

"They don't match their shadows," I struggled to explain. "They don't appear to be human like us." Not that we were really human anymore. Not on the inside where it counted.

"What do they appear to be then?" Luc asked, bewildered and clearly beginning to doubt my sanity.

"Monsters," I said with a shudder. All vampires were monsters, that was a given. But there was something seriously wrong with these people. I could feel it.

"Are you two coming, or are you going to stand there whispering together all night?" the boy called back over his shoulder. He didn't like us having a private conversation, perhaps sensing he was the topic. Increasing our pace, we trudged onwards in morose silence. Luc was giving my visions, or whatever they were, some thought, but he didn't seem to be any closer to understanding them than I was.

Reaching a set of narrow, twisting stairs, we descended two levels and entered a dungeon. Rooms had been carved out of the rock to create crude holding cells. Metal bars prevented any of the penned humans from escaping. The walls, ceiling and floors were made of rock so there was no chance they could dig their way out. Each human had a cell to themselves and there were twenty-five cells on each side of the room.

All fifty humans were naked, malnourished and filthy. They each had a bucket as a toilet and a threadbare blanket for a bed. My withering look told Lord Lucentio what I thought of his description that these poor sods were 'volunteers'. Unfortunately, my blood hunger had to be fed and it wasn't about to pass on a meal. Not even one that was this ragged and dirty.

"Pick anyone you want," the boy invited. Moans and pleas sounded from the cells. Most of the humans clambered to their feet, reaching through the bars with thin arms, pleading for us to choose them. They might not really have volunteered to become vampire food, but this was their existence now. The only pleasure they would be able to feel was the moment when our teeth sheared through their skin.

Half healed bite marks adorned their necks, wrists and even the insides of their thighs. They'd all been bitten so often that their wounds never had a chance to heal properly. Luc pointed at a female without bothering to examine every cage. Like me, he just wanted to get this done.

"Ah, a good choice," the boy said with a giggle as if Luc was choosing from a selection of fine wines. "What about you?" he asked me. I pointed to one of the larger men who seemed like he could withstand another feed without dying on me. "He's a feisty one," the boy warned me, then giggled again. On the floor beside him, his shadow cavorted in apparent glee, clapping its hands soundlessly. *This place is like a mini hell.* Spending a substantial amount of time here would be unbearable. I prayed we could get what we needed from the prophet, then escape from this nightmare quickly.

Unlocking the door to the female's cell, the boy stepped aside as Luc entered. The woman lurched forward with a cry that I took to be happiness. With a few murmured words, Luc calmed her and had her swaying eagerly towards him. Kissing her dirty palm, he turned her wrist and brought it to his mouth. He, at least, had either retained some compassion for humans, or had relearned it over the centuries.

It was over quickly and then the female was shuddering and gasping in pleasure as the vampire cop lowered her to the filthy blanket on the floor. He crouched beside her, murmuring more words. She went to sleep with a smile on her thin, careworn face.

Knowing I could never hope to match Luc's finesse, I waited impatiently for the boy to unlock my victim's door.

With a roar, the freed man leaped forward and caught me in a crushing grip by the shoulders. I captured him with a glance and the fight drained out of him. He was suddenly crushing me to him in a desperate parody of passion instead of defiant rage. He went still when my lips grazed his neck. As gently as I could, I broke his skin and took a few swallows of blood. It was thinner than I was used to from being constantly drained, but it did the job to fill the pit inside me. With an ecstatic smile, the man allowed himself to be placed back in his cell.

Disappointed that we hadn't torn into the pair in a feeding frenzy, the boy petulantly led us back up to the main level. Even his shadow stomped along in a sulk. I felt dirty after drinking from the human slave and not because my meal hadn't bathed in weeks. So far, I hadn't seen any reason why I shouldn't wipe vampires from the face of the earth. If I really was the dreaded Mortis, that was. Despite all the portents and my ability to touch holy objects, I didn't feel all that special.

Leading us down a confusing series of tunnels that varied in height and width, the boy finally halted before an enormous door. Easily twenty feet high and banded in dull, pitted metal, it stood half open. A dark cavern lay on the other side. Gesturing for us to enter, the boy had a final smirk for us. "Vincent awaits you within." *Gee, who could turn down an invitation like that?*

Luc preceded me inside, but only just. I was following him so closely that I was almost stepping on his heels. I jumped when the door boomed shut behind us, closing off any chance of retreat. The cavern stretched off into the distance. It was wide enough that I couldn't see the walls. Torches in crudely made wooden stands marched in a straight line to a throne roughly fifty feet away. If I wasn't mistaken, I believed the figure seated comfortably on the large, gold monstrosity was Vincent. A six foot wide red carpet ran from the door right up to the throne.

"It would appear that Vincent has come up in the world," Luc murmured with quiet sarcasm.

"What do you mean?"

"That," he nodded toward the golden seat, "is the Prophet's throne." After imparting that comforting piece of information, he started forward.

In some of my wildest fantasies, I'd imagined myself floating down a red carpet to a swanky event with a handsome man at my side. Now that it was actually happening, not that this could be described as a swanky event, it felt more like a horrible nightmare than a pleasant dream.

I could sense other vampires huddled together just out of sight. In a cavern this large, hundreds of them could be hiding in the darkness. The torches were spaced out just enough to ruin my night vision. Luc seemed to be at ease, showing no distress at all. Only when I brushed against his arm could I feel how tense he was. I'd hate to play poker with him with his ability to hide his emotions. Unless it was strip poker. *I wouldn't mind playing that with him, heh, heh.* I was lost for a few seconds in a fantasy of our naked limbs entwining. Then Vincent was looming over us and the fantasy disappeared.

Slumped forward with his chin resting on one hand and the other sitting on the armrest, Vincent posed for us, looking a lot like the statue of The Thinker. He'd changed into a deep maroon cloak and had pulled the hood forward so his face was shadowed. Torchlight glinted in his black eyes, giving them a demonic red glow. If I hadn't seen practically every horror movie ever made, I might have been impressed. But it was far too staged to be as scary as he'd intended.

"Have you taken the Prophet's place, Vincent?" Luc asked, getting straight to the point. While I admired his courage, I kind of wished he'd kept his mouth shut. He probably felt it was his right as a Lord to question someone below him on the food chain of vampire royalty. Antagonizing a creature who had an unknown number of servants at his beck and call didn't seem to be very smart. Not that Vincent had offered us any threats. But it was heavily implied in the way he had taken over the throne.

"I am merely keeping his seat warm," Vincent replied. I couldn't see his face clearly, but I heard the smirk well enough. Unseen vampires tittered from the darkness. There seemed to be more than the ten Vincent was entitled to. Maybe a lot more.

"I would like to see the Prophet for myself," Luc said and the unseen throng quieted. They waited with something as close to bated breaths as we creatures could get.

"I am afraid that won't be possible," Vincent replied in tones of false regret. Behind him, his shadow stood and stretched as if cramped from sitting. It turned its head and stared down at us. I sidled closer to Luc, desperately pretending I couldn't see the monstrosity.

"Ah, but it is possible," a new voice called from beyond the lights. Aged, male and heavily accented, it drew closer. "The Prophet is awake and he is asking for Lord Lucentio's guest."

Vincent stood and was swallowed by his shadow. Only his black, beady eyes could be seen for a moment. Then the shadow receded, shrinking back to its normal size. "The Prophet has spoken in his native tongue, Danton?" he demanded.

Clad in a white robe that was very monk-like, the new arrival swept into view. I assumed he was the prophet's protector that Luc had mentioned briefly. "He has said only one word and I believe it is this young vampire's name." Turning to me, excitement shone from his dark eyes. "Is your name Nat?"

"Um. Yes," I said with great reluctance.

"You're named after an insect?" Someone called from the darkness and several vampires sniggered.

"It's short for Natalie," I called back with some asperity.

"She's Australian," Luc pointed out with the faintest of sneers. He was still annoyed with my habit of shortening his name.

"Ah," floated back from the dark, as if that explained it.

As well as the white robe, Danton had a circular fringe of hair that was also very monk-like. If vampires could believe in any kind of religion, I suspected this guy would be their Pope. "If you will follow me?" He bowed to us, then turned his back on Vincent.

Whispers spread out around us. I wondered uneasily just how many vampires were in this place. Now that we were away from the torches, my eyes adjusted to the dark quickly. I saw there were fewer people than I'd thought. There were maybe forty of my new kin watching curiously. Vincent scuttled along behind us like a gigantic cockroach, hurrying to catch up.

Reaching a smaller, but no less impressive door, Danton murmured a few words to a pale blur of a face through a barred window. The door was unlocked and the monk waved us through. Vincent stepped forward with the intention of following, but halted when the monk put his hand on his chest. "Only these two may enter."

I resisted the urge to smirk at Vincent and trotted to keep up with Luc. Danton slipped past us and took the lead down the long tunnel. Another door, also guarded, barred our path after fifty or so feet. A much smaller, cosier cavern waited within.

Chapter Sixteen

Five vampires stood guard around a massive bed. They were dressed in coarse brown robes and were armed with swords. No doubt ancient, the blades were sheathed in plain leather scabbards and hung from rope belts around their waists. They put their hands on the sword hilts and readied themselves for battle as Luc and I approached. At a curt gesture from the monk, they fell back, but their attention remained on us, ready to act.

Thanks to two large fires on either side of the room, it was very nearly stifling in the enclosed space. Chimneys had been carved into the rock, keeping the room mostly smokeless. Beneath the faint traces of smoke that remained, I could smell something sweet that reminded me strongly of cinnamon.

At a faint rustling sound, I turned my attention to the bed. A slight shape made a tiny mound beneath several layers of shabby blankets. A skeletal, wizened hand emerged and pointed unerringly at me. The hand turned over and the finger bent slowly, beckoning me closer. Danton motioned for me to move to the bed, but it was Luc's hand on my back that actually propelled me into action. My feet weren't about to close the distance without assistance.

Rounding the side of the bed, I had my first close look at the prophet we'd travelled so far to see. If a mummy could rise up and come back to life, it would look like this. Sunken eyes, like black raisins, peered at me from a fleshless skull. Fangs stood out starkly from behind shrivelled lips.

As I often did, I spoke without thinking. "No offence, but you look like you could use a good feed."

"I have not fed in over two hundred years," the prophet said in a rusty voice. My ears heard complete gibberish, but my mind translated the words just fine.

"There's fifty people imprisoned in the dungeons below us," I informed the living mummy. "I can get someone to bring you up a snack if you want."

A weird wheezing sound came from the withered chest of the prophet. It took a moment for me to recognize it as laughter. It took another moment to realize the cinnamon smell was wafting from his body. *So, that's what happens when vampires starve themselves. They turn into cinnamon sticks.*

"You," he lifted a bony finger and pointed it at my face, "are the one I have been waiting for."

"Are you sure?" I asked unhappily and took a seat on the bed. All five of the guards hissed in anger, but Danton waved them back. The monk was hanging eagerly on every word we spoke. Not that he would be able to understand his boss.

"Do you bear the holy marks?"

I nodded and clenched my fists. "Yep But I'd rather not reveal them right now." I think we both knew his guards would slay me if they saw them. Since the prophet spoke gibberish, he wasn't in a position to blow the whistle on me. He nodded and his wispy white hair shifted slowly against the pillow like dandelion fluff in the wind. Even if he could have given a warning, I didn't think he would. I wondered exactly who he was a prophet for, if not for God. It didn't seem polite to ask.

"Over two thousand years ago, when I was first afflicted with this gift, I kept a journal of my visions." It took an effort for him to get the words out. He was almost completely drained of vitality. I couldn't seem to last more than a couple of days without feeding, let alone two hundred years. His willpower must have been incredible.

"You are the only one who can read it, but I fear the consequences if my servants were to view the pages." He reached out a palsied hand and put it on my knee. My skin crawled, but I was too polite to leap of the bed with a cry of revulsion. "You must find the journal on the mountain top and read it," he continued. "It will tell you what you must do." He patted my knee and even through the fabric his hand felt dry and papery.

Leaning down, I whispered as quietly as possible. "Shouldn't you be ordering your guards to, uh, rend me in twain?"

His lips moved in a parody of a smile. "Read the journal. My men will not harm you." His eyes closed and he subsided back into his coma. Since he hadn't melted down into a watery stain, I believed he was still unalive. Just how long he could subsist on sheer force of will was a question for another day.

Silence descended, then stretched out painfully. Danton broke it first. "What did the Prophet say?" After guarding the cinnamon stick for a couple of millennia, his curiosity about what he'd had to say must have been enormous. He was all but wringing his hands with the need to know.

Sliding off the bed, I dusted off my clothes. Vacuuming and changing the linens didn't seem to be high on the list of housekeeping chores. Even Luc shifted impatiently when I didn't answer straight away. I was gathering my thoughts, wondering how much to tell them. But the prophet really hadn't had all that much to say. "He said Lord Lucentio and I have to climb to the top of the mountain." Luc gave a brief start at my proper use of his name and title. Hey, I knew when to use discretion. I just ignored the warning signs my brain gave me most of the time. "Apparently, he left something for us up there." I wasn't about to tell them the whole story. Not without talking it over with the vampire cop first.

Puzzling over the news, the monk made a decision. "Then you must act quickly before Vincent discovers your plan and sends his servants after you." Turning to one of the guards, he barked a command in Romanian. I heard it as 'Quickly, show them how to reach the surface'.

At the guard's curt gesture, Luc and I followed him through a smaller door and down a long, skinny tunnel. Turning off into a doorway, our guide entered what turned out to be a storeroom. Luc ducked in after him. Being shorter, I simply walked inside. Old crates and broken furniture had been stacked in haphazard piles. The guard moved a broken, seven-foot tall wardrobe aside to reveal yet another door. Unlocking it, he waved Luc inside.

A ladder that led to the surface awaited us. When the guard closed the door behind me, the shaft became completely lightless. Luc started climbing and I was a few rungs behind him. My night vision kicked in, but there was nothing to see except the ladder and roughly hewn rock.

It took us fifteen minutes to climb to the top. As a human, it would have taken a lot longer and I had my doubts that I'd have made it. As a vampire, I climbed out into the night air without even breathing hard. Or at all for that matter.

Closing the lid that had cleverly been hidden by bushes, Luc scanned the area to get his bearings. We were three quarters of the way up the mountain and the top still towered over us. Spying a dirt track that would take us up to the summit, he took the lead. "What did the Prophet say to you?" he asked after we'd been walking for several minutes.

"He asked if I had the holy marks, then said I had to climb the mountain to get a journal he wrote a couple of thousand years ago."

"You could truly understand his ravings?" He slanted me a doubtful look over his shoulder.

"My ears heard gibberish, but my brain made sense of it," I said with a shrug.

Retreating back into silence, Luc pushed his way through foliage that was making a strong attempt to overgrow the path. Branches slapped at me, hitting me in the chest, face and arms. Growing tired of being attacked by plants in Luc's wake, I dropped back a few feet. After a few seconds, I became aware that we were being followed.

"Um, Luc, I think we're being follo-" was as far as I got before someone jumped on my back. At the high pitched giggle, I knew it was the filthy boy with the cavorting shadow. Thrashing around in a circle, I tried to pry him off, but he clung to me like a super strong monkey.

Luc was fighting his own battle with three other vampires. Clearly, he had some kind of martial arts training. He punched and kicked the vampires away like they were extras in a low budget movie. Every time one went down, someone else from the growing crowd would jump to the attack.

Meanwhile, I was still thrashing around with the filthy vampire on my back. He snapped at my face with his fangs, just missing my eyes every time I turned my head to get a look at him. My sweater began to ride up until the cross at my back became exposed. At the burst of heat against my skin, I figured it had finally made contact with the boy.

Shrieking, he leaped off me and danced around in a distressed circle. Shirtless, he wore only stained, torn pants. Prancing around like that, he reminded me of the little tan dog that had almost become my snack about a thousand lifetimes ago. Except the dog hadn't been wreathed in bright blue flames. A clear imprint of the cross stood out bright red against the stark whiteness of his stomach. Blue flames had sprouted from the imprint and were quickly growing in size and ferocity.

Dropping to the ground, the vamp rolled around in the dirt, trying to put out the fire that was now spreading to his chest and arms. Apart from that first flash of heat, the flames hadn't even touched me. My shirt wasn't even singed, I discovered when I checked that I still had my weapon.

I wasn't the only one to watch as the pretty blue flames bathed the kid. He had an audience of many. He burned a lot faster than Silvius had. Maybe because the fire covered his whole body and not just his hands. He also wasn't vomiting black blood. Was that because I hadn't stabbed him through the heart with the holy symbol? In seconds, his unsettling screams ceased and he began to melt. Luc stood with one hand clamped around a vampire's throat and the other poised to punch. All around us, the creatures stared in horror at their fallen comrade. No one seemed to realize that I had set the kid on fire. *Time to show them what I can do and watch them tremble in fear!*

Pulling the cross free from my waistband, I brandished it. My enemies flinched back in unison, gaping at me in disbelief. Even Luc shied away from the holy object in my hand. "That's what you get," I shrieked in triumph. "Maybe you'll think twice before attacking Mort-" My words were cut off when an object came whistling through the air and punched through my chest.

A rusty, pitted sword sliced through my dead, shrivelled heart and came to a quivering stop. A foot or so of blade stood out from my body. Looking down the weapon numbly, my legs gave way and I was suddenly sitting on the ground. Luc howled in fury and began tossing vampires around like a wolf savaging a bunch of kittens.

This is it. I'm about to die. Again. Staring down at the sword, I waited for my flesh to dissolve, but nothing happened. It didn't even hurt all that much. Eventually, I figured out that I wasn't going to die again and clambered back to my feet. The sword must have missed my heart after all.

A thin, scrawny female vampire leaped at me with a witchlike screech. Sidestepping the attack, I grabbed hold of her arm and twirled in a quick circle. With a sickening crack, she went sailing out into the trees, leaving most of her arm behind. White bone gleamed at me through the coarse sleeve of her dress. Dead blood dripped from the stump. My lips wrinkled back from my teeth in disgust at the sight and smell. *God, that's rank!*

The male vampire who'd wanted to have a taste of me landed in a crouch a couple of feet away. Snarling and squinting horribly, he began to circle around me in a bent over hunch. He held a knife in one warty hand down low, ready to spill my guts out onto my shoes. Since I liked my guts right where they were, I lunged forward and speared him through the chest with the exposed bone of the torn off arm. "Suck that, creep!" I crowed and dusted my hands off when he fell on his back, twitching. Picking up the cross, I turned and the foot of sword still sticking out of me clanged loudly against a tree. It vibrated inside my chest unpleasantly for several seconds.

Luc was surrounded by vampires, almost lost from my sight. They all held rusty, broken weapons and would be only too happy to insert them into my protector. With a pitiful war cry, I brandished the cross and sprinted forward. No one paid me any attention until I set the first few vampires on fire. Then they were screaming and milling to get away from me. I couldn't remember ever being this unpopular before. Not even during the mid-year sale in my previous job when the prices were somehow wrong and I lost about two thousand bucks worth of sales. My assistant had been responsible, but I was the one who was fired for the debacle. That was the one and only time

I'd ever tried being a supervisor. I'd lasted three whole months before being canned.

"Die, vile creature," I screamed and pressed the cross against the vulpine female vampire's head. Instead of catching fire like I expected her to, her head imploded. Drenched in black blood and soupy brains, I stumbled backwards and felt the sword punch into a body. Turning my head, I took in the vampire I'd unwittingly spitted. Slumping forward, he dropped the small axe he'd been about to split my skull open with.

"Look out!" Luc cried in warning. I clumsily turned in time to spit a second vampire on the hilt of my sword. Both were about my height and the pitted metal had found their hearts just fine. They twitched and danced like puppets on strings before becoming dead weight.

With two downed vampires hanging off me like a pair of gigantic Christmas decorations, I was over encumbered and clumsy. Clumsier than usual anyway. Looking around wildly, I searched for more creatures to kill, but the area was now empty. Luc was surrounded by the quickly forming moist patches of our dead kin. He'd apparently torn them to pieces with his bare hands. He was even more drenched in the black gore of the fallen than I was.

"A little help?" I said and gestured at the corpses that were slumped on both ends of the sword.

With a grimace of distaste, Luc stepped forward and peeled first one, then the other off. He tossed their limp corpses aside like garbage. Hitting the ground, they immediately began the process of dissolving. "Can you do something about this?" I pointed at the sword lodged in my chest. He braced a hand on my shoulder and pulled the metal out in one smooth move.

My knees wobbled at the lancing pain, but I didn't go down. It had hurt way more on the way out than it had on the way in. Peeking inside the ragged slit in my clothes, I saw that I'd been right the first time. The blade had gone directly through my heart. "Huh. Look at that," I said in wonder. "Shouldn't I be dead?"

Luc gave me a disturbed glance, but had no answer to explain the mystery of why I was still unalive. He sorted through the puddles until he found a sword that was rusted, but still intact. "Keep your cross handy," he advised, then took off up the path at a run. I noticed that he still hadn't answered my question. Since I was an unliving legend, he probably didn't know why I hadn't died. Maybe the prophet hadn't covered this in his sometimes legible ramblings.

Holding my hands up to shield my face, I let the branches slap away at me and tried to keep up with my ooze drenched companion. I wasn't about to let myself fall behind again. The vamps might get their courage up enough to regroup and make another attempt to attack us.

Wind howled across the top of the mountain when we finally emerged from the trail into a clearing, whipping my hair across my face. I'd expected a horde of crazed vampire minions to be waiting for us, but the area was deserted. Across the clearing was a spire of rock that I estimated to be seventy or so feet high. A jagged opening didn't look inviting, but it was our fate to enter it.

We approached the cave cautiously. Luc held his sword confidently and I clutched my cross nervously. Anything could be inside that hole; bears, wolves, Sasquatch. It was probably a good thing that I wasn't schooled up on what kind of wild animals were native to Romania. My imagination could stretch only so far. Besides, weren't we far more dangerous than any animal could be? Well, Luc was. I'd been more of a liability than of much help during the fracas on the way up the mountain.

Moonlight filtered inside the cave, leaving a silvery imperfect circle of light on the dirt floor. In the centre of the ten foot wide space was a roughly hewn bench seat that had been carved out of rock. A bum shaped groove had been worn in the centre of the seat. A cave wasn't the kind of place I'd feel the need to visit regularly, but maybe that was just me. For all I knew, cave squatting was a favoured vampire past-time.

Circling the seat, I squinted at the gibberish that had been carved into the back of it. Translating the message into English, I hunkered down and examined the dirt.

"What does it say?" Luc asked.

"It says 'Dig'." The message that had been inscribed over two millennia ago wasn't exactly profound, but at least it was to the point. The last thing we needed was to waste time puzzling over a cryptic message.

Luc dropped to his knees beside me and pushed the heavy stone seat away with one hand. My nails were much stronger now, thanks to my transformation to the undead. They cut through the soil easily. Luc dug with stolid determination beside me. His fingers were the first to encounter the wooden box.

Digging it out, he held it up. It was the size of a large envelope and was about two inches thick. The workmanship was pretty good, considering nails and glue hadn't been invented when it had been created. It seemed that the whole thing had been carved out of a single piece of wood. Luc lifted the lid off and we peered in awe at the book inside. The box had been constructed well and no dirt had found its way inside.

Not much larger than a standard paperback novel, we saw that the journal was quite thin when Luc picked it up. It had been bound in the brown skin of an animal, but I didn't know what type. The workmanship wasn't professional, but it did the job of protecting the book well enough. "We will need to get to a place of safety before you try to read this," Luc decided.

"Sounds like a plan to me," I agreed. My curiosity would have to wait. I doubted Vincent would be amenable to us staying beneath the mountain for another night and dawn was on its way.

"Our vehicle will most likely have been rendered useless by now," Luc mused as he placed the journal back in the box, then ducked out of the cave.

"What are we going to do?" I hoped he had a contingency plan because, as usual, I had nothing. Back in my old life, I'd sold clothes for a living. This situation was so far from my old life and world that I might as well have been in another universe.

"We're going to run and hope we find somewhere safe before daylight strikes."

"That's a really shitty plan," I muttered to Luc's back as he darted off into the trees.

We avoided the trail this time. What was left of Vincent's minions would be waiting for us. Instead, we careened down the mountainside in the opposite direction from the castle. Luc gracefully leaped over obstacles with ease. I blundered into them, fell over them and crawled under them about as gracefully as a cow with three broken legs. Panic drove me and made me into a klutz. Or so I told myself. The real reason was that I was moving too fast to control myself properly.

Fleeing became easier when the ground levelled out. We made better time and put as much distance between ourselves and the mountain as we could. After several hours of nonstop running, Luc began angling toward a much smaller hill and I followed him without question. The earth was warming and exhaustion was once again setting in. They were both signs that my lights were about to go out.

Luc ran straight toward the hillside, twisting at the last moment to burst shoulder first through some rotted boards. He then slammed into a metal door and rust flaked off it in clouds. Screeching in protest, the door was ripped clean off its hinges, revealing an old mine tunnel.

Stumbling inside after Luc, I spied a dark side tunnel with rusty rail tracks leading downwards and made for it. I was five steps into the shaft when I lost consciousness.

Chapter Seventeen

Snuggling into my cold, dirt mattress, I kept my eyes determinedly shut. I wasn't even fully awake yet and I knew something was wrong. Cold, dirt mattress just didn't sound right. Neither did the shuffling sound of multiple feet that surrounded me. *Here we go again*, I thought in resignation and opened my eyes to see what misery the night had in store for me this time.

I was unsurprised to see Vincent squatting like an enormous vulture several feet away. He'd changed into a midnight black cloak. The deep hood hid his face so well he almost didn't seem to have one. Like a turtle coming out of its shell, his pale face emerged from the shadows. He smiled nastily when he saw I was awake. His resemblance to my late maker was uncanny. All that was missing was the network of wrinkles. I followed his pointed look to see we were surrounded by vamps. Some of the lackeys held flaming torches. Considering how well we burned, I thought that was a bad idea.

I noticed almost immediately that Luc was being held captive. Two half-naked minions held swords to my companion's throat. A third held his sword ready to skewer his heart. The odds were definitely not in our favour. Luc's stony expression reflected his agreement with my silent assessment of our situation.

"Have I mentioned just how badly death sucks?" I asked the room in general. I didn't expect an answer and wasn't disappointed when I didn't get one.

"Get up," Vincent commanded and rose to his feet. The black cloak didn't suit him, not with his height and pallor. He looked like an overdressed skeleton that someone had brought out early for Halloween.

Flicking a quick look around the area, I saw we were in what had once been a dining room. The place had been abandoned for at least a couple of decades, judging from the dust and dirt coating the wooden tables and benches. Luc must have carried me deeper inside the mine after I'd collapsed for the day. He'd protected me at his own expense yet again. His face was blank, but the knowledge of our almost certain doom lay in his dark eyes.

Standing, I dusted off my hands, then put them on my hips. I counted thirty vampires in the room. Thirty against two, and one of those two was me. *Yep, the odds suck.* I might as well find something sharp, fall onto it and save Vincent the job of ending my miserable existence. Not that that could kill me, as I'd so recently discovered.

"Take your cross out and toss it over there," Vincent instructed me and indicated an area that was clear of his minions. I did so and it landed with a dull thump and a small puff of dirt. Tucked beneath Vincent's arm was the book we'd rescued from the mountain. On the ground behind him, his shadow had the shadow copy of the book open and was turning the pages. Tilting back its misshapen head, it roared silently in frustration, then slapped the book shut and turned to glower at me.

"So," I said into the heavy silence, "what's the plan?"

"The plan," Vincent said as he stalked closer to me, "is to kill you both slowly and painfully."

Personally, I didn't like that plan very much. "I doubt the Prophet will be very happy with that," I hazarded. Several minions shifted uneasily, but none of them were brave enough to voice their agreement.

"The Prophet is dead." I could tell Vincent was lying by the way he cut his eyes to the left. It was a sure sign of untruthfulness. I'd seen that on TV and when was TV ever wrong?

"He is not," I argued.

"He will be soon," Vincent snarled.

"You wish," I muttered. If he was still alive, I hoped he was seeing a vision right now and that he would rise from his coma and send help. The likelihood of that happening was slim to none. Besides, it would take hours for anyone to reach us. We were on our own.

Vincent stalked closer and swished his cloak aside to reveal a long, shiny sword at his waist. "I am going to spit you like the bug you were named for and watch you die," he said with relish. Smiling evilly, he pulled the sword free. So much for his plan to kill me slowly and painfully.

"Someone already tried," my words were cut off as the sword was jammed into my chest, "that," I finished. Vincent took two steps back, presumably to avoid the mess he thought I'd be making in a minute. His expectant look turned to puzzlement when I didn't fall onto my face.

His minions shifted uneasily when I covered a fake yawn with my hand. "Yeah, swords and stakes through the heart don't have much effect on me," I informed him.

Turning, Vincent pointed at Luc. "Kill him!" he yelled, as if that would somehow magically be my undoing.

"Wait," I yelled and the minions froze in mid attack. "I have something to show you."

Peering down his nose at me suspiciously, Vincent held up a hand to stop his vamps from cutting my companion's head off. "What is it?" Considering he looked after the prophet's domain, Vincent didn't seem to know much about Mortis. If he had, he would have been more worried about the fact that I could handle holy objects without bursting into flames and survive a sword through my heart.

"It's...private." The excuse was lame, but it was the best I could come up with on short notice. Truthfully, even if I'd had more notice I probably couldn't have come up with anything better. "The Prophet said I could only show you," I lied, hoping Luc was right about his earlier prediction about my whacky powers. If not, then we were both screwed.

As Vincent moved closer, his shadow leaned forward over his shoulder. Cocking its head to the side, it peered down at me. As he drew closer, the shadow started shaking its head in warning. It knew I was up to something, even if Vincent didn't. "Well, what is it?" Vincent asked. Just as he reached me, his shadow panicked and turned to flee. Connected to its master by the feet, it tripped and fell onto its face. Scrambling in the dirt, it tried to claw its way free unsuccessfully. I was relieved to see it couldn't detach itself entirely.

"Just this," I said and reached up to clap my hands on either side of his face. "Die, arsehole." With these cheerful words, his head imploded with a pop. Brains rained to the dirt floor and Vincent's headless body slumped to its knees. My hands worked just like the cross I'd laid against the vulpine female's forehead.

Holding out my stained hands, I turned to the rest of the crowd. "Ok, which of you buttholes wants a taste of the holy marks? There's plenty to go around." With a mad scramble, the minions fled, shrieking in terror. In seconds, Luc and I were the only ones remaining.

Bending to wipe my hands on Vincent's empty cloak, I straightened up and turned to find Luc standing right in front of me with an unreadable expression. Now that there could be no doubt I was the fabled Mortis, was he finally going to kill me?

"Do you want me to do something about that?" He pointed at the sword still sticking out of my chest.

"Oh. I forgot about that. Yes," he yanked it out and I staggered at the momentary pain, "please," I finished weakly. I doubted I'd ever get used to the feeling of naked steel running through my body. I held onto the small hope that it wouldn't happen so often that I'd have to get used to it.

Luc bent to use Vincent's cloak to clean the sword, then scooped up the journal that had been dropped to the dirt floor. He then loped off toward the entrance. As I scrambled after him, my wound started closing. In minutes, it was gone. The miraculous healing ability was definitely on the plus side of being a monster. I tried to think up other plusses, but the negatives kept popping up instead. Coffee was no longer on my menu. Neither was ice cream. If I'd been able to, I would have shed a tear at the loss of my ability to eat chocolate. Instead, I had a steady diet of blood to look forward to.

It wasn't just food that I'd be missing out on. It might be lame, but I'd secretly dreamed that one day I'd find someone to spend my life with. We'd get married, have a couple of kids and grow old together. Instead, an eternally lonely life loomed ahead of me. Childless and alone, I wouldn't be living, I'd merely be existing. *What do you think you were doing before Silvius jumped you in that alley?* As always, my subconscious had to put its two cents worth in. As usual, I ignored it.

We hiked through a dense forest in silence for a few hours before stumbling across a road. Following it, we moved far more swiftly until we came across a tiny village. With only a small cluster of buildings and one petrol station that doubled as a general store, it could hardly be called a town.

Luc snuck silently up to a beat up old pickup truck that had once been dark green and was now mostly brown with rust. I simply walked up to it. Sneaking wasn't in my repertoire yet. It was after midnight and most of the houses in the town were dark. Unlike us, the townsfolk would be rising with the dawn, or shortly thereafter. Our plan was to be bedded down somewhere safe before we could burst into pretty, yet deadly flames.

Already unlocked, the truck gave itself up without a fight. Luc popped the hood and took a quick inspection of the engine. He determined that it was operational and closed the hood gently. Releasing the handbrake, he pushed the old truck out onto the road, steering with one hand on the wheel through the open window. Between the pair of us, it was easy to trot along pushing the truck.

We had a choice of making either a quick getaway, or a quiet one. We opted for quiet and pushed the vehicle a couple of kilometres away from town before jumping in. Springs poked my butt through the cracked cream vinyl bench seat. A scratchy substance I believe was a mixture of horsehair, as well as other unidentifiable materials, had leaked out. It lay on the seat and floor like coughed up fur balls from a chronically sick cat.

Now far enough away from town that the engine coming to life wouldn't be overheard, Luc reached beneath the dashboard and started fiddling with the wires. He might have been born centuries before cars had even been thought of, but he still knew how to hotwire one. I was impressed, but kept my admiration at his grand theft auto abilities to myself.

Picking up the prophet's journal from where Luc had sat it on the seat, I idly flicked through the pages. Some were illustrated and I could see why the cinnamon stick didn't want his carers to see it. A few glimpses were all I needed to tell me it foretold the coming of the end. I was the vampire equivalent of the apocalypse and I still had no idea why the prophet hadn't turned me in. Did he want our kind to die? Weren't all prophets mad anyway? Receiving divine messages seemed to make them loony.

Although was anxious to take a closer look at the book, being jostled around in the old truck wasn't the best time to do it. The pages were fragile with age and I'd have to be very careful not to tear them. Closing the journal, I sat it on my lap as the engine caught and Luc set us into motion.

Sticking to the smaller dirt roads, we raced against the dawn. Farms became fewer and fewer and I was worried we wouldn't find anywhere to hide from the sun. Topping a small rise, I spotted the vague outline of a building off to the left and pointed to it.

Luc kept the truck at a slow and steady speed while we searched for the driveway. The entrance to the property was almost hidden by scrub, but we nosed our way through. From the overgrown foliage and general disrepair, I wasn't surprised to see the property had been forsaken long ago.

Two stories high, most of the windows in the house were broken and part of the roof was missing. I wasn't sure how much shelter it would offer us from the sun. Anything less than one-hundred per cent just wouldn't do. When we rounded the house and saw the barn, my alarm rose. Only two walls remained. The rest of the creaky old structure had fallen in, taking the roof with it.

Before I could ask if we should search for another place, Luc parked. He climbed out swiftly and strode toward the house. Stopping just short of the crumbling structure, he knelt. A second later, I heard the metallic snap of a padlock breaking. Swinging open a heavy wooden door, he swept his hand toward the dark cellar in invitation. *How could I have doubted him?* He was like a dark hero from a comic book, always coming to the rescue.

Stairs had once led down to the dirt floor, but they were a rotted, broken pile on the ground a few feet below. Leaping down into the dimness, I landed on my feet instead of sprawling on my face as I'd half expected to. Maybe I was finally getting the hang of being the living dead. Luc landed lightly beside me, pulling the trapdoor shut on the way down.

It took a few seconds for my eyes to adjust to the gloom, but there wasn't much to see. Shelves lined two walls. A few jars of what I presumed were preserved fruit had been left behind. Some had shattered, but the contents had dissipated long ago. About twenty feet long by ten wide, the cellar felt like a gigantic grave to me. Beetles scuttled through the dirt, but I was fairly certain they wouldn't try to eat me. Even though I was a corpse, I doubted I'd be very tasty.

Moving to the back of the room, I found a few old hessian sacks and spread them out as a makeshift bed. The boards at my back creaked when I leaned against them and dirt sifted into my hair. I desperately wanted a shower, but that wasn't about to happen.

Luc sat beside me and we both leaned down to look at the book I had open on my lap. "What does it say?" he asked. The clammy skin of his face was only millimetres away from mine. If we'd been human, I would have been able to feel his warmth.

I read the first page all the way through before attempting to translate it. "It's an account of how the first vampire was made." Excitement wormed inside me. This must be how tomb raiders felt when discovering treasures no man or woman had laid eyes on in thousands of years.

Luc's hair brushed against my face as he studied the picture on the right. "Is that what I think it is?" He pointed at a tall, thin and misshapen creature towering over what appeared to be a normal human male. The detail was exquisite. If the prophet hadn't been a vampire, not to mention out of his mind, he could have made it as an artist.

"Yep. That's the thing that created us and its definitely some kind of alien. It says here that dear old Dad used to be powerful, maybe even a kind of demi-deity." The term I wanted to use was demi-god, but I knew it would come out as an embarrassing stutter. "After landing here millions of years ago, its power started to fade and it began to die," I said with a quick glance sideways.

"Indeed," my dark companion inclined his head in agreement. I tore my eyes from his face and forced them back to the book. Sometimes, I forgot how hot Luc was. His lashes were longer than mine, damn it, and framed his dark eyes. His pale skin was flawless and without even a shadow of a beard. I'd always preferred my men to be smoothly shaven. Not that I'd had much choice over the past few years. They hadn't exactly been beating down my door. I really hadn't had much opportunity to meet men between work and spending quality time on my couch with my aching feet up.

"It says the human made a deal with our Father for everlasting life, but not what it would get out of the deal. Shows what a dumbass he was," I murmured. "It's more like everlasting unlife." Everyone knew it was a bad idea to make a deal with the devil. Or a creature very close to being a devil.

Luc shifted a fraction closer and my hunger flared. Sensing it, he went still, then carefully tilted his face towards mine. "Dawn is coming. When you wake, you will need to feed."

Since there wasn't a living human within the nearest hundred miles or so, we both knew what type of feeding he was talking about and it didn't involve blood.

My eyelids were suddenly too heavy to keep open. I fought against it, determined to get my message across. "That's not going to-"

Chapter Eighteen

"Happen," I said and sat up with a start. I'd been in the middle of trying to get some kind of point across to Luc, but I couldn't quite remember what it had been. At least I didn't wake up thinking I'd had a weird dream this time. Reality was turning out to be far stranger than any dream I'd ever had.

Feeling even colder than usual, I looked down to see that I was totally naked. On closer inspection, I amended that to *almost* totally naked. A sack had been wrapped around each of my hands. "What the hell?" *I don't remember putting these on last night.*

Luc, even more naked than me without sacks on his hands, was kneeling beside me. "You must feed and then you can finish reading the journal."

"That's not going to happen," I repeated very succinctly. "What's with the sacks?"

He shrugged a trifle shamefacedly. "I do not want to burn to death from holy fire."

"Since there is no way we are going to have sex, you can take these things off me." I shook the sacks, but they stayed annoyingly in place. He'd used my shoelaces to tie them on. *Very inventive. He's been busy while I was dead.* Accurately reading Luc's expression, I stood up before he could dive on me.

Standing as well and pretending he hadn't been about to pounce, Luc backed me up against the wall. "I handled our first time together badly." He ran a finger lightly down my cheek and I suppressed a shiver. "I wish to make up for that." He smiled suggestively and dropped his gaze to my breasts. My traitorous nipples instantly hardened. They didn't care that I'd made myself a promise. They remembered what it felt like to have Luc's cold mouth on them.

"No." I put my sack enclosed hands out and stopped him from coming any closer. "I'm not going to let you demean yourself again." I was almost in dry tears at the thought of it.

"Let me take care of your hunger, Natalie." He pressed his chest against my hands, bringing our bodies closer together. "As you shall take care of mine."

"I thought you didn't crave flesh anymore," I said in desperation.

"I crave only yours," he said, then closed the distance. His lips touched mine and any thought of further resistance fled. His hands clutched my hips and pulled me closer. My hand slipped off his head instead of tangling in his hair as I'd intended.

"This is ridiculous," I managed, then he lifted me up and pressed me back against the cold wall. Suddenly, it wasn't ridiculous at all. I wrapped my legs around him and put my strangely gloved hands on his shoulders. Luc thrust his tongue in my mouth at the same time as he pierced me below.

"Oh, G-G-G. Shit," I moaned as he kissed my neck and took my breasts in his hands. Then he started thrusting and coherent thought left me. For the first time since I'd died, I was warm. Heat flashed through me from the inside out as he increased his speed and tempo. My whole body tensed and I heard the distinct sound of bones snapping, then I was tipping over the edge into ecstasy.

After a few more thrusts, Luc sagged against me. I was still pinned to the wall as he rested his forehead against mine. My sack covered hands hung limply at my sides. "Did I break something?" I murmured.

"My pelvis. It's already healing." If I hadn't heard the smile in his voice, I would have burst into dry sobs.

"Can you please take the sacks off me now?" I asked dully. The sex had been incredible, but I was left feeling heartsick. I'd promised myself I wouldn't use him like that again. At one sight of his naked body, I'd thrown my promise away. I'd turned into an undead nymphomaniac.

Removing the sacks from my hands, Luc thoughtfully relaced my sneakers while I pulled my clothes back on. I'd left my backpack in Vincent's lair, so I was wearing everything I owned in the world. Finding my cross beneath my sweater, I tucked it into the back of my pants again. This time when we sat, Luc kept a careful distance between us. He must have been under the assumption that my despair was anger.

Instead of reading every word of the journal out loud, I'd read a few pages silently, then gave Luc the gist of it. It was a brief history of vampirekind, beginning with how we came to be. I skipped that part, since we'd covered it yesterday.

"Two thousand years or so ago, the Prophet saw the future of the vampire race," I summed up the pages I'd just read through. "The deal that had been dealt with our Father had a twist. It says here; 'When the light of humankind dies, vampires shall rise.' What do you think he means by that?"

"I believe he is speaking of when the son of Earth's creator died."

"So, vamps were lying low before the big J decided to take the bullet for mankind?" At Luc's nod, I nodded back thoughtfully. Vampire legends had become far more prevalent after Christianity had become so popular. I returned to the journal. "It goes on to say that vampires had begun to turn evil over the millennia. Huh," I mused, "I thought they were born evil."

"Do you feel evil?"

I thought of the naked bout of gymnastics I'd put him through twice now. I also pictured myself snacking on unwilling humans. Unwilling before my vampire mojo took their will away and reduced them to mindless sheep. "Sometimes," I said glumly. After reading through several more pages, I perked up a bit. "Now he's mentioning me." It was weird, I'd been famous two thousand years before I'd even been born.

Leaning down, we studied the picture. Mortis didn't look much like me. We were about the same height, judging her size to those around her. But she was far prettier, with a voluptuous figure that I'd never possess. Standing in a circle of kneeling vampires, she wore a skimpy robe with a plunging neckline and slits to the thigh on both sides. She held her hands up, palm out. The twin crosses stood out clearly. I held my left hand out to compare the imprint against the drawing. They were identical.

"Just for the record, I'm never going to wear an outfit like that," I told Luc solemnly, pointing at the skimpy robe then bent back to the journal. "It says; 'Thus Mortis, destroyer of the damned, shall rise'." I quickly scanned through a few pages. "You were right, I am hard to kill. Apparently, stakes can't kill me, holy water does nothing, holy objects aren't going to be a problem. Fire isn't going to have much effect either." That was good to know even if I had already figured a couple of those out for myself.

"Does it mention sunlight?" Luc asked. It unnerved me a little that he was so interested in finding out what could kill me. I hoped it was simple curiosity.

"Nope. I guess I'd better still avoid that."

Flipping through the pages, I read up on what the prophet predicted was in store for me. None of it made much sense. "It talks about the person who has started killing off the vampires. Apparently, she's convinced herself she's Mortis."

"How can she be when she doesn't bear the signs?" Luc wondered.

"I don't know," I shrugged. "She's probably got a screw loose." I read some more and frowned at the words before relaying them. "There will be a confrontation between us and we'll have to fight to the death." Great, I'd be facing my own impersonator and I had zero fighting skills. Meanwhile, whoever was pretending to be me was killing off our kin left and right with apparent ease.

Luc looked at the far wall of the cellar thoughtfully. "So, the faction behind Mortis is currently working for the impostor without even being aware of it."

"Is that a good thing or a bad thing?"

His answer was a shrug. Personally, I was disturbed by the idea of anyone killing other vampires for me. Even if most of them did deserve it.

"What happens after your battle with the pretender?" Luc asked.

I read through a few more pages and felt a chill run down my spine. "I begin the 'great purge' and start decimating the damned."

After reading through a few more pages, I put on a falsely bright tone. "There is some good news. Apparently, a champion will come forward and stop me before I can utterly destroy vampirekind."

"What do you mean?"

Now it was my turn to shrug. "He'll destroy me, I guess."

With a doubtful frown, Luc stood. "We should put some more distance between us and Vincent's remaining servants." He didn't offer his hand to help me up. He was no doubt scared he'd catch on fire if I touched him now that I bore both of the holy marks.

Before we left the safety of the cellar, I took one last look at the final picture in the journal. I hadn't shown it to the vampire cop and had no intention of ever showing it to him. Tearing it out quickly, I folded it several times and stuffed it into my pocket. Two figures were depicted on the page. A tall, dark haired man stood over a body with a sword in his hand. The dead female, presumably me, lay on the ground with her severed head lying several feet away. Disturbingly, her head seemed to be screaming.

Turning to stare down at me as if he sensed all was not well, Luc gave me a long, unreadable look. The sword he'd pulled from my chest was clasped in his right hand. I didn't need to take another look at the picture to know the weapon was an exact duplicate.

Now that's irony. The man who is trying so hard to protect me will be the one who will eventually chop my head off. That was my luck for you. Just when I'd finally met a hot guy who wanted to have sex with me, it turned out he was destined to kill me.

Chapter Nineteen

While Luc drove, I sulked in silence. I hadn't asked for any of this and now I was going to die. Again. This time, it would be forever. Death might suck, but I was just starting to get used to it.

"We should return to the Court before they send out guards to find us," Luc decided. "I don't want them to become suspicious of us and they need to know of Vincent's treachery."

"What are you going to tell them?"

He spared me a glance. "That he broke the rules and had to be executed. The Councillors will pick someone else to be the Prophet's guardian. Perhaps they will keep a closer eye on Vincent's successor in future."

"Yeah, maybe they'll even install phones," I mumbled to myself. "What are you going to tell them about me?"

"Nothing. They can continue to believe you are my servant and that you are of little consequence."

"But, Danton and his guards know I could understand the Prophet. Word will get back to the Councillors eventually."

"We will be long gone before that happens." Luc gave me a strained smile that I didn't believe for a second. Why would he abandon the Court for me? *He wouldn't. Not after seven hundred years of loyalty.*

"Why are you helping me?" It was a question I'd wanted to ask since we'd met. Now was as good a time as any to voice it.

"Perhaps I hope I can convince you not to destroy our kind," he said lightly and without meeting my eyes.

"Uh huh." I believed that one even less than I believed his smile. Like he'd said the first time we'd met, destiny couldn't be outrun, not even by a creature like me. The only way to avoid the total destruction of our kind was to lop off my head. Well, he had the tool to pull that off now. He just didn't know it yet.

For a change, we stopped in a town and hired a room in a hotel rather than finding a hole in the ground to spend the day in. Compared to the tiny village we'd stolen the truck from, this place was a sprawling metropolis. The hotel Luc chose was on the outskirts of the town. Presumably, this was so we could make an easy getaway to the nearby highway if we were discovered.

Houses were more modern than I'd been expecting in a country like Romania. I'd pictured the entire place being covered in villages of stone and thatch buildings. This town had wood and brick houses, telephone poles and big screen TVs. We could have been in any small town in Australia. Exiting the truck, we headed for the reception desk.

Luc had no trouble procuring a room, once he managed to shake the clerk awake. Sitting up, the clerk blinked at us owlishly. He had a crease mark on one cheek from where it had been lying on a magazine. He was youngish, in his early thirties, and I suspected he'd imbibed an illegal substance before he'd taken his nap. His pupils were huge and his hands shook uncontrollably. Long, unwashed brown hair hung around his face. I could smell the grease from several feet away. Stronger than that was the smell of sweat that stained his grimy red shirt. I was hungry, but not hungry enough to be tempted by this guy. Besides, I'd already had a taste of drug tainted blood and I wasn't about to try it again.

I understood their brief conversation, but couldn't speak Romanian myself, so remained silent. Luc spoke the language fluently, of course. The clerk was probably stoned enough that he wouldn't remember us, but if I spoke English, he might. Taking the key, Luc handed over the required amount of cash and gallantly allowed me to exit first. With no luggage to speak of, we made a strange sight as we trudged down the hall to our room. It was late enough that we didn't run into anyone who might have noticed our lack of belongings.

Our room was sparse and garishly decorated. It was a ghastly combination of colours, but at least the ugly blue curtains were thick enough to keep out the sunlight. The window faced north anyway, so we should be safe enough come morning. The queen-size bed looked lumpy and uncomfortable beneath the eye-searing lime green comforter. A tiny couch, covered in lurid orange fabric, looked even worse.

"Dawn will arrive in an hour," Luc said with a quick look at his watch. "I suggest we both hunt now, so we can get an early start when we rise."

"Ok." *Yeah, the sooner we get back to the Court, the safer I'll feel. Not.* I kept my misgivings to myself and quietly followed Luc to the exit at the far end of the hall. He left the door open a crack for a silent re-entry. Even someone as stoned as the clerk would be suspicious if he saw us leaving the hotel at this hour. Most stores would be shut, so what reason could we have to leave our room? A romantic pre-dawn walk? *Not likely.*

Luc melted away into the night and I was left to fend for myself. Two blocks away from the motel and deeper into the town, I revised my thought that I could be in any small town in Australia. We didn't have many cobbled streets back home. I could swear I heard a horse clomping by a couple of streets away. For a minute, I was scared I'd been warped back in time. The sight of bright electric lights shining through the windows of a tavern ahead eased my mind.

Three levels high, the pub had been around for at least a few hundred years. White paint had been applied so many times that it would be impossible to strip it back to the original stone beneath. Cracks ran in haphazard patterns in several places and had been inexpertly patched. The windows were large and dirty, but I could make out a few diehard drunks inside.

I wasn't in the mood to search further, so I hung around the tavern and waited for a victim to stumble into my trap. With time running out, I mentally urged one of the men to leave. It was spooky standing all alone in the shadows. A low, dense mist began to rise, adding to the eerie atmosphere. I had to remind myself that I was the scariest monster in the area.

My patience was rewarded after about half an hour as two men exited the tavern. Speaking quietly, they stuck to the street lights and avoided the shadows. Following in increasing frustration, I was about to jump them both when they parted. One continued down the main street. The other trotted down a dim alley. "Big mistake," I whispered with a grin and hustled after him.

Either my undead feet scuffed the ground, or he sensed me closing in on him. Sending a look of pure terror at me over his shoulder, he took off with a cry of, "Aiiiieeee!"

"People really say that?" I muttered. "Hey, you! Get back here! You can't resist my evil allure!" I whisper-shouted after his retreating back.

I had to give my fleeing meal credit, he *allll*most made it to the safety of his home. His key was jittering in the lock when I yanked him backwards into the bushes. We'd made a bit of noise during our chase and I didn't want anyone seeing me snacking on him. It seemed prudent to get out of sight quickly.

He was a big guy, broad through the shoulders and a good foot taller than me. Unfortunately for him, I'd gained considerable strength as the unliving and held him down easily.

When I angled my head so he could see my eyes, he squeezed his own shut so he wouldn't be caught in my spell. *Damn, the food is wily around these parts.* I didn't want to hurt him, but I also didn't want him to remember the encounter. Holding him down with a hand over his mouth, I reached down and grabbed hold of his nuts. As expected, his eyes popped open. "You are a she-devil." His horrified whisper was muffled behind my hand, but it was still audible.

"Buddy, you have no idea," I sighed without any actual air escaping from my lungs. Now that our eyes were locked, I had him under my control. "Sleep," I commanded, then bit down on a tasty spot on his neck as his head sagged to the side. He'd wake up sometime later in the bushes, thinking he'd stumbled into them drunk before passing out. From the trampled look of the shrubbery, it wouldn't be the first time it had happened.

Getting my bearings, I scurried off toward the hotel. I'd run quite a distance during the chase and dawn had to be close now. Full of blood, I couldn't sense the arrival of the sun as easily as I usually could. Thanks to the alcohol in my meal's system, I felt a little drunk myself.

"I am surprised you did not unleash your flesh hunger on the hapless man after snaring him so…handily," Luc said from right behind me.

Staggering sideways, I put a hand on my unbeating heart. "Cripes! Don't do that."

"Has your flesh hunger risen yet?" he asked me pleasantly.

"Nope," I lied. It reared its ugly head every time Luc cocked an eyebrow in my direction.

"Pity." With a sly glance at me, he indicated we'd arrived at the hotel with a nod. He pulled the still unlocked back door open and gestured for me to enter first. Manners sure had changed over the past few hundred years. Men rarely held doors open for women anymore. If they did, they'd get an affronted stare half the time. I'd never minded gallantry. Not when it saved me from opening the door myself.

Luc locked our door after a quick glance around to make sure no intruders had snuck into the room, then began stripping immediately. His eyebrows rose when I didn't emulate him. Tugging the curtains closed so there was no possibility of the sun getting in, I took a seat on the couch.

"There is plenty of room in the bed," he pointed out.

"I'm fine here." I'd also be away from the temptation of using his body to sate my flesh hunger on. It would be far too easy to take advantage of him again if I woke up naked in his arms. Taking my shoes off, I lay down. It was immediately obvious that the couch was far too small. Bringing my knees up to my chest, I turned my face away from the window and snuggled into the coarse orange fabric. It was dusty and smelled like old farts and cabbage. *Cabbage farts. Wonderful.*

Rustling came from the bed as my companion made himself comfortable. He made several satisfied sounds to let me know just how comfy he was. Clenching my hands tightly, I ignored him as best as I could. My fingernails bit into the twin holy marks as I worried about my impending death. Just how long did I have left before my head became separated from the rest of my body?

Dawn came before I had my answer and I sank into its dark embrace willingly.

Chapter Twenty

When I woke, I checked to see whether my hands were covered in makeshift gloves like plastic bags or socks. They were unadorned with the exception of the holy marks. Lying scrunched up on the couch, I was still fully clothed.

Luc sat on the edge of the bed, grimly checking the edge of the sword. *I hope it'll be sharp when he hacks my head off with it,* I thought morosely. If I had to die, I'd prefer one blow to do the job rather than several. The idea of Luc needing to take a few swings to get the job done didn't fill me with delight.

I received a sardonic look from him at my rather obvious whole body inspection and chose to ignore it. Leaving the hideous couch, I headed for the tiny bathroom. Turning the water on full blast, I took care of the flesh hunger Luc knew full well was raging through me as quietly as possible. After one good orgasm, I was good to go. Of course, I had to bite my hand to muffle the sounds. Forgetting my new strength, I bit right through to the bone. My blood had definitely changed, but it wasn't quite as acidic and horrible as Silvius' had been. Luckily, the bite marks had healed by the time I finished blow drying my hair.

"Shall we?" I said snidely to my sombre companion and picked up the book from where I'd left it on the coffee table. With my cross in place and book in hand, I was ready to leave.

Narrowing his eyes, Luc studied me, then shook his head. I was a puzzle he'd never be able to solve. Hell, even I didn't know how I worked. I didn't have the uncontrollable hungers normal fledgling vampires had. I felt sorry for my meals. I didn't particularly want to kill anyone. What sort of vampire was I? A fairly lame one so far.

It would take too long to drive back to France, so we headed for the nearest airport instead. Luc stopped long enough to buy a long black coat to conceal the sword that would be the instrument of my death. I could imagine the screams of panic if we entered the airport sans coat.

Leaving the beat up old truck at the far end of the short term parking lot, we hurried toward the small airport. It was still early enough for it to be crowded. Luc drew stares either from his constant frown, or his brooding good looks. He scanned the flight boards and located the next plane to France. "We must hurry," he said. "The flight is scheduled to leave in twenty minutes."

"That's cutting it close," I murmured. We still had to buy the tickets and make it through the x-ray machines before we could board the flight.

Smiling down at me and making me feel all fluttery in the stomach, Luc winked. "Trust me, Natalie. We will make it."

My heart also tried to flutter, but couldn't since it was dead and shrivelled. I hid my dismay that we would be back at the Court in just a few short hours. "My hero," I said in a high pitched falsetto tone and batted my eyelashes. This earned me another small smile as we reached the end of the ticket line.

We once again had space around us that separated us from the rest of the people in line. I was glad we'd eaten before we went to bed. Hunger hovered somewhere in my subconscious, but it wasn't demanding fulfilment yet.

Luc handed over a credit card to the guy behind the counter and nabbed us two seats on the flight to France. The card surprised me even after having seen him hotwire the truck. He was very progressive for someone who had died not long after the dark ages had happened. If I were to live for seven hundred years, what would I see? A list flew through my head; hover cars, teleportation instead of airplanes, telepathy instead of telephones, instant meals in pill form. Again, my imagination stumped me. *I need to read more sci-fi books.* Then again, why bother to read them when I could potentially live to see mankind's most farfetched ideas come to life?

Leaving the desk with our tickets in hand, Luc's coat momentarily flashed open. A young woman passing by saw the sword. Her mouth opened to scream and she made the mistake of glancing up at Luc's face. He bamboozled her with his vampire magic and leaned down as he passed. "You didn't see anything troubling," he whispered silkily into her ear.

"No," she agreed in a wooden voice, "I saw nothing at all." She continued on without raising the alarm.

"Neat," I murmured, impressed again by how good my new and only friend was at being a vampire. Maybe I'd be that smooth one day. *Don't kid yourself,* my subconscious scoffed. It clearly knew me better than I did.

It was my turn to use my strange powers of allure at the x-ray machines. I might not be smooth like Luc, but I was able to capture the eye of the guard easily enough. While I had the unfortunate sap under my spell, Luc went into action. He quickly removed his coat and hid the blade in the folds before placing it on the conveyor belt. I took my time piling my belongings into a plastic container, earning grumbles from the people in line behind me. It was hard to keep my eyes on the guard's and strip off my shoes at the same time, but I managed it without falling over.

Luc made it through the metal detector and retrieved his coat and sword without drawing attention. I released the guard's gaze with relief and put my shoes, cross and the prophet's journal in the plastic tray. It took practice to bamboozle people for more than a few seconds at a time.

"Finally!" An elderly man in the line behind me muttered in a foreign language I couldn't place. I rolled my eyes, but refrained from saying anything childish in return.

Hurrying through the metal detector, I rescued my belongings and quickly reshod myself. My cross received a grimace from Luc as I stuffed it back into my pants and out of sight.

We made the flight just as they were giving the final boarding call. Again, we were separated during the trip. Luc took the window seat this time. I'd have liked to have seen him try to explain away the sword if he'd been in my seat. Was it even possible to hypnotise a bunch of people at once?

This time I was trapped between two people in the middle section of the plane. On my right was a woman about my age. She gave me a quick smile, then pulled a book from her handbag. On my left was a teenage boy. His look was surly and lingered on my chest. My cool stare had him flushing and turning away, pretending he hadn't been caught staring at my boobs.

A few minutes after the plane took off, I gingerly opened the journal and began reading through it again. I caught the woman to my right staring in open mouthed fascination at one of the illustrated pages. It was a picture of me slaying a bunch of grovelling vampires. Luckily, the Mortis in the pictures really did look nothing like me. Angling the book away from my fellow passenger and into the light more, I noticed something I'd missed last night. The shadows cringing on the ground in the pictures looked different from their masters. *So, it wasn't just my imagination. The Prophet saw it, too.* But what did it mean? I had no answer for that one and the prophet had relapsed back into his coma, so I could hardly go back and ask him.

Again, our flight was over six hours long, but there were no delays this time and we landed well before dawn. I waited for Luc to reach my row before squeezing into the line behind him. He kept his hand on the pommel of the sword to stop it catching on the seats, or banging into anyone's legs.

We made it through customs with practiced ease and stood indecisively off to the side out of the flow of foot traffic.

"I guess the guards aren't waiting for us this time," I said after a couple of minutes of waiting.

"It would appear not," was Luc's disturbed answer. He might be fairly progressive for the ancient undead, but he didn't seem to have a cell phone. He motioned for me to follow him and headed for a bank of pay phones. Dialling a number, his expression turned dark when the phone rang out.

"Something is wrong," he said after hanging up. "No one is answering the phone."

"I thought the Comtesse didn't like phones." I almost called her the praying mantis again, but you never knew who was watching, or listening so I quenched the urge. *Great, now I'm becoming paranoid.* Hadn't I heard somewhere that you weren't paranoid if people really were watching you?

"While the Comtesse does not approve, she understands that it is a useful tool. A telephone was installed several decades ago and someone always monitors it."

"So, it's a bad sign that no one is monitoring it right now, huh?" My question was rhetorical and I didn't receive an answer. Our eyes met and we came to the same conclusion. The impostor me must have made a trip to the Court and not just for a friendly cup of tea. I wasn't entirely unhappy at the thought of hordes of vampires being slaughtered like cattle. Practically speaking, it just meant less vamps for me to take down later on. "What do you think we should do?" I asked. As I'd suspected, he already had a plan in mind.

"I must see if there are any survivors." I'd almost forgotten for a moment there that Lord Lucentio was the vampire equivalent of a cop. Of course he'd need to investigate what had happened. It was his duty and obligation. Now, if I could just wait somewhere safe while he went about his investigating, I'd be much happier.

"Are you sure that's a good idea?" I asked. "What if my impersonator is still there?"

"Then," he said after a short pause, "you shall battle as the Prophet predicted."

"Great," I muttered without enthusiasm as he headed for the rental car desk. I might be the favourite to win the battle ahead, but that didn't mean I was looking forward to it. I especially wasn't looking forward to what the journal said would happen after I slaughtered my way through the bulk of vampires in the world.

"We should feed and find a place to hide during daylight hours," Luc decided.

"Good idea." Any plan that would prolong the moment I had to face my nemesis had to be a good one.

"I'll meet you at the rental car desk in twenty minutes," he said, already turning away to find his victim.

Scanning the airport, I was frozen with indecision. I had only a short time to find a meal and I had no idea where to start. Then I spotted a likely victim and knew how a lion felt when picking a vulnerable calf out of a herd of water buffalo. A cleaner was heading for a maintenance closet to stash his tools away after a hard night of work. Pushing a plastic trolley full of cleaning products, his attention was on the floor and his steps were weary. A peek at his face indicated he was half asleep.

Glancing around casually to make sure I was unobserved, I closed in on my target. He had the trolley most of the way into the closet when I pounced. Pushing him inside, I pulled the door shut after me.

"What's going on?" he asked in French. It was completely lightless inside the small room.

"Sorry," I said as he fumbled for the light switch, "I thought this was the bathroom." I had no idea if he could understand me or not, but it didn't matter once the light bloomed. As soon as it came on, my eyes caught his and he was lost.

My nose was clogged with the overpowering smells of cleaning products, but that didn't deter me from biting into his neck. The taste of blood drowned out the scent of harsh bleach and lemon cleanser. The cleaner sank to the floor wearing a happy smile when I was done with him.

Opening the door cautiously, I made sure the coast was clear before switching off the light and pulling the door closed. My watch said I still had ten minutes left as I sauntered towards the rental car desk. My self-satisfied smile turned into a scowl when I found Luc already leaning against the counter, waiting for me. "That must have been a quick snack," he said with a gleam in his dark eyes.

"I've always been partial to fast food," I said with a casual shrug.

Leaning over, he brushed his thumb over my bottom lip, then brought it to his mouth and delicately licked it clean. "You missed a bit," he said with a smile.

Mesmerized by his charm like a defenceless human, it took the pointed throat clearing of the rental car woman to snap me out of it. Luc smirked, then turned to take the keys.

"Where are we going?" I asked when we were nosing out of the airport grounds.

"To a safe house."

"Are you sure it's still safe?" My query was dubious considering the lack of response he'd had from the mansion.

He inclined his head. "Yes. People I trust have already taken up residence in the house." So, he'd had time to find a meal and to make another call before I'd met him back at the rental car desk. Centuries of practice must make perfect. I didn't bother to ask who we would be meeting at the safe house. If Luc trusted them, then I'd just have to trust them, too. He'd managed to keep me unalive this long, hadn't he? My insidious subconscious tried to bring up the fact that Luc would also be the one to end my life, but I ignored it. There was no use dwelling on something that I couldn't change. My demise had been prophesized and that was the end of it. *Really? You're just going to give up without a fight?* The thought was too loud to ignore successfully this time.

We drove through dark countryside in the general direction of the Court mansion, but pulled up several kilometres short. The narrow road we turned onto took us to a small country town. As we drove through it, I wondered how many of these unsuspecting townsfolk had served as vampire chow over the past few centuries.

Our safe house turned out to be a rustic old farmhouse. Two levels high, it was made of a combination of brick and wood. Smoke flowed from its four chimneys, a sure sign it was a vampire abode. It could be the middle of summer and the fires would probably still be lit.

Luc pulled into a four car garage with a dirt floor that had only one other car in it. The vehicle was black and strangely familiar. I saw why when a door leading to the house opened. Igor, who had chauffeured us from the airport to the mansion and back, nodded curtly in greeting. He and Luc immediately began exchanging quiet conversation. I followed behind them as they entered the house.

I heard every word of their conversation and translated it without hassle. Apparently, my impersonator had burst into the Court mansion two nights ago. She had cut a swathe through several guards before being surrounded. The Comtesse and other Councillors had been whisked away by more guards who had apparently been prepared for a quick escape.

Maybe the impostor wasn't as skilled as I'd thought if she'd already been captured. Igor shattered my illusions by going on to say that she had then struck down twenty guards. The rest had fled before she could skewer them with her weapon of choice, a spear. She had disappeared into the night and no one had any idea where she'd gone.

"Does she bear the signs?" Luc asked quietly.

Igor paused with his hand on a door leading deeper into the farmhouse and shrugged. "I was outside when she invaded the mansion. I heard this from several of the survivors. But," he added, "I heard from a reliable source that she does have some strange marks on her hands."

Sharing a disturbed look, Luc and I followed him through the door.

Chapter Twenty-One

It was late and the men decided to postpone any further conversation until we rose for the night. "The bedrooms are upstairs," Igor said in English with the thickest accent I'd ever heard. It would have been easier to translate his words from Russian, or whatever nationality he was, in my head.

Luc nodded, he'd been there before. The directions were for me. I smiled my thanks and trailed up a staircase after my companion. The room I chose was small, with a double bed that was piled high with blankets. After a quick shower in the tiny bathroom down the hall, I stripped down to my t-shirt and climbed between the sheets. Exhaustion pulled me down into oblivion.

Opening my eyes just after the sun went down, I started back when I saw a familiar face a few inches away from mine. It wasn't a face I expected, or particularly wanted to see first thing after waking up. My only consolation was that he lay on top of the blankets rather than beneath them.

"Hello, *chérie*," Geordie murmured. His hand *was* under the blankets and on my butt. He squeezed to test the muscle tone. "Would you care to share your flesh hunger with me?" At his sly smile, I planted a hand on his face and shoved him as hard as I could.

Cartwheeling through the air, he hit the wall and slid down to land on his face. "I'll take that as a no," he mumbled into the carpet. Sitting up, I pulled the sheet up to my chin, amazed at my own strength. I was ready to launch him through the air again if he came near me. Luc burst through the door, sword in hand. He took in the situation and rolled his eyes when he spotted Geordie climbing to his feet. With a fatalistic shrug, the boy ambled out, straightening his clothes with quiet dignity. "Perhaps some other time," he said with a grin. A faint impression of his body had been stamped into the wall. If he'd been human, he'd have been a mess of broken bones and internal injuries.

"Someone should neuter that kid," I said as he disappeared from the room.

"Geordie is over two hundred years old," Luc told me. "He has not been a child in a very long time."

As far as I was concerned, he'd always be a kid to me. Now Luc, he was definitely a man. There was nothing boyish about him at all. I drank in his leanly muscled form as he stalked out the door. I wondered if I would be able to jump his bones a few more times before he killed me.

Dressing, I left the bedroom to seek the others out. I passed a couple more bedrooms before finding the stairs. At the bottom, I followed voices into a dining room. It was spacious, with heavy oak furniture on display. A worn rug in patterns of red and royal blue covered the floor beneath the large dining table. There were enough seats for a dozen people. It looked far too big but Igor, Geordie and Luc sitting around it. They were deep in discussion about our situation.

While the menfolk spoke boring strategy, I took a tour through the house. Floral wallpaper in shades of light yellow and peach predominated. It was very girly and didn't match the picture of a vampire safe house that I'd conjured up. I'd been expecting a dank cave somewhere deep underground, with heavy metal doors for fortification. The shutters on the windows was the only indication that creatures who were allergic to sunlight lived here. Heavy curtains, also in floral patterns, could be drawn across the shutters. No stray rays of sunlight were going to penetrate this house. It was weird how hyper alert I was about windows and curtains now.

Vampires didn't eat, yet the kitchen was fully stocked with modern appliances. The fridge and shelves were empty and the appliances were just for show. I didn't find any doors to a hidden cellar, or hear the cries of kidnapped humans who could provide us with meals.

Searching the bedrooms, I found a clean white t-shirt and red sweater that were several sizes too big for me. My own jeans and underwear would have to do for now. Borrowing a large brown leather handbag that had been left behind by someone with horrible taste, I stuffed my old clothes inside. Backtracking to my bedroom, I fished the journal out from beneath the mattress and hid it inside the bag.

I ambled back into the dining room just as the men were pushing their chairs back. A course of action must have been agreed upon. I didn't bother to ask where we were going. I was just supposed to be Luc's servant, after all. My plan was to follow along meekly and to keep my mouth shut until I had to step up and duke it out with the imposter.

Leaving the rental car behind, we climbed into Igor's black car. Geordie was silent beside me in the back, prudently leaving any wisecracks unspoken. After a few minutes of quiet, I realized everyone in the car was frightened. Especially me.

All three men, and I hesitated to put Geordie in that category despite his longevity, had brought weapons along. Igor had a nasty looking curved dagger about the length of his forearm. Geordie had a meat cleaver clutched in his slightly trembling hand. Luc had his trusty sword. As far as two people in the car knew, I was weapon-less. I was banking on the cross stuffed down the back of my pants and the imprints on my hands being a surprise to any enemies we encountered. The longer I managed to hide them, the longer I would remain insignificant.

When we arrived at the mansion, there were no lights shining through the windows. I couldn't hear any sounds of voices or movement. The place was empty of the living dead and was as dark and quiet as a tomb.

Staying in pairs, we split up to search the ground floor. Igor grabbed hold of Geordie before he could trail after me and dragged the grumbling boy off to the east wing. In room after room, all Luc and I found were a few stains on the ground and discarded clothing that had once been our kin. Furniture was broken, or knocked over and the floor was scuffed from the battle.

Meeting Igor and Geordie back at the stairs, we headed up to the second floor. I half expected a tumbleweed to roll across the ballroom floor when I saw the stark emptiness. Damp patches and empty clothing, the remains of fallen vampire guards, marked the polished wooden floor. I tried to avoid them, but it was impossible when there were so many. My sneakers started making sucking noises from the goo sticking to their bottoms. Geordie walked on his toes and made disgusted faces at the sounds his cheap tennis shoes made.

There were no mystical etchings drawn in blood instructing us where to go next. The members of the Court had fled. Only God, and possibly Luc, knew where they'd gone.

When Luc and Igor moved aside to discuss our next move, Geordie sidled up to me, meat cleaver at the ready. I thought he was going to hit on me again, but he surprised me with his seriousness. "I do not like this, *chérie*," he whispered, eyeing the shadows skittishly. We were in trouble if he was looking to me for comfort. Unfortunately, his instincts were true. Soft, stealthy footsteps sounded below, then began making their way upstairs towards us.

Luc and Igor exchanged a wary look, then moved to join us again. We stood four in a row like gunslingers of old, minus guns or the skills to use them. All three men brandished their weapons. I slipped my hands into my back pockets, hiding the holy marks. If anyone caught a glimpse of them, the handy ruse that I was merely Luc's servant would be shattered and the element of surprise would be lost. With my lack of fighting skills, I needed an edge and they were the only one I had.

Ten vampires entered the room one by one. They were dressed in jeans, slacks, jackets or sweaters. At a glance, they could pass for human. Their unnaturally dark eyes were the only thing that gave them away. Plus the fact that they weren't breathing. They carried weapons ranging from crossbows, to knives and swords.

Their leader, a squat, wide shouldered vamp with a shaved head, stepped forward. "Lord Lucentio," he said and inclined his head in respect. His weapon of choice was a curved scimitar.

"Martin," Luc responded with a distant nod.

"May I ask which side you are on, my Lord?"

Igor, Geordie and I exchanged frowns. None of us had any idea which side these guys were on, or who the sides even belonged to. Luc didn't seem surprised, he had already figured it out. My belated guess was that they might belong to the faction that supported my imposter. Luc cut his eyes to me and gave me a slight nod. It was spooky how he seemed to be able to read my thoughts.

Before I could speak, my attention was drawn to the shadow of a vampire that stood next to a window. The curtain had been ripped down, allowing silvery moonlight to filter inside. While he stood up straight with his hands clasped on his weapon, his bored shadow was slumped against the wall, picking its nose.

So far, my interaction with vampires whose shadows acted independently of their owners had not been friendly. In fact, you could say they had been decidedly unfriendly, since they had all ended up trying to kill me. Silvius had succeeded, hence my new identity as the scourge of vampirekind.

Two more vampires entered, carrying crudely made torches. All twelve of their shadows suddenly loomed against the wall or floor. Some twitched uneasily, turning their heads to take us in. A couple sank onto their haunches and held a soundless conversation with each other. One was making animal shapes on the wall with its hands. None were acting like normal shadows and that told me the vamps were the bad guys.

Aren't we all the bad guys, my subconscious said. *Worse guys than us then,* I corrected myself absently.

Luc was stalling, weighing up how badly we were outnumbered. Leaning backwards a bit, he caught my eye again. We had a choice to make. If we wanted them, we could have twelve supporters on our side. Or my side anyway. I thought about it for a second, then shrugged and stepped forward.

"Hi. You don't know me, but I have something to show you that you might find-" my words were cut off when a crossbow bolt thudded into my chest, "interesting," I finished lamely before I could raise my hands and show them the holy marks. *Getting speared through the chest is really starting to get old.*

With a roar, Igor and Luc leaped forward to do battle. Geordie danced on the spot like a frightened poodle, then scampered forward to help. He was screaming as shrilly as a hysterical teenage girl at her favourite rock star's concert.

As for me, I tugged vainly at the bolt lodged in my chest for a few moments before deciding it wasn't going anywhere. Sidling around the edges of the melee, I picked up a machete that had been dropped and waded into the fray. It didn't surprise me that I was screaming just as shrilly as Geordie.

Chapter Twenty-Two

Lunging, slicing and chopping with precision, it was clear Luc had far more skill with a weapon than the rest of us. Geordie stayed low, dodging in to hamstring anyone who came too close. Igor grimly swung his dagger with enthusiasm, if not skill.

Servants rather than soldiers, the impersonator's supporters fought little better than Igor and Geordie. We'd have been overwhelmed fairly quickly if they'd had any training. I was being completely ignored, so I took the opportunity to step up and swing my machete at an exposed neck. My target caught the movement from the corner of his eye and ducked, but not quite quickly enough. The machete thunked into his head and lodged there.

Turning burning eyes on me, he started toward me, grinning evilly. He thought I was unarmed and hence vulnerable. Before I could reach for my secret weapon lodged in the back of my pants, Luc's sword appeared through the vamp's chest. Pulling it free, he whirled back around in time to block a sword blow. Their weapons clanged loudly, then Luc spitted his opponent.

Geordie squealed and I turned to see him clutching at a bolt someone had shot at him. Luckily, it was lodged in his shoulder instead of his heart. *Aw, we have matching accessories.* Grimly searching for the crossbow wielding vampire, I discovered him crouching low near the wall. He was nearly hidden from me by his shadow. It was hunched forward, hiding all but his eyes and the wicked looking crossbow in his hands. Teeth gleamed in a bloodthirsty grin as the vampire quickly loaded another bolt.

Surreptitiously making sure I wasn't being watched, I pulled my cross free and speared it across the room. The shadow saw it coming. Standing, it tried to bat the cross out of the air, but failed. It recoiled as the metal passed through it and wedged in the vampire's forehead.

Thrashing like a squashed cockroach with its guts hanging out that just wouldn't die, the shadow snarled silently at me when I approached. It snapped at me more and more weakly with elongated teeth as its master kicked his feet, then was still. The shadow shrank into nothingness as the vampire died. Pulling the cross free before it could sink into the quickly spreading puddle of ooze, I wiped it clean on the dead vamp's now empty sweater and searched for my next victim.

Five of the twelve vampires were down. The remaining seven were still ignoring me, concentrating mostly on Luc. Bloodied and wounded, my pretend maker stood with Igor at his back and Geordie crouching nearby. They were surrounded by enemies and I didn't like their chances of coming out of the fight unharmed. It was a miracle none of us had lost any limbs so far.

Picking up the discarded crossbow, I pointed it at one of the bad guys and pulled the trigger. The bolt thumped into his back, missing his heart, but doing a good job of distracting him. Jerking, he turned, spotted me and disengaged from the fight. He stomped toward me as I frantically searched for another bolt. In the flickering torchlight, his shadow hulked large and glared at me menacingly. Now only three feet away, he raised his sword over his head.

Instead of simply splitting my head open, he drew out the moment in evil pleasure, enjoying my terror. In desperation, I grabbed the bolt sticking out of my chest and yanked it free in a surge of fear. The shaft was coated in my thickening blood. The vampire's pleasure instantly turned to alarm now that I was armed. He ceased grandstanding and his sword swung downwards. I plunged the bolt into his chest, then rolled to the side as his sword descended. With a loud clang that faded into the general cacophony, it hit the wooden floor. I slid a finger through a cut in the sleeve of my borrowed sweater. *Man, that was close.* I was pretty sure even I wouldn't survive a severe blow to the head.

My terror fled and terrible anger was replacing it. I was supposed to be their damned leader and they were trying to kill me. Snatching up the fallen sword, I decided it was time to teach them a lesson. I might be newly made, but that didn't mean I was entirely useless.

Choosing my target, I carefully aimed the sword, waited for him to pause, then rammed the blade through his back where his heart should be. I had better luck this time and hit my target. Luc's expression reflected his surprised when the vampire fell and he saw me standing there. I didn't have time to bask in his shock that I wasn't standing on the sidelines, fainting from terror. Two of the men on either side of me lunged forward. I dropped to my knees and they stabbed each other through the stomach. *Idiots,* I thought snidely. Igor calmly pierced one through the heart as Geordie leaped to his feet to chop his cleaver into the other guy's neck.

Luc bellowed a war cry that raised the hairs on my arms and lashed out at the remaining enemies. With eight of them now down, the last four broke and turned to flee. I tripped one as he tried to leap over me. Landing on his face, he skidded a few feet across the floor. I had my knees planted on his back before he had a chance to scramble up. A momentary view of the side of his face told me I'd nabbed Martin, the leader of the small group.

My borrowed sword sliced through Martin's back, piercing his heart. Suddenly, his shadow burst up and twisted around to face me. Black arms snaked out and wrapped around me firmly. They should have been insubstantial, yet they pinned me in place as if they were manacles made of iron. My strength began to seep away as cold filled me. Martin continued to struggle despite the sword through his heart. My life was being drained by the shadow to keep its owner alive. How, I didn't know. Shadows weren't supposed to be sentient, yet theirs were. Somehow, they had gained a form of life.

Luc, Igor and Geordie moved to surround me. They stared at the vampire twitching between my knees. "Why is he still alive?" Geordie asked. "It should not be possible."

His tone and expression were disturbed, yet reluctantly curious.

"That is a good question," Luc replied and knelt beside me. Still wrapped in the shadow's arms, I could barely turn my head. "What is wrong, Natalie?"

"His shadow," I whispered, cold to my very bones.

"Shadow?" Geordie asked, looking around. "What shadow?"

"You can see his shadow?" Luc asked me quietly.

"It's…draining me," I gasped out and my vision began to go dark.

Standing, Luc twirled his sword overhead, then brought it down across the pinned vampire's neck. As Martin's severed head rolled across the floor, the shadow released me, wailing soundlessly in dismay before fading. I couldn't remember reading anything about this in the journal. Whoever or whatever gave the prophet his visions had missed a few important details.

Free from the icy embrace, I fell gracelessly onto my side, shivering in cold and reaction. Geordie knelt beside me, reaching for my hands. I clenched them into fists before he could see the holy marks. Uselessly trying to warm my hands with his room temperature ones, at least he didn't try to cop a feel. Maybe not all vampires were all bad. At least not all the time.

Drawing Luc aside, Igor spoke to him quietly in French. "What just happened?"

Through my peripheral vision, I watched Luc hesitate, then shrug. "She was hallucinating. This is not the first time she claims to have seen strange shadows. Natalie is new to our world. What seems normal to us is abnormal to her. Perhaps this is her mind's way of coping with the stress."

Unbeknownst to him, my usual way of dealing with stress was to go shopping. I'd end up taking most of the items back because I couldn't afford them, but it was the actual buying of frivolous things that made me feel better. I'd never hallucinated in my life. Why would I begin to hallucinate now that I was undead? I hoped he was making this up and that he didn't truly believe what he was saying. If he did, then that meant he thought I had a few screws loose.

Igor didn't look convinced. Unable to come up with any other explanation, he had to let it go.

"We should get out of here," Geordie said quietly, looking over his shoulder to make sure no more of the imposter's army were creeping up on us. I had warmed back up to room temperature again and climbed to my feet. At Luc's enquiring look, I nodded that I was good to go.

Chapter Twenty-Three

In morose silence, we headed back to the safe house. We were all filthy and stained by the ooze of the fallen, and from the wounds that we'd received. My first order of business was to take a shower. My wounds had healed by now, so at least the water didn't sting when it hit my skin.

Clean again, I dressed in my old clothes, having depleted the safe house of anything else that would even remotely fit me. There didn't seem to be a washing machine on the premises. Not that I had much to wash.

It occurred to me that Luc might have a change of clothes that I could borrow. They would be far too large for me, but I'd be able to live with that until I could find something more suitable. I could hear him moving around in the room next to mine. *No time like the present,* I thought.

Knocking lightly, I entered at Luc's quiet, "It's open."

"I was wondering if," my words trailed off at the sight of Luc wearing a pair of pants and nothing else. A knowing grin slid into place when he saw my attention wander to his chest. "Do you have any spare clothes?" I finished up, forcing my eyes back to his face.

"Check the dresser," he indicated a chest of drawers, then slid his thumbs into his waistband. I turned away after a flash of white flesh, glad my face couldn't flame red anymore. Luc's pants dropped to the floor and he entered the bathroom. Trust him to have his own ensuite.

Opening a drawer at random, I pulled out a black t-shirt and sweater as the shower started. Resisting the urge to join Luc, my eyes fell on the keys to his rental car. They sat on the bedside table, unused and possibly feeling lonely. *Maybe I should pop downstairs and warm the car up,* I mused. *Maybe I should even take it for a short drive, just to make sure the engine doesn't seize up from lack of use.*

Convinced by my own desperate logic, I snatched up the keys and tiptoed back to my room. I didn't really need to take the prophet's journal on my short journey, but it seemed safer to take it with me than to leave it lying around. Igor or Geordie might stumble across it, then explanations would have to be given.

Moving quickly but quietly, I made my way downstairs. I held the borrowed handbag stuffed with Luc's fresh clothes to my side tightly so it wouldn't make a noise and betray my presence. Igor and Geordie's voices were a low murmur coming from the dining room. The front door was in their line of sight, so I sidled over to a window, not wanting to interrupt their urgent conversation. The window slid up silently and I slipped outside.

Luc's rental car was sitting where we'd left it in the garage. Taking a seat behind the wheel, I put the key in the ignition, then just sat there for a few seconds. During the fight with the imposter's minions, one thought had kept coming back to me; I was going to die. With Martin's shadowy arms wrapped around me, sucking my energy away, it had finally hit home. There was no way for me to survive after I took down the imposter then 'decimated the damned'.

Or was there? A crazy new thought had been plaguing me. One that I hadn't allowed to surface until a couple of minutes ago. *What if I didn't face the imposter at all? What if I just…ran away?* Luc hadn't seen the last page of the journal. He had no idea that he would take my life. *What he doesn't know can't hurt me,* I decided.

It seemed like sound reasoning to me. Running away might not be the noblest thing to do, but self-preservation was far more important to me right now. The key turned, the engine caught and I put my foot down. Dirt spurted from beneath the tyres, hitting the underside of the car as I reversed out of the garage. Cowardly fleeing for my life, I almost hit the door on the way out.

Peeking in the rear view mirror, I saw a face appear in one of the unshuttered downstairs windows as I took off. It looked like Geordie, but the image dwindled too rapidly for me to be certain. Luc would be sure to follow me and I had to get far away as quickly as possible. I kept my foot to the floor and I also kept the lights off to make it harder for him to tail me. My night vision was good enough that I didn't need headlights anyway.

Finding a highway that led north, I swung onto it and started passing traffic. Startled stares followed me when my fellow motorists spotted my lightless car zooming past. If any cops started chasing me, I'd just keep driving. I could take an exit and evade them fairly easily without any lights blazing to give away my position. I'd never been an overly confident driver before, but necessity had turned me into a speed demon.

I drove until I felt the pull of dawn tugging at my mind, making me drowsy. Picking an exit, I wove a random path until I found an underground parking area. Taking the ticket that popped out when I pushed the button at the gate, I wondered how I was going to pay to get out when I didn't have any money. *Worry about that later,* I instructed myself. Dawn was coming and I had to take steps to ensure my safety.

Driving two levels down to where the sun's rays shouldn't be able to reach me, I picked a spot at the back of the lot and reversed the car into the slot. My much sharper senses told me that no one was around when I exited the car. Opening the trunk, I boosted myself inside, then pulled the lid down, enclosing myself inside a handy metal coffin.

It was possible the car would be discovered and towed away while I fell into the temporary daylight death of a night dwelling monster. My chances of remaining undiscovered were higher if I hid in the trunk. It seemed safer than sleeping on the back seat.

Lying in the stuffy confines, I wriggled into a more comfortable position and tried to come up with a plan. I had no money, only one change of clothes and nowhere to go. In effect, I was in the same position I'd been left in after dispatching Silvius. Except this time, I was in a foreign country where English wasn't the national language. I might not have trouble understanding foreign languages now, but I still wouldn't be able to communicate with most of the population.

That decided me, I'd have to go someplace where English *was* the national language. Australia was too far away. I had zero confidence I'd be able to make it all the way home without either burning to death from the sun, or being discovered as a non-human entity. *What about England?* It was close and they definitely spoke English there.

I fell unconscious with the idea of driving north until I ran out of road and hit the English Channel. Once there, I would cross over to the land of my distant ancestors.

Chapter Twenty-Four

Waking, I stretched muscles that didn't really need to be stretched since they weren't cramped and my hands encountered metal walls. Before I could spiral into panic I remembered I was in the trunk of Luc's rental car. Outside my stolen vehicle, shoes clicked on concrete, car doors slammed, engines coughed to life, then the cars drove away. I waited for the noise to abate before popping the trunk open and climbing out.

An elevator over to the right dinged and a lone man disembarked from the depths. Dressed in a dark, sombre suit, he carried a briefcase and spoke rapidly into a cell phone. Finishing his quiet conversation, he slipped the phone into his pocket and strode towards the few remaining cars. I was moving before conscious thought told me to. My stomach didn't rumble, I didn't think it was capable of that anymore, but it was insisting that it was dinner time.

I waited until my meal had unlocked his car and deposited his briefcase inside before striking. Tapping him on the shoulder, I hid a grin at his decidedly unmanly squeak. He whirled around with his hands raised defensively, expecting an attack of some kind. His alarm changed to relief when he saw presumably harmless little me standing there.

Putting a hand over his heart, he laughed then spoke rapidly in French. "You scared the devil out of me!" I translated his words mentally and laughed with him. Then our eyes locked and he was mine.

He wasn't bad looking, with light brown hair and blue eyes. The body beneath the suit spoke of hours spent in the gym. My flesh hunger rose up and warred briefly with my blood hunger. *Do you really want to have sex with this stranger,* I asked myself incredulously. The answer was no, definitely not. But it wouldn't bother me much to take half a pint of his blood.

Swaying toward me at my unspoken command, his hands found my hips and gripped hard as I went up to my tippy toes. A shudder ran through him when my lips touched his neck. From afar, we would have resembled a couple locked in a passionate embrace. Up close, it was a horror story of my unnatural hunger for the sweet and salty substance that powered all humans.

My teeth broke through his skin and found the vein unerringly. I took as much blood as I could stomach, then eased him down before his legs could give out. He was sitting on his briefcase, but by his bemused expression, I doubted he even felt it.

After a surreptitious look around, I determined that our exchange had gone unnoticed and scurried back to my car.

Driving towards the exit, I spied the metal bar preventing me from leaving and remembered that I didn't have any money. Payment could be made by inserting a credit card into a slot, but I didn't have one handy. Fortunately, there were no ticket guards to ask me uncomfortable questions about how I preferred to pay. There was, however, a security camera perched over the exit. I had stopped just out of range more by accident than design.

Knowing that Luc could be close on my trail, I felt an urgent need to get back on the road. Reversing back a bit, I parked the car again, remaining close enough that I could make a quick getaway. Sticking to the shadows, I approached the camera with caution. A car pulled up at the gate and I shrank back behind a concrete column. The female driver inserted a card in the slot and drove off when the bar rose. I stared after her enviously. If I'd had any brains, I would have searched my snack for a credit card. My hunger had momentarily taken control of my ability to think.

Judging the angle of the security camera, I sidled up to it, doing my best to stay out of the range of the lens. What I was about to attempt couldn't be seen by humans. It would advertise the fact that there really were supernatural creatures living among them. Since advertising our presence was against the rules, I'd do my best to remain undetected. I didn't want to give the Councillors any reason to begin hunting me down. Staying under their radar had become my number one goal.

Making one more sweep of the car park for witnesses, I bent my knees, then launched myself into the air. Like a basket-baller making the greatest slam dunk of my life, I reached the level of the camera and swatted it to death.

Unfortunately, I put too much power into the jump and smacked my head into the concrete ceiling.

"Ow! Shiiiittttt!!" Landing awkwardly, I put my hands on my head just in case my brains were trying to leak out. The skin wasn't broken, but the bones shifted around unpleasantly beneath my palms. I'd cracked my skull in several places, but it was already starting to knit back together.

With the pain rapidly fading, I scurried into action. The camera was out of operation. Hanging from a couple of wires, it was spitting sparks angrily. Small pieces of plastic and metal littered the ground. I kicked them out of the way so they wouldn't puncture my tyres.

Jogging over to the barrier, I pushed it up, heard something snap and kept pushing until it bent backwards then gave an ominous crack. It would be just my luck if the barrier fell on my stolen car when I drove through. With that in mind, I ripped the bar off completely and threw it aside. Hurrying to my ride, I climbed in, then rapidly made my escape from the car park.

I was hit with the giggles as I found the highway and resumed my trek north. The picture of me launching into the air and crunching against the concrete ceiling was stuck in my head. Maybe I should get in some practice before trying something like that again. I was still so new to being a vampire that I didn't know my own strength.

It took me most of the night to reach the northern tip of France, due to traffic and getting lost and having to backtrack a few times. I managed to get turned around on the streets of Paris and gaped at the Eiffel Tower on my way past. Twice. It was almost worth being made into the undead to see the tall metal tower all lit up at night.

Fighting my way through the clogged traffic, I made it through the busiest streets and kept going north. The later it became, the less traffic I had to contend with. Stopping to fill up the tank before it ran completely dry, it took only one brief glance at a fellow customer to bamboozle him into giving me all the cash in his wallet. It amounted to just enough to pay for the petrol.

I finally reached Calais after getting lost a couple more times, then drove around looking for another underground parking lot to hide in. I wasn't about to attempt crossing the Channel with so little time left before dawn.

Locating a likely car park, I nosed the car inside and headed for the next level down. Securing myself in the trunk again after choosing a parking spot, I mulled over what I knew about the English Channel. I'd heard people crossed it all the time and that it could take twenty-odd hours to cross, depending on the weather and skill level of the swimmer. I wasn't a very strong swimmer, but I was hoping that wouldn't matter much now that I could no longer drown. The problem was that I would have less than twelve hours of darkness to make the crossing before dawn. Travelling to England by ferry or train was out. Someone might remember me. I didn't want to leave a clear trail of where I was going and make it easier for Luc to follow me. If he could track Silvius halfway across the world and right to the mausoleum where he'd met his timely death, he could track me easily enough.

It was a relief when I sank into sleep and could put my concerns away for the day.

Come nightfall, I woke to the comforting, if not comfortable confines of the trunk. It was hard to believe that I'd had a home and an actual bed once. It felt like my old life had happened a long time ago in a land far, far away. *Australia is far, far away, stupid.* I was allowing myself to grow maudlin and I couldn't afford the distraction right now.

Leaving the car in the parking lot, I scrounged for a plastic bag that wasn't full of holes and found one in a bin on the street. The lot I'd chosen was in an area that didn't see much foot traffic, so no one saw me scrounging around in the trash. Wrapping the journal and cross in plastic securely, I debated whether it would be good enough. I didn't want the journal to be water damaged, so I found another bag and wrapped the bundle inside it. It should be water tight now.

My nose led me to the water, past a shopping district that was probably quaint by day, but was mostly deserted now. I was tempted to break into a clothing store for supplies, but my time was limited.

The smell of salt water grew stronger until I could see the dark water lapping at the shore. I heard a ruckus as I approached the Channel and watched from a distance as a man in his early twenties slapped his arms and chest in an effort to psych himself up to make the crossing. He had a support team around him offering advice and encouragement. I looked around for my own support team and saw a lone cat sitting on a low stone wall, staring at me impassively. With a disdainful sniff, it jumped to the ground and sauntered off. *So much for my support team,* I thought forlornly.

Keeping my distance from the small crowd, I made my way down to the water. I clambered over slippery rocks, wrinkling my nose at the strong smells of salt and sewage. Water slopped into my shoes as I neared the Channel and my toes shrank back from the cold. As the support team raised a cheer for their champion, I stuck the journal and cross down the front of my pants, braced myself and plunged into the water.

It wasn't just cold, the water was very nearly freezing. While my competitor wore an insulated wetsuit, I wore jeans and a sweater. My teeth started chattering and didn't stop. I thought the exercise would warm me, but I was wrong. You needed live blood pumping through your veins for that to happen. I wished there had been some way to bring the spare change of clothes with me, but I hadn't been able to find any more plastic bags. Now I wouldn't have a dry change of clothes once I reached the other side.

Pacing myself several hundred yards away from my competition, I realized after about ten minutes that he was holding me back. My stroke might not be as smooth as his, but I also wasn't getting tired. Putting my face down into the water, I put on a burst of speed and trusted my hearing to keep me out of trouble.

A ferry was crossing the river somewhere in the distance. Smaller vessels chugged backwards and forwards. At one point, I had to dive as a boat approached. I surfaced when it was gone and continued my swim. It was a moonless night. Cloud cover helped to ensure that no one saw me cutting through the water.

Water lapping against rocks warned me that I'd made it to the other side. My watch told me I'd broken all the records, I'd only taken five and a half hours to make the crossing. If I hadn't been so frigging cold, I might have felt proud of my efforts. Sure, I'd only managed to cross so quickly because I was the living dead, but it had still been an accomplishment.

Clambering up the rocks, I steered clear of the crowd that had gathered to greet my competition. I'd left him behind long ago and they would be waiting for a long time for him to arrive. Spying a few chairs that had been brought along for the lazy to sit on, I crept up and nabbed a couple of blankets that had fallen to the ground.

Two old ladies, mostly drunk from the sounds of it, laughed raucously. I caught the tail end of a filthy joke and shook my head. Women could be very dirty when there were no guys around to hear them. Figuring I needed the blankets far more than they did, I snuck away into the night. Drinking alcohol was something I'd done fairly infrequently when I'd been alive. It was doubtful it would have the same ability to warm me inside now as it once had.

Wrapped in the blankets, I searched for somewhere safe to stay. Gone were the days when I could have booked a room in a hotel. I had no money, no identification and I didn't trust the staff not to come in and clean even if I put the 'Do Not Disturb' sign on the door. I had to find someplace away from the sun where I would remain undiscovered. I reluctantly thought of finding a cemetery and borrowing a mausoleum for the night. My mind rebelled at the idea. *Been there, done that, not doing it again.*

My foot caught on something and I lurched forward a couple of steps. *Graceful as a gazelle,* I mocked my clumsiness, glad no other vampires were around to witness my stumble. Glancing back to see what I'd tripped over, I spotted a manhole. The lid was raised slightly and blended in so well with the road that I hadn't even seen it.

Hmm, the sewers, I mused. They would be dark and deserted. Being beneath the roads would be safer than wandering the streets with increasing desperation. Kneeling beside the lid, I checked the street to make sure I was still alone. Lifting the lid as easily as I'd have once lifted a cup of coffee, I peered down into the shaft. A rusty ladder led down to water that glinted below.

Wrinkling my nose at the smell that wafted out, I climbed inside and pulled the lid shut behind me. I made sure it was properly closed this time so no other rogue vampires might stumble over it. Sliding quickly to the bottom, I wiped my hands on a blanket to get rid of the rust, moisture and slimy feeling. The tunnel was completely lightless. There were no markings to indicate which would the best direction to head in.

Choosing the left tunnel simply because I couldn't stand there for what remained of the night, I headed deeper into the sewer.

The odour of human waste was overpowering and I seriously had to rethink the idea of hiding out down here. *What safer place could there be? Humans won't come down here.* Except for the occasional maintenance crew, my assumption was probably correct. I saw no signs of recent human activity on the slime and moss encrusted walkways that ran alongside the sewer channels.

Passing the occasional grate that let street crud and water in, I knew I'd have to find somewhere better than one of the surface tunnels to bunk down in. Sunlight would still be able to find me here. Reaching an intersection, I now had four directions to choose from. I let my instincts take over and guide me.

Taking tunnels at random, I eventually found one that ended in a cul-de-sac. There were no grates to let in the killing light and I deemed I'd be safe enough for one night. The blankets I'd pilfered had helped to soak up some of the damp, but I still felt chilled. A meal might have warmed me up, but it had been the longest night of my new life so far and I frankly just wanted it to be over.

Curling up against a wall on one of the blankets, I huddled into a ball with the other one tucked around me. I was so wide awake I thought I'd never fall asleep, but when my watch said it was close to dawn, my eyes began to close. I gave up without a fight and subsided into welcome nothingness.

Chapter Twenty-Five

As soon as I became conscious the next night, I was on the move. I had no idea if Luc had bothered to follow me or not, but I had to assume he would. Dover was too small to hide a lone vampire for long. What I needed was a place with millions of people living in it where I could easily hide. London was my best bet. Now, what would be the best way to get there?

Emerging from the sewers near a park, I brushed myself off as best as I could, dumped the blankets on a bench, then headed for the nearest main road. With my journal and cross hidden beneath my sweater down the front of my jeans, my luggage was light. Being a smallish woman all on my own, I figured I looked like a low risk hitchhiker.

Walking down the road, I waited for a sucker to come along. Within minutes, a vehicle approached. Turning around, I walked backwards with my thumb stuck out in the universal sign that I needed a ride. A dark grey van swerved over to pick me up. No woman in her right mind would have gotten into the van after taking a look at the driver. He had wild ginger hair, a matching beard and the deadest eyes I'd ever seen on a live person.

"Where are you headed, love?" His voice was deep, inflectionless and as empty of life as his eyes.

"As far as you can take me," I replied.

After a deep, considering look, he nodded at the passenger door. "Hop in then and I'll take you for the ride of your life." His smile was wide and would have been utterly terrifying if I'd still been human. If he'd known what I was, he would have been the one to run screaming.

Accepting the invitation, I climbed inside and pulled the door closed. I was expecting the move even before he made it and was ready as his fist came hurtling toward my face. I caught his hand and yanked the hairy monster closer to me. His eyes opened wide in surprise with the beginnings of fear. I bet he hadn't been scared of another person in a long time, if ever. After a longer than usual staring match, he succumbed to my mojo. The usual dreamy blankness took over and he was ready for my command.

"Take me to London," I ordered and let his hand go. I wiped my palm on my jeans in an effort to rid myself of the soiled feeling touching him had given me. Hypnotised by the dark powers that animated my corpse, he took off smoothly. His driving skills apparently weren't affected by being beneath my spell. He made no objection when I turned the heater on full blast. Within minutes, sweat trickled down his face, but I was still shivering.

We made good time along the highways and byways. I was mildly disturbed that he hadn't fallen instantly beneath my power. Maybe it didn't work so easily on the deranged.

They should hand out leaflets when they make new vampires. A guide to being undead would have come in handy over the past couple of weeks.

I had plenty of time to examine the van, which I named the Lair of The Ginger Monster in my head. The smell of old blood, excrement, urine and perfume was strong. A human might not be able to smell it, but I could. I made an educated guess that the ginger psycho had murdered at least several people in the back of his ride. There was no obvious visible evidence of this, but I was betting a black light that forensic cops used would make the dark grey carpet glow violet from the overlapping bloodstains.

Was I concerned as I rode beside the murderer of an unknown number of people? Not really. Not for my sake anyway. I could easily snap him in half like the wishbone of a chicken if I wanted to. But I did get to thinking about the poor sods who had suffered at his hands. His big, ginger, meaty hands with their unwashed nails and rough callouses.

"How many women have you killed back there?" I asked him at one point. For all I knew, he might be perfectly innocent and I was just jumping to false conclusions.

"Thirty-two," was his serene answer. *Definitely not jumping to false conclusions then.* I turned to him slowly with my upper lip wrinkled in shocked disgust. "Also, twelve men and five children," he tacked on just to add to my revulsion.

"Why?" I had to know what would drive a person to end so many lives.

"It's fun. I like to hear their muffled screams as I slice them apart." He gave me a slow, insane smile, then subsided back into silence.

I might be able to squash the ginger giant like a bug, but I spent the rest of the trip with my attention on him to make sure he didn't suddenly snap out of the spell I'd put him under.

When the signs told me I was on the outskirts of London, I instructed the psycho to pull into a narrow alley. It was very late, but there was still a fair amount of traffic on the main roads. The alley was currently deserted, but that could change at any moment.

"Stop here," I ordered and the Lair of The Ginger Monster pulled smoothly to a stop. "Give me your wallet," was my next order. I felt no guilt or compunction against robbing the human killer at all and emptied his wallet of cash when he handed it over. Stuffing the bills into my pockets, I didn't bother to count them. I just wanted to get out of the van. If any shops were still open when I woke, I'd hunt for some more clothes.

I could order the psycho not to kill anyone else, but I doubted the hypnotism would last past dawn. Once I died for the day, I was fairly certain my hold over him would cease. There was only one way to make sure he didn't end any more lives prematurely. Reaching over, I took hold of his unwashed ginger mop and reefed his head around sharply. The sickening crack of bones and tearing of tendons wasn't pleasant, but I felt my duty was done. The thought of munching on the freak wasn't appetising, dead or alive, so I left him there with his head on backwards, staring at the headrest. The cops would have a hard time working that one out. Once they figured out they had a serial killer on their hands, they wouldn't shed any tears for him.

It was back to the sewers again for me, at least for now. Maybe I'd be able to think of a better solution when I had a chance to really ponder my future. Right now, I was on the run from my destiny.

Locating a manhole to the sewers was easy enough, they were spaced out fairly regularly. Picking one, I climbed inside and slid down the ladder. It was way smellier in this sewer than it had been in Dover. Globs and smears of excrement decorated the walls and narrow walkway beside the drains. Wads of toilet paper and worse things floated past in a steady stream, including the waterlogged corpse of a cat.

Choosing a direction that seemed to be heading north, I moved deeper beneath London. I trudged for a couple of hours with dawn drawing ever closer. Finding somewhere safe, and less stinky, was a priority, so I picked up my pace.

Modern concrete and metal pipes slowly began to give way to far older, crumbling concrete and possibly clay pipes as I took a smaller than usual tunnel. I wasn't an expert on sewer architecture, but I could tell that I was in a far older section of the sewers and that it was leading downwards. Down was good so I continued on.

I knew I was in an abandoned section of the sewers when the smells began to fade. The slime and moss dried up and it became warmer, dryer and almost cosy. Light bloomed in an intersection ahead and I was suddenly wary. Who or what could possibly be down here besides me?

Making as little noise as possible, I crept up to the intersection and peeked around the corner. I spied two crude beds made out of flattened cardboard boxes and a couple of blankets. The light came from a fire that had been set in a metal drum. *Could some hobos have found their way down here?* I wondered doubtfully. The idea that any human would have the guts to travel so far into the bowels of London was ludicrous.

"Ello, ello, ello," a voice suddenly boomed from behind me. "What have we here?" I jumped and both feet actually left the ground for a second. Whirling, I discovered that two men had crept up behind me while I'd been trying to creep up on them. Both wore filthy, ragged clothing and hadn't bathed in months, if not years. They were too dirt encrusted to tell much about them, apart from the fact that they were vampires. *Vampire hobos. Now I've seen everything.*

"This here is our lair, missy," the other guy said. His accent was so thick I could barely understand him even if he was technically speaking English.

"Who do you fink you are coming into our home like this?" the first vamp demanded. They were slowly herding me toward the fire and I let them. If this was going to turn ugly, I'd rather have room to move than to be trapped in the narrow tunnel.

"I was just looking for somewhere safe to spend the day," I explained, trying to reason with them, yet knowing it was pointless. They were predators and I was the prey. Or so they thought.

Exchanging a glance, their eyebrows went up. "Somewhere to spend the day?" the one on the left repeated in amusement.

"So she says," answered his buddy.

"Listen, girly," spat the one on the left, "we ain't running a hotel for vampire waifs here." His friend nodded in agreement. "Why don't you run along back to your master before he finds you missing?" As if they had any intention of letting me go. My self-preservation senses were in full operation and they were screaming that I was in danger.

I backed out of the tunnel into their lair. They followed me, fanning out to cover the only exit. The fire at my back did two things; it helped to take some of the chill out of my bones and it also threw their shadows onto the rough stone walls.

My heart tried to sink when I saw their silhouettes. The one on the left was scratching its head in puzzlement, while its master stood with his hands by his sides. The shadow on the right giggled soundlessly into its hands as its master furtively pulled something long and sharp from behind his back. What sort of vampire carried around an instrument that could kill its own kind? *A crazy one, of course.*

"I can't go back to my master," I said to stall them as I prepared myself for battle.

"Ooh, ran away, did you? Naughty girl," the vampire on the left giggled. As he did, the one on the right closed in.

"No," I responded and wiped sweatless hands on my jeans, "I killed him." That brought me a split second of hesitation from the vampire with a stake in his hand. Then it was hurtling through the air, aimed at my chest. It thudded into my heart just like all the other projectiles that had been thrown at me lately. It had the same effect as all the rest; none at all. I left it where it was.

I didn't have enough time to reach for my cross, but I had two other weapons at my disposal. Darting forward, I grabbed the face of the vampire who'd staked me. His flesh began to sizzle and his garbled screams were muffled by my palm.

"What are you doing to David?" the other vampire thug screamed before launching himself at me. Airborne, he was far more graceful than I'd been while trying to smack the security camera down. Pushing the other vamp away, I turned and received a punch to the face. Seeing stars, I reached out blindly and caught his hand in mine. Now it was his turn to scream. Gibbering in pain, he tried to yank his sizzling hand free. Grimly holding on, I pulled myself closer and slapped my free hand on his forehead.

He immediately began to melt, so I sprang clear. Both vampires stumbled around, flesh running down their clothes to puddle on the floor. They ran into each other, fell over, then rolled around on the floor in agony. I could see it was going to take a long time for them to die this way. It must take both holy marks to make their heads implode instantly. Unwilling to listen to the screams any longer, I avoided their ooze and hunkered down beside them both. Laying my hands on them like the healing hands of a devout preacher, I ended them both one after the other.

Now that I was alone again, I pulled the stake out of my heart and dropped it to the ground. The wood was stained a grim dark red. Wiping my hands clean on the now empty and filthy jacket of one of the deceased, I shook my head at the mess. Trust me to stumble into the lair of a couple of crazy vampire hobos. "It's my lair now," I muttered and couldn't dredge up any excitement about my new abode.

Wishing I hadn't left my pilfered blankets behind in Dover, I shook the dirt off the dead vamp's blankets and tried to ignore the smell. Doubling up the cardboard provided me with a very uncomfortable mattress. It was better than lying on the bare floor, but not by much.

I'd had another long night, but I wasn't weary in the physical sense. I was more tired in mind than anything else. Lying on my side, I drew the blankets over me and realized I was homesick, not just for my bed, but for my entire old life. The job I'd spent a good part of my time mentally complaining about seemed ideal to me now. Sure, I might have only had one toilet break during the day, but it'd had a few perks. One of them was that I'd had a whole shop of clothes to pick and choose from at cheaper prices than my customers had to pay. I might not have been living in the lap of luxury, but compared to where I was living now, my small apartment had been more than adequate to suit my needs.

What did I have now? A pair of jeans, a sweater, t-shirt and undies. All were in dire need of a wash. My bed was pathetic. I had nothing to occupy my time. I had no friends or family. *That part hasn't actually changed. You haven't had friends since moving to Queensland from New South Wales eight years ago.* That was true. Also, my family were all dead. I'd always expected to join them in whatever afterlife there was, if there was one. I was now living my afterlife and so far, I hadn't seen any sign of my dearly departed.

If this was going to be how I spent the rest of my unnaturally long life, then I'd quickly become bored with it. Reaching beneath my sweater, I set the cross on the ground close by and made sure the journal was still intact.

I'd slipped the page that I'd torn out of the book back into the journal during my trip across the Channel. Taking it out, I fell asleep studying the picture of my prophesized doom. The scream on my detached head was haunting.

My life might be meaningless now, but the alternative was unthinkable. *What happens to vampires after they die*

227

anyway? I had absolutely no desire to find that out for myself.

Chapter Twenty-Six

I didn't feel brave enough to go shopping when I rose the next night. Facing humans in my dishevelled state would be sure to draw unwanted attention. Cleaning up first would be a good idea. I decided to go on the hunt for fresh water so I could at least wash the dirt off my face and hands.

Luc kept popping into my head like an annoying song I couldn't help memorizing the words to as I searched the tunnels. I felt guilty that I'd abandoned him to the imposter. Had I broken the prophesy when I'd run away? He was supposed to kill me, but if I'd changed my fate, was it possible that he might be slain by the imposter now?

Deep in the bowels of London, I tried not to think of Luc and to concentrate on investigating the latest tunnel I'd found. This one was even older than the others. It was so cramped that I had to duck, or risk scalping myself on the rough rock ceiling. Hearing a noise somewhere in the distance, I stopped to listen. *Rat,* I decided and continued on. Once upon a time, coming across a rat in a sewer would have filled me with the utmost terror. Now I didn't give a crap. An army of rats could try to overwhelm me and I'd flick them off like nits. *Nothing in these sewers can hurt me,* I had just finished thinking when I stepped out of the tunnel directly into an ambush.

All the stealthy noises I'd heard during my exploration suddenly made sense. It hadn't been rats at all, but creatures far more cunning and deadly. A glance backwards showed me I was completely surrounded. Sly, crafty and tricky, ten vampires blocked the intersection and my escape. These vampires were a far cry from the pair I'd dispatched last night. They were clean, well dressed and worryingly organized.

A guy who might have been twenty when he'd been turned stepped forward. His coat was black, hung almost to the floor and looked warm. I envied him. My clothes were still slightly damp from my dip in the water last night. His black hair was trendily cut, if you were a fan of the eighties. He sported several piercings through his eyebrows and ears. "Who are you?" he asked in a cultured, proper English accent.

"Nat," I replied then corrected myself when I saw mouths open, "Natalie Pierce." I didn't want to go through the whole 'you were named after an insect' saga again.

"She's an Aussie," someone muttered.

"What? Who turned one of *them* into one of *us*?" The question was full of loathing and not aimed at anyone in particular. *Frigging poms,* I thought in disgust at their snobby attitudes. *Bunch of bloody whingers.* They'd always treated

Australians like distant and embarrassing cousins they'd rather pretend didn't exist.

"What are you doing here, Natalie Pierce?" the once trendy and now sadly behind the times vamp asked. The murmurs quietened.

"Um, hiding from the Councillors," I hazarded. Astonished whispers spread through the group. If this wasn't a pack of rebels, then my take on vampires was all wrong. Maybe they were even a band of my supporters. I decided it would be smarter to wait for proof of that before showing my holy marks to anyone.

"I am Ty," the black haired vamp said with a short bow. "We have been watching you as you have explored our tunnels." *Gee, that's not disturbing at all.* More disturbing was the fact that I hadn't known I was being stalked.

"We want to know what happened to John and David," a short, pixie like girl demanded. Most of the vamps were wearing black, but she was dressed in a red blazer and purple jeans. Her hair had been dyed the same shade of red as her top. She clearly liked to stand out. Maybe she hadn't learned the value of blending in yet. To be noticed by these creatures was not necessarily a good thing.

"They attacked me and I defended myself." I kept my answer as short as possible. The more I kept my mouth shut, the less trouble I could get myself into.

"*You* killed John and David?" a tall, wide shouldered male vamp said in clear disbelief.

Ty silenced them all with a frown. "Come with us, please. There is someone I'd like you to meet." Surrounded as I was, I had zero choice, no matter how polite they were acting. Silently cursing that I'd so handily fallen into their trap, I followed behind Ty as we traversed even deeper beneath London.

After nearly an hour of making our way through low tunnels, we stepped out into a wide cavern. The top was lost above the electric lights that had been rigged up at a ten foot height around the perimeter of the circular space. A group of around forty vampires, ceased their conversations as Ty led me to a long table in the centre of the room. It could seat twenty and had two long bench seats and one regular wooden chair. The dark wood was faded from age and the surface was scarred from rough treatment. Conversation picked up again, but it was hushed and interspersed with frequent peeks in my direction.

A man who I assumed was the leader of this tribe sat on the lone chair. His attention was directed at the book that he was hunched over. Something about the book gave off ominous vibes. It was a lot bigger than the journal that was currently stuffed down my pants. It was about a foot long, six inches wide, but only a centimetre deep. The pages were thick and weren't made from conventional paper. The book was far too old for that. Even from a distance I could see that the writing was in a language that no one in this day and age would be able to read. Only an ancient vampire would be able to decipher the words. And me, of course.

As the page turned, I caught sight of a drawing. It was strikingly similar to the one at the beginning of the prophet's journal. The demi-god, tall, thin and in no way resembling any creature that had walked the earth before stood next to a human, offering its wrist. *Who are these people,* I wondered. *More to the point, what do they want with me?* Unease skittered down my spine.

"Alexander?" Ty addressed his leader. When he looked up, Ty stepped forward and bowed respectfully.

"Who do you have there, Ty?" The question was in French. I pretended not to understand and examined him curiously. Around fifty in mortal years, Alexander was probably much, much older than that. His suit had gone out of fashion around two hundred years ago. His white shirt had lace at the collar and cuffs. No man in their right mind would wear lace these days. Silver hair was swept back from his forehead. He had few lines on his face and could have been considered handsome if meeting his eyes hadn't been like staring into the pits of hell.

"Her name is Natalie Pierce. We found her wandering the tunnels." Ty spoke rapidly and seemed nervous.

"So," Alexander stood and approached me, "this is the intruder who so rudely dispatched John and David, our faithful watchdogs." I kept my face bland and interested, giving away no clue that I could understand everything they were saying.

Staring into my face, Alexander did his best to psych me into blurting out something stupid. Little did he know that I'd faced creatures that were far more dangerous and crazy than him. Silvius had kidnapped me and made me what I was. Vincent had stabbed me through the heart with the sword that was destined to take my head. One had killed me and the other had tried to finish the job properly. What was Alexander going to do to me? What could he do that hadn't already been tried before? That was a question I didn't really want an answer to.

"Where is your maker, girl?" he asked me in lightly accented English.

"Dead." No one was shocked by the knowledge. "A Court guard came to Australia and killed him." I wasn't about to mention names, not unless I had to. "He brought me back to France and introduced me to the Court. They expected me to bow and scrape to them, but that just isn't my style. So, I took off and ended up here."

After another lengthy stare, Alexander nodded and stepped back. "You are welcome to join our little family," he indicated the group of vampires who had drawn closer to watch the exchange. "Stay as long as you like."

I had the feeling this was an invitation I couldn't refuse. Everyone looked at me curiously, almost as if I was a new species. Compared to them, I guessed I was.

Ty drew me aside as their leader returned to his book. "Roxie," he gestured to the pixie girl. She scowled then ambled over. "Show Natalie to the sleeping chamber," he instructed.

With a bad tempered jerk of her head, Roxie stomped off toward a wider tunnel. We headed upwards and the passage emptied out into an abandoned subway station. A few carriages had been left behind when the station had ceased to be operational. There were five in total. They were made of wood and the paint long ago faded, or peeled off. It was like stepping back in time before everything had been made of metal or plastic.

Roxie headed past the first four carriages to the last one in the row. Climbing the narrow stairs after her, I saw that the carriage had been converted into a sleeping area. The seats had been removed and bunk beds had been installed in their place.

"Pick a bed that doesn't already have blankets," Roxie said without a speck of graciousness. "Blankets are in the box up the front." I followed the finger she pointed with and saw the box in question. It was a beat up old trunk that was covered in scratches.

"Thanks." My reply was about as gracious as her offer had been. I retrieved a couple of moth eaten blankets from the trunk and chose the top bunk right at the back of the train. Roxie watched me with all the welcome of a dog hunkered over a rotten bone.

"So," I said when my bed was made, "what do you all do here?" I was trying to make idle conversation and was doing a dismal job of it. Something about these vamps, about this whole place had my fight or flight instincts jockeying for position. Vampires were everywhere, watching me, watching Roxie, watching each other. It would be impossible to leave without being noticed.

"We eat, we sleep, we fuck," Roxie said with a sneer. "What else does our kind do?" On that note, she turned and stomped back toward the main cavern.

"Ok, then," I mumbled to myself. While eating, sleeping and fucking were all enjoyable to some extent, it just wasn't enough for me. There had to be more to this existence than satiating our hungers. Was that why I was so different from other vampires? Because I had retained my favourite pastime of reading? Because I missed my old life?

Walking back to the main cavern slowly, I reviewed what I knew of vampires in general. I hadn't spent enough time in their company to know what habits they had. Luc and I had been on the move so much that we hadn't had time to chat about what we liked to do in our spare time.

Thinking of him brought another flash of shame. I was startled to realize I missed him. Out of all the vamps I'd met so far, Luc was easily the nicest. *You just miss his body,* my mind whispered snidely. That was true. I hadn't fed my flesh hunger in a while now. I wasn't the least bit tempted to bounce on any other vampire I'd met. Ty was cute in a pierced, bad boy kind of way, but I just couldn't see myself getting naked with him.

Conversation paused as I made my reappearance, then quickly resumed again. I was a five second wonder. Sidelong looks were sent my way, but heads turned away when I tried to catch anyone's eye. After a few minutes of this, it dawned on me that almost all of the vampires here were terrified. From the way their gazes repeatedly returned to Alexander before skittering away again, I deduced that he was the source of their fear.

Standing on the fringes, I watched them all watching their supreme leader. It was one tiny mistake that gave Alexander away. He sat at the table, once more hunched over the book. His silhouette lay on the floor beside him, reading its own shadow copy of the book at a shadow table. Alexander raised a hand and scratched his nose. His shadow didn't. It was good. Very good. But the silhouette wasn't quite paying enough attention.

Every vampire I'd met who had a shadow that could think for itself had tried to kill me. I was under no illusions that Alexander would be any different. So far, none of the vamps had seemed to be aware of what their shadows were up to. Sentient shadows were a mystery that I just didn't have an answer for. One thing was certain, in my efforts to avoid my destiny, I'd landed in the den of yet another evil being. More evil than the average vampire, that was.

A group of four rebels standing nearby exchanged whispers, taking turns to stare openly at me. After a heated discussion, they sauntered over with exaggerated casualness. Three were male and one was female. They wore black coats like Ty's and had almost as many piercings. The female's eye makeup was gothic and made her skin seem almost translucently pale. Her pale yellow hair was cut short, like a boy's.

"So, what part of Australia are you from?" one of the guys asked. His accent was more Irish or Scottish than English.

"Brisbane, Queensland."

"Queensland is supposed to be the 'sunshine state' isn't it?" another male said. "You don't have much of a tan, do you?" he sniggered.

"I don't get much sun these days," I reminded him. I'd have one hell of a tan for approximately a nanosecond before I disintegrated. The others sniggered some more.

"How long have you been one of the nocturnal?" the girl asked. Her accent was almost as cultured as Ty's. I judged her to be the oldest of the four, in vampire years. They all looked to be around their early to mid-twenties.

They wouldn't believe me if I told them I'd been turned less than three weeks ago. I should still be a ravenous, sex starved lunatic from what Luc had told me. "Almost a year," I lied.

"If you need to screw, I'm up for it," offered the third guy. His teeth overlapped when he grinned. How he could take a bite from a human and not tear out their jugular by accident was a mystery.

"I'll keep that in mind," I responded as politely as possible.

Ty kept his eye on me from a distance during our conversation. He didn't make it obvious that he was watching me, but I was aware of his scrutiny.

Several other small groups approached me to make inane conversation. They sized me up and offered their services if my flesh hunger got out of control. Most of them were jittery and their attention constantly flitted to Alexander. The man himself kept his focus on the book, flipping through it and reading pages seemingly at random.

I wondered how fifty-odd vampires could live in one place without being discovered. Even in a city the size of London, surely they would be noticed. *That's not my problem,* I told myself. *I need to concentrate on getting out of here.* That was true and it was becoming clearer to me as each minute passed with excruciating slowness. I didn't want to live in fear of a man who wasn't even my master. If I had to live as a monster, then I'd rather do it on my own than in company such as this.

As the hours passed, I tried to blend in and to watch the group as a whole. Patrols of two came and went regularly. They reported to Ty each time they returned. He listened gravely, nodded then sent another pair out into the tunnels. I'd had no chance of remaining undetected in the lair that had so temporarily been my home.

Dawn neared and vamps began drifting off toward the railway tunnel. I hadn't had enough time to work out whether there were any patterns to the patrols yet, but I wasn't going to stay here much longer. Come nightfall, I was going to make a break for it. I had a bad feeling about these sewer vamps, especially about their leader. My hope was, if he really was up to something, he would let me settle in for a few nights before he did anything unpleasant to me. As a newcomer and someone who had killed two of his watchdogs, I wasn't going to be held in very high regard.

Following the small pockets of huddled groups, I trudged to the last train and made my way to my chosen bunk. Copying the others who had the top bunk, I vaulted up and lay down. This time, I managed not to smash my head into the ceiling. Not only would that have been embarrassing, it would have been difficult to explain. Vampires were many things, but they were rarely clumsy.

I didn't want to accidentally roll over when I woke and risk crushing the journal. Thinking of a hiding place that might work, I removed it and the cross from their place of concealment beneath my clothes.

Slitting a hole in the side of the mattress facing the back wall, I winced at the low tearing noise and slid my belongings inside. A thorough search would uncover them easily enough, but I was hoping it wouldn't come to that. *This time tomorrow, I'll be far away, sleeping somewhere safe,* I told myself. I just hoped I wasn't kidding myself.

Chapter Twenty-Seven

Waking with unaccustomed alertness, I lay utterly still, filled with the knowledge that something was seriously wrong. This had happened to me numerous times lately, but this time it was worse than usual. The lumpy mattress I'd been lying on had mysteriously changed into a cold, hard surface. I'd also managed to acquire bracelets around my wrists and ankles while I slept. If I wasn't mistaken, they were the kind of bracelets that had chains attached to them. They were too heavy to be made of anything but strong steel or iron.

Knowing I couldn't put it off forever, I opened my eyes to see what kind of trouble I'd landed myself in while I'd been dead to the world.

I'd been transferred from my not so comfortable mattress to a far less comfortable stone slab. The stone was deep black and had been polished to an almost mirror like sheen. The word 'altar' sprang to mind. This conjured up images of black and white movies where the hapless damsels were rescued in the nick of time by their burly boyfriends. I didn't have a boyfriend of any description, let alone a burly one. Luc and I had slept together a couple of times, but we weren't exactly dating.

Disappearing beneath the altar, the thick chains were secured somewhere out of my sight. My hands were clenched tightly into fists, hiding the twin holy marks. Had my body managed to protect itself while I was being carried away in an unanimated state? It must have, or I wouldn't have woken at all. The vamps would have taken drastic action to end my life if they knew who and what I was.

Six of my kin stood a few feet back from the altar. Dressed in black cloaks with the hoods up to hide their faces, they were mostly anonymous. Despite his disguise, I recognized Ty from his general shape and size. Not to mention from the glint of metal I spied from his piercings beneath his hood. They stood silently, waiting for something. Or someone.

Torchlight flickered unsteadily on the walls. There were too few to illuminate the area very well, not that any of us really needed the light. We were in a natural cave, judging by the roughly formed rock walls and dirt floor. Moisture ran down the walls and gathered in tiny streams that flowed into a crack in the floor. The monotonous plinking sound of dripping water echoed from within one of the four tunnels that branched off to the sides. I sensed we were deeper beneath the earth now, but I didn't know just how far down we were.

A small table sat at the base of the altar. It had been carved from the same black stone as the smooth slab that I lay on. The workmanship was functional rather than decorative. It had been designed for one purpose and that wasn't to dazzle people with its beauty.

A small bowl was centred on the table. Made of plain brown clay, it had been stained almost black from repeated usage. Some type of thick, dark liquid had spilled over the sides. Sitting beside it was the book Alexander had been reading. This was clearly a room where dark rituals were performed. Since I was the helpless damsel in distress who was currently chained to the altar, it wasn't hard to guess that I was going to be the star of the next ritual.

Muffled footsteps sounded in the distance, quickly drawing closer. My anxiety grew. If my heart had been able to beat, it would have been working at triple time.

Alexander's shadow preceded him as he emerged from one of the smaller tunnels and strode into the room. It turned its head and studied me for a long moment before suddenly falling back behind its master. Instead of retreating to the floor like everyone else's shadows, it took up a spot on the wall so it could watch the proceedings.

Why no one else could see the moving silhouettes was an ongoing puzzle to me. I knew it wasn't just a figment of my imagination because of the shadow that had tried to suck my energy dry. The sentient shadows were real, but I was the only one who ever saw them in their unnatural action. Sometimes, it really sucked being Mortis.

Alexander wore a cloak of deep maroon. He threw the hood back dramatically to reveal his solemn expression. The leader of the sewer vamps obviously saw no reason to hide his face from me. Why would he when I would be dead soon? His eyes, black, inhuman and as insane as my maker's had been, raked over me.

Fear crawled from my stomach upwards and lodged in my throat. What was it with ancient vampires? Were they all crazy? Maybe that's what happened to beings that lived for thousands of years. Their minds couldn't cope with a life that never ended. I wasn't sure I wanted to live for another hundred years, let alone a thousand.

"Good, you are awake," he said with a small, polite smile.

"I have to say, I'm not impressed with your hospitality so far," I replied, hiding the quiver in my voice. It was highly unlikely I could kill these creatures with shame, but I'd give it a try anyway. "I thought Europeans were raised better than that."

"You murdered two of our…associates," Alexander pointed out as he rounded the table and picked up the book. It was a weak excuse to chain me up and kill me and we both knew it. "If you were expecting hospitality, then you should have found somewhere else to cower during the daylight hours."

Gee, I guess I've been told. "How can I murder someone if they're already dead?" I muttered. I hadn't been cowering in the lair I'd so briefly occupied. I'd been shivering with cold. There was a big difference.

Alexander raised his head and his silver hair glinted in the torchlight. "You will very shortly find that out for yourself, my dear." He smiled to display just how delighted he would be at having the chance to show me.

"What exactly are you planning to do to me?" I wasn't expecting a detailed answer and was unpleasantly surprised when I received one.

"I am going to cut open your chest and pour my blood directly onto your heart." Alexander didn't bother to look up from the book as he gave his off-hand reply. Now I knew what the black crud in the bowl was, although I'd already had my suspicions. Two of the black hooded vampire lackeys shifted uncomfortably at the pronouncement of my doom.

Not everyone was happy about participating in this ritual. Maybe because it had been practiced on members of their dysfunctional family before. Random disappearances within their ranks would explain why the others were so nervous and scared. Deep down, they knew Alexander was responsible. With nowhere else to go and without anyone else to lead them, they stuck around and hoped they wouldn't be the next to disappear.

"What purpose is that possibly going to serve?" I asked.

This time, Alexander looked up from the book and I wished he hadn't. His eyes glowed with almost religious fervour. "I pride myself on being somewhat of a scientist. You will help me to perform an experiment. This book," he held it up and I saw a detailed drawing of our Father on the crudely made leather cover, "is incredibly ancient and was passed down to me from my maker. It foretells our ascendance to a greater state than we currently occupy, yet it does not indicate exactly how this will happen. And so, I experiment on trespassers in an effort to discover how to make this happen." Yep, that was definitely religious fervour all right. Did I even want to know what kind of religion an ancient vampire followed? Nope. Not in the least. My curiosity on that subject was non-existent.

"Ok, so you want to experiment on me. What result is the experiment supposed to have?"

A crafty look slid over his face, he didn't want to divulge his reasoning to his followers, but he also didn't want to give up an opportunity to gloat. Gloating won out, as I'd suspected it would. "As the book foretells, I am trying to create a new breed of vampire. One that is stronger, faster and superior in every way. We will finally become what we were meant to be, instead of the pitiful creatures we currently are." If he'd been human, spittle would have flown from his lips with the force of his conviction.

I almost didn't need him to say the rest. On some level, I knew where he was going with his experiment. "And what are we meant to be?"

"Divinities!" Alexander gazed at the cover of the book, then gently lay it down. "Or as close to divinities as we can become." The word he wanted to call us was 'gods', he just couldn't say it without stuttering.

"You want to rule the earth, enslave mankind, etcetera, etcetera?" That was usually what the vampires ultimately wanted in the movies. I didn't see the sense in it myself. Humans were unpredictable and extremely inventive. They'd find a way to overthrow their evil masters. Even if some of the oldest vampires could stay awake during sunlight hours, they were still extremely vulnerable to it. One shaft of sunlight would be their undoing. There were a lot more humans than there were vampires. Surely, they would overwhelm us and drag us either kicking and screaming, or dead to the world from our daytime hiding spots.

"Naturally," Alexander's smile was courteous and he even managed a twinkle in his eye. "Why should we hide out here in the bowels of the earth when we should be living high above the humans?"

You couldn't argue with a madman and Alexander had left sanity behind a long, long time ago. I chose to remain silent.

Luc had told me the first night we'd met that to drink the blood of our kind would kill us. I didn't suppose having it poured onto my heart would be a fun experience. In fact, it was almost certain to be excruciatingly painful and end in my death. Pretty soon, I'd be just one more blemish to be wiped off the altar.

"I take it you've tried this experiment before?" I made one last ditch effort to escape using the power of persuasion. It had never been my strong suit before, but maybe I'd gained the ability when I'd joined the exclusive undead club.

"Many times," Alexander replied, flicking through the book again.

"And you've failed each time," I pointed out. "What makes you think I'll be any different?" Ok, my argument was weak and far from persuasive. It was the best I could come up with considering I was chained down and was looking at a vastly shortened life span.

"I don't," was his reply. Stopping at the page he wanted, Alexander put the book down and pulled a knife from his robes. It was a foot long and gleamed sharply in the flickering torchlight. "You are an unknown, a rogue vampire without a master. For all I know, you might be a spy sent by the Councillors." A sardonic lifting of the eyebrow was a sign he didn't really believe that. It was simply another convenient excuse to execute me. "Killing you is only prudent. Killing you by this method will also aid my research."

Now would be a good time for Luc to jump out of the shadows and rescue me. I waited hopefully while Alexander bowed his head and mumbled some kind of dark prayer. Luc didn't appear and the fact that I was in serious trouble finally sank in. If my hands were free there would be no problem. I'd turn Alexander and his minions into stinky puddles and waltz right out of there. Testing the chains, I had only enough room to raise my hands a few inches off the slab. Unless the vamps bent down within my range, I wasn't going to be able to use the holy marks on them.

Finished intoning his prayer, Alexander picked up the bowl and sauntered over. At a flick of his silver maned head, four of the lackeys stepped forward and placed their hands on me. They held me down by my shoulders, forearms, thighs and calves. Two minions remained in the background, presumably to act as backup in case something went wrong.

One of the lackeys on my left shifted enough to let Alexander through. He placed the empty bowl between my knees. If there had been any give in the ankle bracelets, I would have tried to smash the bowl. There was none and my legs were chained down firmly. The move would have been petty, but maybe it would have slowed the ritual down. How many old clay bowls could they possibly have lying around? A Tupperware dish wouldn't have had the same menacing effect.

Alexander's shadow had been behaving itself well up to now, but it couldn't contain itself any longer. It stood unnaturally tall behind its master when it should have been lying flat on the ground. Leaning forward, it hunched over Alexander's shoulder. Without clear features to read, it was difficult to tell what emotions it might be feeling. I nevertheless sensed that it was enjoying this even more than the head vamp was.

Holding the knife up so I could admire it for a couple of seconds, Alexander went to work. Bending, he delicately sliced my sweater open. The blade cut through the fabric with disturbing ease. My t-shirt and bra went next. Now half naked, I tried hard to ignore the avid stares of the henchmen that were huddled around me.

"You know this is going to be a waste of time," I said, striving to sound reasonable. Reason was the last thing I was feeling. Gibbering terror would be closer to the mark. But I was damned if I would add to this freak's enjoyment. And he *was* enjoying it, that much was obvious. Alexander's face was practically alight with happiness. He'd probably been the world's oldest serial killer before he'd been turned, however long ago that had been. "Nothing is going to happen."

"Oh," his grin was monstrous in its pleasure now, "but something *will* happen. You will die, very painfully and very slowly." That part I didn't need to know. "Once my blood touches your heart," he went on to explain, "it will begin to poison you. I am much, much older than you and far more powerful. Your body will have no resistance against my blood."

I opened my mouth to tell him that I wasn't quite as pitiful and powerless as he thought, but it was too late. The knife descended and plunged into my chest.

Chapter Twenty-Eight

It happened so fast that at first there was no pain. I'd had objects thrust through my chest too many times for my liking. This time, my chest was hacked open inch by painful inch and I didn't get a chance to heal.

Thick, dark and disturbingly sluggish, blood ran from the wound and soaked into my ruined clothes. I screamed, long and loud, but it did nothing to diminish the agony. When Alexander deemed that the cut was long enough, he raised the knife to shoulder height, then slammed it down into my rib cage.

My bones cracked and splintered. Shards were driven into my heart and lungs. The pain was exquisite and almost beyond description. My screams changed, becoming deeper, almost guttural. My fangs descended, shredding my bottom lip. The minion holding my right wrist down slackened his grip momentarily. The instant the pressure left my arm, I jerked it up and the chain snapped like it was made of dental floss.

"Hold her!" Alexander screamed and the pressure came back twofold. Excitement shone from the insane leader of the London sewer vampires. He was encountering something new and his experiment had barely begun. If he hadn't been out of his mind, he might have thought twice before continuing on with it. What sort of scientist didn't think their way carefully through their experiments? *Um, crazy ones,* I replied to my own question. Instead of taking care and feeling his way with caution, he reached into my chest and yanked my ribs apart.

Shrieking in agony, I bolted upright despite the pair of vamps holding my upper body down. The chain around my left wrist snapped with a sound like a gunshot. The two lackeys hung off me like leeches. I wasn't the only one screaming. Panic spread through them and the other two backup henchmen jumped into the fray. The sheer weight of numbers drove me back down.

"This time it will work!" Alexander crowed. Delirious with joy, he pushed back the left sleeve of his robe and cut deeply into his own wrist. Squeezing the rent flesh, he forced a rivulet of dead blood into the bowl.

If Alexander managed to finish his ritual and pour his blood on my heart, I was no longer positive that I would die. I was scared that if he poured his diseased ooze into me, I wouldn't die at all. I might become something even worse than I already was. Wasn't being Mortis, death of the vampire race, already enough to contend with?

Lifting the bowl, Alexander elbowed his minions out of the way and raised the clay vessel above my chest. "Dark Father, I offer you this sacrifice made of blood taken from my own body." I heaved, lifting off the table a few inches before being slammed back down again. "Take her and show me what we can become!" The bowl tipped and foul, black crud splashed into the open cavity that had been carved into my chest.

Hydrochloric acid would have hurt less than Alexander's noxious blood did when it splashed onto my heart. Thrashing in torment, I jerked left and right, trying to escape from the altar. My body lifted off the table again and this time it couldn't be forced back down. Only my head and heels still touched the smooth black stone. A blood curdling shriek burst from my fanged mouth and rebounded around the chamber.

After an eternity of agony, my brain tried to shut down, but couldn't quite manage it. I went limp and my head lolled to the side. It was as close to fainting as I could get. My heart sizzled and lurched, pumped a few times, then expired once more. For a moment there, I had almost been...well, not alive, but slightly less undead.

"Is that it?" Ty whispered. "Is it over?" He sounded shaken and he wasn't the only one. Feet shuffled and disturbed murmurs swept through the small group. Some were on the edge of fleeing.

Alexander brushed his minions aside and thumbed open my half closed eyelids one after the other. Whatever it was he was looking for, he didn't see it. "No. No! There has to be more!" The insane leader of the sewer vamps was truly distressed that his experiment had failed once again. Truthfully, I'd also expected something a bit more dramatic than a near fainting spell after the torment I'd just suffered through.

"Uh, Alexander?" One of the lackeys was brave enough to tug on his sleeve to gain his attention. "Should she be able to heal like that?"

Staring down at my chest, Alexander prodded the now unbroken flesh with a finger. I'd felt the wound rapidly knitting back together. Bones, veins and flesh had realigned back to their original positions. It had happened in seconds and it hadn't hurt at all. It was a bit like having ants crawling all over my rent flesh, ticklish and unpleasant.

"I think we should get out of here," someone muttered nervously, "before something bad happens."

Alexander's shadow seemed to agree. It was hunched down, shielding itself from me while timidly peering over the vamp's shoulder. It sensed my dazed gaze and flinched away. Now that the pain was gone I was beginning to focus again. The thought uppermost in my mind was that the chains on my wrists had broken. *I'm free!* This was very good news for me, but not so good for Alexander and his band of frightened men. It was time for them to reap the brunt of my wrath. And I was feeling very wrathful indeed.

Seven startled vampires gaped at me when I sat up. My fangs were still out and my grin had to stretch around them. Thankfully, my lower lip had healed along with my ribs. "You know," I said into the silence, "I feel pretty good, considering I just had my chest hacked open." Turning my head, I met and caught Alexander's eyes. "Now, why don't I chain you down, cut you open and pour some of *my* blood into *you*?"

"What are you?" whispered one of the minions who had backed away from the slab.

"Who, me?" I said with feigned innocence around the forest of teeth that had sprouted in my mouth. "I guess I haven't formally introduced myself." Holding both hands up, I showed them the twin holy marks that were branded on my palms. "My friends call me Natalie, but you gents can call me Mortis."

For the count of three seconds, all was still. Then I was swamped by vampires. Alexander stabbed at me with the knife again. I lifted my arm and the blade clanged against the metal cuff around my wrist. Sparks flew as the blade snapped off. A minion jumped on my back and I peeled him off like a scab. Just like the ginger psycho, I wrenched the vamp's head around until it was staring backwards. Unlike the ginger psycho, the undead henchman didn't die. He tumbled off the table to the ground with his head flopping on his broken neck. Screaming, he scrabbled through the dirt on his hands and knees.

Distracted by the injured lackey, I failed to block the blade of the knife that Alexander had scooped up. It punctured my poor, ill-used heart and lodged there. I'd lost count of how many times I'd been stabbed in the heart now. Based on past experiences, it wouldn't harm me, but they didn't know that. In fact, I now had the perfect opportunity to free myself completely from the altar.

Howling and clutching at the snapped off blade, I rolled off the table. With two loud pops, the chains on my ankles snapped. I crouched down out of sight, side by side with the vamp whose head I had rearranged for him. His back was to me, but our eyes met anyway. It was one of the creepiest things I'd ever seen. Before he could give me away, I yanked the knife out of my chest and rammed it into his back. My fingers were sliced to the bone by the blade, but the flesh knitted back together almost instantly. It was eerie how fast I was able to heal now.

"Check to make sure she's really dead," Alexander ordered in an unsteady voice. His plans had gone badly awry so far and they were about to get a whole lot worse. An evil grin sprouted on my face and I stifled the urge to cackle in triumph. Having open heart surgery performed on me against my will had made me very cranky.

Ty was the one who was pushed forward to be the sacrifice. Creeping around the altar, the first thing he saw was the empty clothes of the vamp that I'd just stabbed. His remains were just starting to seep out in a wide circle. Then he spotted me hiding in the shadow of the black stone slab. Since I wasn't a damp patch on the ground, he correctly deduced that I wasn't dead.

Scuttling around him, keeping out of sight of the others, I was on my feet before he could issue a warning. The knife I'd rescued from the dead minion found his heart and he jittered on his feet, mouth opening and closing in silent screams. He dropped to his knees, revealing me to the five remaining vampires. If they'd had any brains, the whole lot of them would have fled for their lives. They'd all heard of Mortis, but none seemed to grasp what that meant. I was their nemesis, the long awaited doom of their kind. But, did that stop them from attacking me again? Nope.

The four remaining lackeys rushed me. They'd managed to overwhelm me with sheer numbers before, but I wasn't chained to the altar this time. I clamped my hands on the head of the first vamp to reach me. It imploded with a wet popping sound. Frenzied with terror, the other three kicked his already melting body out of the way and began to attack me with their bare hands. Their long nails tore my flesh open, but I barely felt it. My wounds healed in an instant anyway.

Using both hands, I palmed a pair of faces away and shrieks of agony pealed out. Their deaths would be slow, but I was beyond caring. Swiping out a hand, I batted at the head of the last minion. His face showed horrified surprise when his head detached from his neck and went spiralling off into a nearby tunnel. His body turned into liquid almost as soon as it hit the ground. Beheading a vampire seemed to be the quickest way by far to kill them. I filed the knowledge away for future use.

Alexander backed away from me when I turned to confront him. Even for a long dead vampire, his face was ashen. Any blood he had consumed lately had been drawn deep within his cold body. His shadow gibbered silently, pawing at his shoulder and pointing at me in terror.

"You shouldn't have tried to be a scientist, Alex," I advised him, advancing slowly. I didn't bother to cover my bare chest, my hands would shortly be required for another job. "You have no idea what you've unleashed." Neither did I, but my warning sounded suitably ominous.

"But, I did this for the Dark Father," Alexander stammered. "If you are Mortis, then surely you should be on my side." He was speaking in a language that had been lost long ago. It wasn't Latin, but something even older. I believed it was the spoken version of what had been written in the book.

"I would never stand with a madman who worships an evil alien," I informed him coldly.

Wailing at the knowledge that it was about to die, his silhouette suddenly rushed forward to engulf Alexander. I was momentarily disconcerted to hear the shadow's screeches clearly in my head. Alexander was almost jerked off his feet as his shadow possessed him. "You know nothing of our kind, pitiful creature!" it spat, using Alexander's mouth to speak to me. "We were once more powerful than you can even conceive of." Hatred poured from it in icy waves. "Our time will come again. Even now, we work to return to our rightful place. There is nothing you can do to stop us."

Using Alexander's body, it laughed. The laughter turned into howls that were primordial and savage. No human could hear a sound like that and remain sane. Luckily for me, I was no longer human. I was far more than that. Not even just a simple vampire, I was Mortis, death of the damned. *It's time to end this shadow*, I thought with grim satisfaction.

Leaping forward, I caught the dark silhouette off guard. It lifted both hands to ward me off, but I was already too close for it to stop me. I crashed into Alexander's body and he tumbled backwards. Falling with him, I reached through the shadow's head to the flesh and blood of the body beneath. The shadow wrapped its arms around me, but I was ready for the attack this time. Shudders wracked me as my already low body temperature plummeted. Once Alexander was dead, I knew that the shadow had to follow him into oblivion, even if this silhouette seemed to be more powerful than any I'd encountered before.

Feeling silver hair beneath my fingers, I struggled to get a decent grip. The shadow was forcing me backwards, pushing against me with all of its will. I slipped and lost my hold. Frustrated, I slapped at the shadow and my hand passed through its head. It shrieked in pain and loosened its grip a touch. Apparently, the holy marks could also hurt the dark shades. Seizing the moment, I leaned forward with all of my weight and ignored the cold that had seeped into my bones. My fingers found and closed around Alexander's ears.

Piercing shrieks drilled into my head as the holy marks began melting the vampire leader's ears off. When they were just warm rivers of melted flesh, my palms met the sides of his head without resistance. I turned my face away just as his head imploded in my hands. Goo splattered my chest and shredded clothes, but missed my eyes.

Squirming in pain and torment, the shadow released its hold on me and began to shrink. Tearing at its hair, it wailed as its master began to melt. It finally dissipated when there was no solid flesh left.

Straddling the spreading stain that had been Alexander, I shook with the cold that would have drained me completely if it had gone on for much longer. It wasn't safe for me to remain in the cavern. Someone could come looking for Alexander and his minions at any moment. It felt like it had been hours since I'd woken up chained to the altar, but my watch said it had been less than one.

Pushing myself to my feet, I stripped off my torn sweater and shirt and used them to clean off as much of the goo from my skin as possible. I then searched the discarded clothing for replacements. I found a sweater and long black coat that weren't too badly stained and pulled them on. The arms were too long and I had to fold them back several times. I looked like a kid wearing her father's clothes.

Before leaving, I picked up Alexander's book from the table. It was far too big to hide down my jeans, so I stuck it beneath the jacket, holding it close to my body. It was easy enough to locate the correct exit. It was the tunnel with the most footprints in the dirt.

Following the tracks upwards, I soon found myself back in the populated areas. I received curious glances, but no one ran screaming from me. The dark experiments Alexander had performed in the cavern below had been a secret. Not a very well-kept secret, going by the terrified stares the vamps had once given their now departed leader.

When Alexander and Ty didn't come back, the shit would be sure to hit the fan. I wanted to be long gone by then. Heading straight for the sleeping quarters, I retrieved my cross and journal. The cross went into a pocket of the jacket for easy access. One of the blankets served as a carry bag for the books after knotting it securely. The torn page was back in my pocket. If anyone managed to wrest the books away from me, at least they wouldn't be able to see my final demise.

I roughly remembered the path we'd taken when I'd first been invited to join the group and headed back to the main tunnel with the intention of retracing my steps. With the package slung nonchalantly over my shoulder, I strode into the hall and into confusion. Minions milled in small groups, worriedly searching the tunnels for signs of Alexander or Ty. They were used to being led, but I couldn't dredge up any concern for what would happen to them now. I'd worry about that in the future. Right now, I just wanted to get the hell out of there alive and intact.

Roxie took in my change of wardrobe and glared at me with suspicion. She started in my direction as I made my way through the throng toward the tunnel I recognized as being the entry point. Someone grabbed her arm and whispered something urgent. She scowled at me, then turned and ran off back towards the sleeping area. I forced out a sigh of relief. If she'd questioned me and found my answers lacking, I would have been in deep trouble. I had no illusions that I'd be able to fight my way to freedom through fifty or so vampires.

Mostly ignored by everyone else, I slipped into the tunnel and began to jog. I'd never had a great memory or sense of direction as a human, but I found my way back to the lair that had so briefly been my home. There was nothing of any value to salvage there. Orienting myself, I chose a direction and began to run.

Chapter Twenty-Nine

Staying in the sewers was now out. Alexander's minions might put two and two together and figure out that I'd had something to do with their leader's death. My new plan was to get to the surface and to find somewhere secure to hide for the day. London had soured for me. I'd have to find somewhere else to live.

Making turns at random, I made my way back up to the surface tunnels. I stopped when the noises of cars and people on the street above became muted with distance. Finding a rusty metal ladder, I climbed up to the manhole and listened for the sounds of activity. I heard no footsteps, or signs of life. Metal grated loudly when I pushed the manhole up. There was no one around to hear me as I scrambled out and dropped the lid back into place.

Dawn was still a few hours away. There was plenty of time to put some distance between myself and this place. A wave of homesickness and despair hit me. I was stuck in a foreign land with nowhere to go and no one to turn to.

Every time I turned around, someone tried to kill me. I hadn't asked to be turned into the living dead or to become the dreaded Mortis. But it was a gig I was stuck with, permanently. *It's not going to be very permanent if you're going to end up dead.* Sometimes I hated my snide subconscious.

Footsteps far down the street drew me out of my self-pity. Maybe a meal would lift my spirits. I'd need energy if I was to make my escape from the city. It was a good enough excuse, so I hustled stealthily after the unsuspecting prey.

A tall, dark haired man, clothed in a long black coat, strolled along the footpath. He sensed nothing as I crept up behind him. He heard nothing as I launched myself through the air before landing on his back. Tilting his head sharply to the side, I was about to bite into his neck when he spoke. "I would not do that if I were you, Natalie. It would be very bad for your health." His tone was calm and his voice was familiar.

Rolling my eyes upwards from the vulnerable stretch of neck I'd been about to munch on, I saw a profile that I would have recognized anywhere. "Luc?" At his nod, I let go of him and dropped to the ground in disgust. "Great," I muttered, "I'm dying for a feed and *you* have to come along and ruin it." Beneath my disgust was silent relief that I had stumbled across a friendly face.

Turning, Luc watched me gravely. "I have been searching for you."

Under any other circumstances, having a hot guy looking for me would have made my night. The circumstances being what they were, the prospect filled me with dread. . I knew he was some kind of world-class tracker, but how had he managed to stumble across me in a city this size? Maybe it was just random chance.

"Why?" I heard the whine in my voice and I didn't care. "Why couldn't you just leave me alone?" I kicked a stray brick in annoyance. It hurtled through the air and smashed into the back window of a parked car. Glass shattered, the alarm went off and dogs up and down the street began to howl. Pretty soon, there was a barking frenzy as dogs in neighbouring streets became caught up in the excitement.

"Perhaps we should discuss this somewhere more private," Luc suggested. Lights were turned on, windows were shoved open and irate humans began screaming for someone to turn the alarm off.

For a moment, I struggled against my destiny. It had found me once more and had wrapped its tentacles around me firmly. I'd escaped for a brief time, but I was now back in its clutches and it wouldn't let go of me again. "Fine. Whatever," I replied ungraciously.

We hurried off before we could be discovered by the angry owner of the car. Luc kept his left hand at waist height and it dawned on me that he wore his sword beneath the coat. It was bad enough knowing my fate without having a constant reminder of it in my face all the time.

Luc led me to a black sedan that he'd probably stolen, since it didn't have a rental car sticker on it. We drove away and ended up in the parking lot of a small rundown hotel. The lobby was shabby and had been decorated in tones of grey. It was depressing and did nothing to lift my mood.

Luc's room also turned out to be grey. A queen-size bed took up most of the room. A small couch sat in front of an old boxy TV. Tucked in the corner was an utterly useless kitchenette. Useless to us anyway. Locking the door, Luc engaged the safety chain to keep staff out if they were rude enough to ignore the sign he put on the door warning them to keep out. He gave me a guarded look, then pointed to a small suitcase at the foot of the bed. "There are several changes of clothes inside, if you wish to freshen up."

Guilt crashed down on me again. I'd run away and left Luc to deal with the imposter on his own and he had still thought of my comfort. Dropping my gaze, I mumbled my thanks.

The suitcase held four changes of jeans, shirts, sweaters and underwear. They were in my size and still had the tags on them. Picking clothes at random, I locked myself in the bathroom. I left the blanket wrapped bundle just outside the door. Steam probably wouldn't be good for the ancient books. I kept the picture of my eventual beheading close. Luc was under enough stress already, he didn't need to see that.

After taking the longest shower in history, I could no longer hide myself in the bathroom. The room was full of steam and my skin was wrinkled. I managed to delay the inevitable a few minutes longer by blow drying my hair. Clean and almost warm for the first time in days, I braced myself for an unpleasant confrontation and left the bathroom.

Luc sat on the bed, flicking through the book I'd pilfered from Alexander's torture chamber. His expression was faintly disturbed. "Have you read this?" he asked without looking up.

"Not yet." I hadn't exactly had time to since fleeing for my life from the sewers.

"It is similar to the Prophet's journal, but seems to tell the tale from a different perspective." I'd expected anger from Luc once he caught up to me, but he was acting as if I hadn't cowardly run out on him.

"Aren't you pissed at me?" I asked.

"No," he replied, flicking to the next page.

"Why not?"

At my persistence, Luc shut the book. "You do not come from my world," he said and I saw something like compassion in his dark eyes. "You do not understand vampire politics and you do not care about them." This was true and I didn't bother to deny it. "Not only have you been turned into a creature you previously had no belief in, you have been made into our doom." He shuddered and glanced at the prophet's journal where my story was written and illustrated. "You may be our doom, but you are also our hope."

"How do you figure that?"

Taking my hand, he carefully avoided the holy mark and drew me closer. "You read the Prophet's journal and know what he foresaw. You shall decimate us, but 'a remnant shall remain'." At my puzzled look, he elaborated. "We are the only two who know of this. The woman impersonating you does not."

It finally dawned on me then. "You mean, if I don't fight her to the death, she'll end up killing all vampires?"

He nodded and pointed at Alexander's book. "I am very interested in what this book has to say."

I wasn't, but gave in with good grace and took a seat beside Luc. Touching the pages made me feel unclean even after my lengthy shower. Ignoring the lurid pictures of humans being flayed open and eaten by vampires, I quickly read through the first few pages.

"It's an account of how we came to be, just like the Prophet's journal." Reading a few more pages, I was relieved to see this book didn't mention me at all. My relief was quickly replaced by unease. "It rambles on about the alien who gave its blood to change us into vampires. It says that vampires will ascend into 'greater beings', but a price must be paid and the human who started all this had no idea what the price would be."

Alexander's book was larger than the prophet's journal, but it lacked a lot of content, apart from pictures of death and dismemberment. The last page captured our attention. A vampire was kneeling on the ground with his head touching the ground. His shadow, which should have been behind him, according to the placement of the torches, stood over him instead. A triumphant expression had been drawn within the inky face.

Luc stared at the picture, puzzled. "What does it mean?" he asked. The explanation danced at the back of my mind then my eyes dropped to his mouth. I'd forgotten how full and tasty his lips were. "Natalie?" He reached out and shook my shoulder. My gaze lifted to his eyes and he grew wary. "When did you last feed your flesh hunger?"

My tongue felt thick in my mouth and my words were slurred. "I can't remember. When did we last, er, get naked together?"

Surprise and alarm chased across Luc's features, then his eyes dropped to my chest. He had no idea that a few short hours ago, my chest had been a hacked open ruin. "We should probably take care of your hunger." He tried to sound unwilling and failed.

"Yep. We'll be able to concentrate better then." I dimly remembered promising myself I'd never use Luc again, but the promise melted away as my hunger rose.

Luc placed the books on the floor, then we were tearing our clothes off. His pants went first and he was still struggling with his shirt when I tackled him. He was standing at attention and I couldn't wait any longer. His shout of pleasure was muffled by his shirt when I shoved myself onto him.

Tearing the shirt in half, he flung the pieces aside, then grabbed my hips. I rode him hard and the bedsprings protested in metallic shrieks at my intense speed. Luc's hands rose and cupped my breasts, fingers toying with my nipples. I moaned at the sensation and increased my speed until I felt fire blooming in my girly parts. My orgasm hit me, my back arched and my legs clenched.

Luc swore as a bone in his leg snapped. Then he pulled me down, rolled us over and it was his turn to be on top. His broken femur didn't slow him down at all as he plunged inside me. His eyes were wide, wild and dazed as he reached his own utopia and finally collapsed on me.

Neither of us was breathing hard, or at all for that matter. If we'd been alive, we might have passed out after exerting ourselves like that. Rolling onto his side, Luc contemplated me. I lay on my back, staring at the ceiling. Thoughts of doom were knocking on the door to my subconscious and I didn't want to let them in.

"What happened in the sewers, Natalie?" Luc asked me. "I had a feeling the rebels would either find you, or you them. I was about to begin searching the tunnels when I heard a panicked frenzy beneath the streets."

"Do you know Alexander? The leader of the sewer vamps?" He nodded and I wasn't surprised. The Councillors probably knew of all the small and not so small pockets of resistance out there that thought they were so well hidden. "He thought he was some kind of scientist. He was performing experiments on any stray vamps that made the mistake of wandering into the city."

"He tried to experiment on you?" Luc sat up, completely at ease with his nakedness. I wasn't and began to search for my clothes.

"He didn't just try, he succeeded." I described the dark ritual as I dressed. Luc saw there wasn't going to be a repeat of bedroom acrobatics and put his pants back on. Scratches I'd made on his pale flesh were beginning to fade. His bare chest was a distraction, so I hunted up a fresh shirt for him and tossed it over.

"Alexander poured his blood directly onto your heart and you survived?" Luc repeated as he pulled his shirt on. He couldn't seem to get past that fact. "What does this mean?"

"You're asking me?" I shook my head in bewilderment. "I have no idea. The experiment wasn't covered in either of the books. I'm pretty sure it was something he thought up all on his own, the sick freak." He was a dead freak now, but I was afraid the damage had already been done. For once, it would be nice to kill my enemies before they managed to torture me.

"Alexander was attempting to speed up the process," Luc mused. "You said that his shadow possessed him?" He seemed incredulous at my impatient nod. "If they have the power to take over their master's bodies, why have they not done so before now?"

Frustrated, I threw my hands up. "I don't know. I don't know why I'm the only one who can see them, either." I pointed at him when his eyebrow quirked. "I am not crazy!"

"I did not say that you were."

"Your face said it." He frowned at that, but wisely said nothing. Pacing up and down beside the bed, I came to the conclusion I'd been so desperately trying to avoid. I might be Mortis, the doom of vampirekind, but I had a responsibility as well. If I did nothing, the imposter could wipe out all of my strange new kin. If I stepped in, most of 'the damned' would die, but a few would be saved. A tiny voice in the back of my head reminded me that Luc would live. He had to, because he was the one who would eventually kill me. "All right," I finally gave in for good. "Let's go and find the crazy bitch so I can kill her."

Chapter Thirty

Energized either from the sex, or from my ungracious acceptance of my dreaded fate, Luc reached into his pocket and pulled out a cell phone. He quickly scrolled through the numbers stored on it and chose one.

"I didn't think you had a phone." I diplomatically refrained from saying I didn't think he would actually know how to use one.

"The Comtesse frowns on us blatantly using technology she doesn't understand," he said as the phone rang on the other end. "But that doesn't mean we don't use it when we are out of the range of her influence." He smirked, then his expression grew grave when a voice answered.

My keen hearing made out Igor's voice from a few feet away. "Have you found her?" His question was gruff and to the point, very Igor-like.

"I have." At the cautious look thrown in my direction, I deduced that they were talking about me. "She is well and was waiting where we'd arranged to meet. Do you have a lead on the imposter yet?" *I don't remember arranging to meet with him.* I did remember running away and hoping he wouldn't find me. It was admirable how Luc switched topics so smoothly, though.

"She has crossed the Channel and is making her way north, killing any of our kin who are unfortunate enough to cross her path."

"Where was she last seen?"

"At McIver's estate," was the grim reply.

"That is only a few hours south of London," Luc mused. "Natalie and I will head there as soon as we rise. With luck, we will run across the imposter during our journey." *Luck? That's not what I'd call it.*

Igor mentioned something about trying to meet up with us then they both hung up.

"What did you tell Igor and Geordie about my…disappearance?" The guilt came back and I dropped my gaze to avoid his.

"That I predicted your impersonator would soon head to London. I told them I sent you ahead and that I would be joining you shortly."

"How did you know I'd come here?" Was he a mind reader?

Luc shrugged. "It was the most obvious city for you to hide in."

Nice to know I'm so predictable. "Is McIver an actual person, or is that just the name of the estate?" I asked to fill the uncomfortable silence.

"Gregor McIver is a very old, very powerful vampire. He was offered a seat as a Councillor when the Court was first formed, but refused the honour."

I detected respect in Luc's tone and was intrigued by it. "I bet that made him unpopular."

Luc inclined his head. "Indeed. I believe he abhors what we are and wants no part of our lifestyle or politics." At least there was one other vampire on earth I had something in common with. "He has never made a servant, choosing to employ masterless vampires as guards instead. They are loyal and dedicated to him as he treats them like valued employees rather than useful tools that can be discarded at a whim." Now I sensed bitterness at how his former master had treated him. It was weird calling a female his master instead of mistress, but it seemed to be part of their tradition.

"And now they're probably all dead," I said morosely.

"Gregor is a crafty old monster," Luc disagreed. "I would not be surprised if he has survived."

With an hour or so left before dawn, we sat on the bed, studying the two books. Luc asked me to translate passages for him now and again. He drew his own conclusions to the sometimes cryptic passages. All we really learned was that the demi-god that had created the first vampires had a master plan that no one had figured out yet. Most of it sounded like wishful thinking to me, but it was a disturbing read anyway.

Luc had already drawn the curtains against the death rays of the sun. I would begin to feel sleepy any minute now. Stripping down to my t-shirt, I climbed into bed. The couch was far too small to attempt to sleep on this time. Luc took a shower and came out minutes later wearing black boxer shorts. He folded his clothes neatly on the couch, then lifted one eyebrow at me suggestively.

"What? You want permission to have sex with me once I turn into a lifeless corpse?" I said crankily, knowing full well he could stay awake after the sun rose if he had to, at least for a while.

Grimacing, Luc gave up and climbed in beside me. "I am not into necrophilia."

I remembered waking before him when we'd spent the night in the back of a rental car. He'd been without a doubt, stone cold dead. He was normally a very sexy man, but not when he lay there unmoving like the corpse he was. I had to assume I was just as unappealing when I was dead to the world.

Sudden brightness hit the window and flared in a thin line against the wall. I scrunched my eyes shut against the painful glare. "What the hell is going on out there?" Was someone shining a powerful light in through our window?

Turning to Luc when he didn't respond, I did a double take. All animation had left him. His face was still handsome, but it was slack, white and lifeless. *Ok, any second now I'll fall unconscious.* I waited expectantly, but nothing happened. Shifting onto my side, I stared at Luc's corpse and willed myself to sleep.

Ten minutes later, I threw back the blankets in disgust. "It's too bright in here," I complained. Only the tiniest trace of sunlight was filtering inside, but it was enough to ensure I couldn't fall unconscious. Once it was dim enough, I was confident I'd go down for the day.

Approaching the window was like walking toward a furnace. Heat was coming off the curtain in waves. A tiny tent had formed in the fabric, allowing the bar of light to enter the room. I could almost imagine the paint was sizzling where the ray touched the wall. The heat was all in my head, of course, but that didn't make it any less real.

Turning my face away from the light, I reached out and poked the fabric flat. As I did, the tip of my pointer finger was exposed to sunlight for a fraction of a second. Pain, intense and excruciating, thundered into my hand. I snatched it away from the window and inspected my finger. Half of it was gone, or nearly gone. The meat had been burned to ash and fell to the carpet like a cigarette that had been left to burn on its own. Stark white bone lay exposed without flesh to cover it. I wiggled my finger bone and managed to gross myself out. *I guess this means I'm definitely allergic to sunlight then.* I'd held onto the hope that this might not be the case, since I was the much unanticipated Mortis. The hope now withered and died.

It took hours for my finger to regenerate. I tossed and turned beside the unmoving body of my companion as the flesh grew back around the bone. I envied Luc his oblivion. At last, I grew sleepy and closed my eyes.

I dreamt that I was standing in the throne room of a magnificent castle crafted from white marble. Deep red curtains that were long enough to brush against the floor covered the windows. A blood red strip of carpet ran from the doorway where I stood right up to a delicate gold throne. A woman with white hair sat on the highly polished seat. Up close, I knew she would be light blonde. The Comtesse, also known as the praying mantis, eyed me haughtily, then dismissed me as being beneath her notice. The other Councillors were huddled behind her, cowering in fear.

Guards surrounded the throne, preventing anyone from the Court from coming too close. Stains were scattered on the floor and empty clothing marked where the dead had fallen. Scores of vampires, dressed in their finest, were bunched against the walls. Their attention was on the solitary figure that stood defiantly before the throne.

Walking down the red carpet, I crept up on the lone figure that was dressed in a tight black leather outfit. She held a spear in her right hand. The long blade was covered in the black goo of dead vampires. As I reached her, she whirled around to face me and I started back. Instead of having a normal human face, hers was made of shadow. "You cannot win against me, puny vampire," she spat, then rammed her spear into my stomach.

Waking with a shout, my hands scrambled to hold my intestines in. It took me a moment to realise I was still in bed. Halfway through pulling a shirt on, Luc stared at me in astonishment.

"I thought I was back in the sewers for a second there," was my lame excuse for my reaction. I already saw shadows that moved that no one else could see. If I told Luc that I could now dream, it would make me look like an even bigger freak. *Why am I suddenly dreaming again? How is it even possible?* Alexander's grim experiment, that was how. By mingling his blood with mine, he had initiated changes in my vampire makeup. I didn't know what this meant, but instead of dying when the sun came up I now slept like a normal human. It also had to be why I'd heard the shadow talking in my head.

A quick shower did nothing to wake me up properly. I almost felt like I had a hangover and deduced that I hadn't slept enough. It was an affliction I never thought I'd have again. Like eating solid food, sleep should have been beyond me now. Bleary eyed, I dressed and joined Luc in the bedroom.

Luc retrieved his small suitcase from within the closet. I didn't need to look inside to know all of his clothes would be black. They always were. The books were safely ensconced in my equally tiny suitcase.

"Are you ready, Natalie?" he asked me with a touch of concern.

He probably thinks I'm going to run out on him again. "Let's go," I replied and was a step behind him when he opened the door.

We attracted little attention as we made our way to the car. Luc kept to the speed limit, stopping only long enough for us both to grab a snack. We'd need our strength just in case we did run into the crazy cow who thought she was me. After the nightmare I'd had, I would be only too happy to postpone the introductions.

After driving for several hours, we entered a picturesque area of large estates and manor houses. Not that I could see much from the road even with my heightened vision. Then we were pulling into a driveway and halting before an imposing set of gates. Made of grey stone and iron bars, they were wide enough to fit two cars through abreast. A vampire guard approached the car with a sword in his hand. "State your business," he grated, glancing in through the window to examine us thoroughly. It was encouraging to see anyone was still left unalive.

"I am Lord Lucentio," Luc said and I almost sniggered at how pompous he sounded. I reminded myself I was supposed to be his servant and stifled my laughter. "Is

275

Gregor in attendance?" That was a diplomatic way of asking if the old vampire had kicked the bucket.

"He is, but he isn't taking callers," the guard replied.

"I hear you had an unexpected visitor last night," Luc said mildly. "The Councillors have sent me to make sure she never bothers anyone again. Are you sure Gregor won't take any callers?"

Shifting from foot to foot indecisively, the guard made a stay put motion with his hand. "Wait here." Unlike the liveried servants in France, this guy wore a black sweater and cargo pants. It gave the impression of being a military uniform without actually being one. The modern clothes and old fashioned weapon were a disconcerting contradiction.

Luc waited confidently as the guard strode over to a speaker set into the stone gate. Moments later, the gate opened and we were waved through.

I stared at the grounds in wonder as we sped up the gravel drive. Hedges had been shaped into animal figures; horses, rabbits, lions, bears and even pigs cavorted on an immaculate lawn. It amazed me that someone who had been dead for as long as Gregor was purported to have been could have an interest in topiary.

We pulled up in front of the three story mansion. It was just as elegant and breath-taking as the Court mansion in France had been. Inside, it had been decorated with far greater taste than the one in France. The colour scheme ran more to blues and neutral tones rather than to blood red. The guard who had met us at the steps showed us through into a library that was larger than my whole apartment had been. I goggled at the sheer number of books that lined the shelves until Luc elbowed me in the side.

Gregor McIver sat on a comfortable looking antique chase lounge that had been pulled over to within a few feet of the fireplace. It would be toasty warm on the lounge. I wished I could spend a few days just sitting there reading. But new vampires didn't care about books. They cared only for feeding their hungers. Until told otherwise, I would continue to pretend to be the perfect servant. Or rather a passable servant.

Standing, Gregor turned out to be a couple of inches taller than Luc. He had probably been in his late forties when he'd been turned. His face was craggy and lined and his brows were heavy enough to cast his eyes into shadow. A mane of dark blond hair framed his compelling face.

I met his eyes and had the uncanny feeling that he knew I wasn't just an average, ordinary vampire. I sensed he was far more ancient than Luc, but he was wearing an expensive modern suit. It was dark grey and was matched up with a snowy white shirt and silvery tie. He wore a heavy twill coat in dark brown, which would have been too warm for a human in spring.

"Lucentio," he said and offered his hand. "It has been a long time, my friend." The men shook hands warmly. "Who is your lovely companion?" he said and turned to inspect me keenly.

Sensing the ploy that I was his servant wouldn't work, Luc altered the story on the spot. "This is Natalie Pierce. We met a short time ago in Australia after her master was killed. She is new and I could not abandon her to life without a master in a country where they do not believe in our kind."

"How kind of you," Gregor said shrewdly as he waved his guard to leave the room. The vampire left reluctantly with backward glares warning us to behave. "Now, would you care to tell me the real story?" Gregor said once the vamp's footsteps faded away.

Chapter Thirty-One

Luc and I exchanged looks as Gregor gestured to another set of couches further away from the fireplace. These were dark brown leather rather than the pale cream of the delicate lounge. I shrugged to let Luc know I was ok with whatever story he wanted to tell him as we followed our host to the couches.

Taking a seat, Luc leaned forward and glanced around to make sure we weren't being overheard. "What can you tell me about the woman who attacked your estate last night?"

Sitting back, Gregor crossed his arms. "She is not Mortis, I can tell you that much."

"How do you know that?" I asked, then wished I hadn't when his piercing eyes fell on me again.

"Because, my dear," he said then moved too quickly for me to track and grabbed my hands, "she did not wear these." We both looked down at the holy marks on my palms. Luc made no overt move towards his sword that rested against the arm of the couch, but he was sitting very still and was ready for action.

"How did you know?" I whispered.

"The books." Gregor nodded at the volumes surrounding us. "No vampire under a hundred cares for anything, but food. Or sex," he added and squeezed my fingers. "If you were truly newly made, you would have shown no interest at all in my collection. Therefore, you must be a very unusual member of our species."

Luc gave Gregor a hard stare and the older vampire released me, then sat back again. I was frankly wondering why he wasn't cowering away from me and screaming for his guards. "Will I ever understand vampire politics?" I asked the room.

"No," both men responded automatically and shared a chuckle.

"Can you tell us what happened last night, Gregor?" Luc asked.

The tension had relaxed a little and Gregor nodded. "The madwoman showed up at the gate and slaughtered my guards. She cut a path to my doorway, but she was not prepared for the defences I have put in place against such an attack." His grin was crafty and imminently pleased with himself.

"What sort of defences?" I had to ask.

"I have containers of holy water ready to douse the unwary with from windows on the second floor. It is dangerous for my men to handle them, but they take precautions."

"I take it your men did not make an end to the imposter," Luc said.

"No," Gregor shook his head regretfully. "One of my men spilled the holy water before he was fully ready. The imposter, as you call her, took off running as soon as the first drops touched her."

"That proves she really is an imposter then," I decided.

"How so?" Gregor asked.

"Because I'm supposed to be immune to holy water. I bet she also can't do this." I pulled the cross from the back of my jeans and held it up. Both men cringed away until I made the cross disappear again. "I'm not positive about the holy water, though. I haven't come across any lately to test the theory."

"I can assist you with that," Gregor offered. Reaching for a metal flask on the small end-table to his right, he carefully uncapped the lid, then offered it to me.

I took the flask, shrugged and swallowed down a mouthful. Luc gave a shout of alarm and batted the flask out of my hand. Gregor cursed as a few droplets splashed onto his coat. Steam rose immediately and he quickly stripped it off.

Wiping dribbles of liquid off my chin, I rolled my eyes at their theatrics. "You two need to get a grip."

Luc seized my chin in his hand and examined my face. "You are not injured." It was a statement, not a question. Releasing me, he sat back on the couch, shaken. Since neither of the men could touch the flask now that it was dribbling water onto the rug, I picked it up and recapped it.

"Despite the signs that she bears," Gregor said as he folded his smoking coat and placed it over the arm of the couch, "you did not truly believe." The accusation was directed at Luc, but it might as well have been aimed at me. The whole deal about me being Mortis was hard to believe. How could *I*, Natalie Pierce, clothing store manager, be the worst of all monsters? I couldn't shake the feeling that someone, somewhere, had made a terrible mistake when they'd chosen me for this gig.

"And is it so easy for you to believe, old friend?" Luc said with some bitterness. "The prophecy has finally come true and I was the one to unleash it amongst us." *It? I'm an it now?*

"You're not responsible, Lucentio," Gregor argued. "Who was Natalie's maker?"

"Silvius," Luc and I said together.

Gregor nodded thoughtfully. "Yes, I could believe Silvius capable of bringing forth the greatest danger to our kind that was ever conceived of." He chuckled and I shot a glance at Luc. Gregor's shadow had been acting normally, but now I wondered if the ancient vampire was just as crazy as the others I'd met. "Tell me, my dear," he said suddenly, "are you harbouring an urge to stake me through the heart?"

Put on the spot like that, I felt awkward and exposed. "Um, no." Not yet anyway. There was always a chance I'd change my mind once I got to know him a little better.

"That is why I am less concerned about you than I am about your imposter," he said and leaned back against the couch. He certainly seemed relaxed. "She believes she is on a holy mission and feels no compunction at all about ending our existence."

"Who does she think she is?" I burst out. "I mean, I know who she thinks she is, but what the hell makes her think she's really me?"

"Did she bear the holy marks on her hands?" Luc asked.

"She had marks that are in the shape of a cross," Gregor admitted. "But they are plain compared to Natalie's. As for who she might really be, I can't say. Her face was masked. I saw only her eyes, but I believe she might be oriental."

Both men exchanged a meaningful look. "What? Does that mean something?" I switched my attention between them in confusion.

"There is long standing bad blood between the European and Japanese vampires," Luc explained. "Both have tried to take over as absolute rulers of our kind over the past twenty thousand years or so. We have settled into an uneasy truce, but I would advise against travelling to Japan. Any emissaries we send do not tend to come back."

"I would not put it past their Emperor to have staged your imposter," Gregor said. "It would give him great amusement to upset the Councillors and to disrupt the Court."

I thought about it for a minute, ignoring the fact that the Japanese vampires had an actual emperor in charge. Although it was a fascinating fact, it had little bearing on our problem right now. "You think they might have taken a normal human, scarred her hands with cross marks, turned her into a vampire and trained her into a killing machine?"

"Yes," Luc said and casually brushed lint off his pants. I guessed once you'd been unalive for a few centuries, nothing much surprised you.

"So, I'm up against someone who has been training to kill us for G-G-G," closing my eyes for a second in frustration, I tried another word, "the Lord knows how long? Maybe hundreds of years?"

"I do not think you have anything to fear, Natalie," Gregor said with a small smile.

"Why?" I asked grumpily. There was plenty to fear. Oodles to fear. There were so many things to fear, I couldn't even list them all.

"Because very little on this earth has the power to harm you."

"I know that," I said in exasperation.

"What is bothering you then?" Luc asked.

I squirmed, not wanting to answer. "She's going to seriously kick my arse before I finally kill her," I blurted. That was my greatest fear, apart from my predicted beheading. I knew she would kick my butt, there was no question about it. We hadn't even met yet and I already felt embarrassed about the future arse kicking I'd be forced to suffer at her hands. "I'm going to look like an idiot."

Tucking the flask of holy water into my back pocket, I covered my face with my hands. The holy marks felt slightly rough against my skin, almost like I'd worked up a good set of calluses. *I wish.* Calluses had the capacity to be worn down. My holy marks were there to stay.

Gregor chuckled and even Luc's lips twitched at my outburst. "We promise we won't laugh if she 'kicks your arse'," Gregor said in a fair imitation of an Australian accent.

"So, old friend, will you be joining us?" Luc sat forward and stared at Gregor intently.

Nodding thoughtfully, Gregor indicated me with a graceful gesture. "I do not think that remaining neutral will be possible. It is better to be on the side that you know will win than to be on the losing side."

He has no idea that I'm going to end up in two pieces once this is all done. The thought depressed me, but I tried to hide it. I wasn't about to turn down help from a possible ally.

"Where do you think she'll head next?" Luc asked.

"She's been heading due north for the past few days," Gregor mused. "Isabella's estate would be the next logical target for her if she remains on this course."

"Great, give Isabella a call and see if the imposter has come knocking," I suggested and received twin wry looks in response.

"Isabella does not use a telephone," Luc said, as if I should have known this.

Of course not, that would be too convenient. "Don't tell me," I held up a hand to stop any explanations from being voiced. "She's as ancient as dirt and doesn't believe in using modern technology like electricity and plumbing."

"Correct," Gregor said with a nod. "If we hurry, we can make it to her estate within two hours."

"I suggest we leave immediately," Luc responded and stood. He retrieved his sword while Gregor called for a guard. He asked for a replacement coat and for a vehicle to be readied. The guard gave a curt nod and a quick salute then took off at a run.

"To the Batmobile," I muttered quietly and hurried after the two men when they headed for the door.

Chapter Thirty-Two

Luc and I sat in our car and waited for Gregor to reappear. He'd disappeared around the side of the mansion, followed by a couple of guards. After a short wait, our ally made his appearance in the front passenger seat of a van. My acute hearing told me the black vehicle was crammed full of guards. The window tinting was dark enough that I could only just make out the curtains that had been hung on the inside. Even the windscreen had a curtain ready to be drawn against the sun's deadly rays.

There were no such handy precautions in our car. We were hoping to search Isabella's place, take care of the imposter, then hole up somewhere before dawn could arrive and strike us down. I had serious doubts we'd catch up to her so quickly, but we had to be prepared for a confrontation.

Luc took the lead and Gregor's van followed closely behind. "Why do you trust Gregor?" I asked to break a silence that was quickly becoming monotonous. The country road we were on was rough and full of potholes. The car sank into a dip, then bounced back out again. I came close to biting the tip of my tongue off.

"We have a long history," Luc explained unhelpfully and swerved to avoid the next divot.

"Try not to overwhelm me with information, Luc."

He slanted a look at me, then returned his attention to the road. "When my master was…killed, I needed some time away from the Court. I'd met Gregor several times when he was forced to attend meetings held by the Councillors. Usually, they were in relation to the Japanese vampires. Gregor saw how I was treated and offered me refuge if I ever won my way free."

"Who killed your master?" I asked for the second time. There had been something fishy about the way he'd said that that raised my curiosity.

"The Comtesse," he said in a clipped tone.

"Surprise, surprise," I murmured, completely unsurprised. I was surprised that he'd answered me honestly this time. "Why did she kill her?"

"For treason." From the way his lips thinned, I guessed I wouldn't get much more about that particular subject from him.

"So, after your master died, you went to visit Gregor and he let you stay with him for a while?"

"Yes," Luc inclined his head. "He showed me what life could be like outside of the Court. It doesn't all have to be about blood and sex."

"You gave up the sex part," I remembered.

"And I am glad it is part of my life once more," he said silkily. Picking up my hand by the fingertips, he carefully avoided my palm and placed a kiss on the back of it.

"You're smooth," I complimented him and wished we could pull over for a quickie. If Gregor and his van full of guards hadn't been right behind us, I might have suggested it.

"Centuries of practice," he said, then his mood turned dark again.

"What happens after I kill the imposter?"

Startled at the turn of conversation, Luc frowned at the road ahead. "I really have no idea what the future will hold for either of us once you have accomplished that task."

"If I'm supposed to be the doom of us all, does that mean I'll go on a vampire killing spree?" I didn't feel in a very killing spree sort of mood right now, but I couldn't read the future either. Something bad could happen that might change my mind and make killing anything that sprouted fangs seem like a good idea.

"Let's just take one step at a time," Luc suggested.

Against my will, my head turned until I was looking at the back seat. Luc's sword, shiny and silver, lay there waiting to be used. *Hi there, Nat,* I could almost hear it thinking with cheerful malevolence. *We have an appointment to keep and I'm really looking forward to it!*

I tried to tell myself that I had years, possibly centuries before my head would depart from my neck. It would take time to track down most of the vampires in the world and turn them into puddles of slime. So why did I feel like the end was lurking just around the corner?

Chapter Thirty-Three

Isabella's estate was a smaller version of Gregor's. Her mansion was similar to his, but had only two stories instead of three. It was ominously quiet and no movement could be seen from the building or grounds as we pulled into the driveway. Gregor's van followed us closely enough that I could see his concerned expression when I turned to stare over my shoulder. His driver's face was stony and grim.

Up way past their bedtime, crows lined the low stone fence that ran down either side of the driveway. They seemed to stare right at me as we drove past. A stiff breeze ruffled their feathers. One gave a low caw that sounded like a prophecy of doom.

Shivering, I turned my attention to the grounds. They were well kept, but no late night gardeners toiled away at their duties. Twice, we drove over suspicious dark spots on the gravel driveway. The remains of vampire guards? I was pretty sure they weren't simply oil slicks from leaking cars.

Not with the empty clothing and dropped weapons that accompanied the stains.

Twin doors made of dark red wood that might have been mahogany, stood open in a parody of invitation. As we stepped out of the car, we spied more suspicious moist patches on the driveway and steps. Gregor joined us as we hesitated at the entrance. His brows drew down and he shook his head as his contingent of guards drew short swords. "That will not be necessary, gentlemen," he told his uneasy men. "I fear the damage has already been done and the culprit is long gone."

I agreed with his assessment of the situation. If anyone had survived, they had fled from the scene. Luc and I followed Gregor when he stepped inside. Signs of battle could be seen throughout the entryway. The imposter had fought her way into the mansion and up the staircase, going by the gouges and tears in the wallpaper where stray sword blows had landed. The wooden balustrades had been splintered and hacked. Puddles and empty clothing of the fallen marked the carpeted staircases as we made our way up to the second floor.

We followed the path of destruction to the end of a hallway. Several vampires had tried to guard the bedchamber of the mistress of the estate and had died defending her. Pushing open the remaining half of the door, Luc stepped over their vestiges and into the ornate bedroom. The furniture was a bit girly and fussy for me. My tastes didn't tend toward so much pink and pillows with frills on them. Isabella's clearly had.

A gigantic four poster bed showed clear signs of a struggle. Feathers littered the bed and floor from a pale pink pillow that had been stabbed to death. Satin sheets in hot pink had been sliced right through to the mattress. A filmy nightie, pink of course, lay in the middle of the bed. Streaks of black gore splattered the walls. The spreading blemish on the linen must have belonged to the late Isabella. A heavy gold necklace and multitudes of rings were scattered throughout the mess.

"Isabella put up a hell of a fight," Gregor said and I believed I detected grief in his gaze before he averted his face.

"Where would she head next?" Luc asked grimly. His hand was clenched around his sword hilt in a white knuckled grip.

Rousing himself from his despair, Gregor didn't have to contemplate long. "The Stravovsky estate would be the next place to attack."

"I don't suppose *they* have a phone?" I muttered.

"As a matter of fact, he does" Luc said as he pulled his phone out of his pocket. "I only hope our warning will not come too late."

Gregor and I listened in on the conversation, able to hear both sides easily enough. Luc warned a guard at Stravovsky's place that the imposter was on her way. Fortunately, she hadn't arrived yet. It was too late for her to attack now, dawn was too close. She would arrive not long after nightfall was his guess. The guard replied that he would make sure the place was fortified and that they would try to hold on until we got there.

Igor arrived as the conversation wound down. He gave me a curt nod and Gregor a more respectful one. Geordie was nowhere to be seen. He was probably hiding out in the car. I wished I could join him and leave the hunt up to people who were better equipped to deal with it than I was.

"We missed her," Igor said flatly as Luc hung up the phone.

"We'll get her tomorrow," was Luc's grave promise. A glance was enough to warn Gregor to keep my identity a secret. Everyone would find out about me soon enough. Too soon for my liking if we caught up with the imposter tomorrow night. Then the screaming and fleeing would begin. Gregor's lips twisted wryly, indicating that he would keep his peace, for now.

We all chose bedrooms in Isabella's empty mansion to spend the day in. Luc didn't follow me into the room I'd picked as I'd secretly hoped he would. He gave me a distracted smile and headed down the corridor. He obviously wasn't in the mood for naked acrobatics.

Shutting the door, I slid the bolt home, then wondered if I should leave it unlocked in case he changed his mind. The thought that Geordie was slinking somewhere around the mansion prevented me from unbolting it. I didn't want to wake up with him in my bed again. Once had been enough.

Tired, but restless, I wandered over to the window and drew the curtain. Boards had been nailed over the glass from the inside. I remembered seeing shutters on the outside as we'd driven up. Isabella hadn't taken any chances. The curtain was thick and was backed by heavy sun-blocking fabric. After one quick peek, I'd picked this room because it didn't have girly frills. It was decorated in shades of soothing green. I could use some soothing right about now. It had been sorely lacking in my life lately.

I felt dawn coming and hurried over to the bed. Stripping down to my shirt, I slid beneath the covers and waited for sleep to claim me. The sun rose, heat baked against the triple layer of protection on the window, but I didn't drift off. Lying there, wide awake, I wondered what the hell was going on. Just like an ancient vampire, I could now resist the magic that made us die at dawn. It hadn't just been a once off as I'd hoped.

For several hours, I lay in bed, worrying about the future. Growing bored, I closed my eyes and tried to will myself to sleep. It worked and I fell into a doze. A dark and disturbing dream followed me down into unconsciousness.

Luc stood before me wearing an expression of misery. His sword was in his hand with the tip resting on the floor. He said something to me, but it came out without sound. Then the silver blade was in the air, swinging at me in a deadly arc. It moved too fast to be avoided even if I hadn't been rooted to the ground with shock.

The blade connected and my head flew through the air. It bounced on a white marbled floor and rolled for a few feet before coming to rest at an angle where I could see my body. I watched as my body fell to its knees in slow motion. Several vampire lackeys fell on it with their swords swinging. Dark red blood flew as they dismembered my limbs. My mouth opened, but the scream that I wanted to voice remained silent.

Choking on my dream scream, I started at a knock. "Natalie, it is time to go," Luc said through the door.

"Be there in a minute," I called back, forgetting that yelling wasn't necessary with our enhanced hearing. By the time I was dressed, I had calmed down. *It's just a dream. There's no way that is going to happen to you.* Luc might be destined to behead me, but I was fairly certain he wouldn't let anyone hack my body to pieces afterwards.

Geordie made an appearance when we gathered in a large dining hall on the first floor. He looked as sullen as ever, but flicked me a small smile. He'd upgraded his weapon from a meat cleaver to a short sword, but he didn't handle it with any more confidence.

"We will head directly to Strovovsky's estate," Luc was saying to the gathering. "It should only take us an hour to travel there. If we are lucky, we will find the imposter still on the grounds."

"Why do you call her that?" one of Gregor's men asked. "I saw the holy marks on her hands. She is Mortis." Superstitious fright ran through the crowd. I felt the beginnings of panic stirring amongst them.

"I assure you, she is not," Gregor said and put a hand on the frightened man's shoulder. "She has only one of the signs and they could be easily manufactured." The vamp allowed himself to be soothed and relaxed under the calm stare of his boss. "She ran from holy water just as fast as you or I would."

"You mean the real Mortis is immune to holy water?" one of the other men asked in dismay. *I sure am,* I thought cheerfully, but hid my private glee. *There are lots of things that don't hurt me.* The couple of things that could hurt me very badly were sunlight and having my head chopped off. My brief good mood evaporated at the reminder.

"Yes," Luc responded. "She will also be able to handle holy objects and fire will have no effect on her."

"How do you know this?" the second guard asked.

"He has read the same texts that I have," Gregor interjected smoothly. "The Prophet's ramblings have been documented on the few occasions he has made sense. The Councillors have copies and make them available to Lords and Ladies who wish to read them."

I hid my amusement at the paltry explanation. I had possession of a text that no man, save Luc, had ever seen. The prophet's journal was currently hidden in the trunk of Luc's car, alongside the book about the demi-god. Something fluttered at the back of my mind about Alexander's book. An idea had been niggling me for a while now. It tried once more to form, but then we were on the move and I had to shelve it. If it was important, it would come back to me. We had a more immediate problem to deal with right now. *It's time to take down the imposter.* I mentally cracked my knuckles in nervous preparation.

By sticking to twenty kilometres above the speed limit, we made it to Strovovsky's place in less than an hour. Sounds of mayhem reached us as our vehicles bolted through the open gates one after the other. A fight was raging within the mansion. Luc slammed on the brakes and we skidded to a halt on the loose gravel. He was leaping out of the car and opening the back door to reach for his weapon before I'd even unbuckled myself. Sword in hand, he was first through the smashed front doors.

Following much more slowly, Geordie and I allowed the group to precede us and brought up the rear. Eyes wide and solemn, Geordie looked more human than vampire in his fright and even younger than his mortal years. "I do not like this, *chérie*," he whispered and huddled closer to me.

"Neither do I," I replied. Since I was almost twice his age in mortal years, I felt as though I should at least try to be braver than he was and headed inside.

Noisome blotches, empty clothing and dropped weapons made temporary headstones where the inhabitants had fallen. Entering a large sitting room that was decorated with impressive antique furniture, I halted at the sight of our quarry. Luc, Igor, Gregor and his six men surrounded a lone female. *So, that's my imposter,* I thought with grim fascination.

We were exactly the same height, I noticed straight away. She was as slender as me, but infinitely more deadly. Dressed from head to toe in black leather, she looked like a fifteen year old boy's wet dream. Long midnight black hair was held back in a high ponytail. Throwing knives hung from a belt slung low over her hips. I was relieved to see my dream had been only partially true; her black leather suit was the same, but her face wasn't made of shadow. Her famous spear twirled in a deadly circle as she dared the men to close in.

Luc lunged forward, then danced back as the wickedly sharp spear suddenly swung in his direction. Igor dived in and slashed at the imposter. With a girlish laugh, she back-flipped gracefully out of his reach, then playfully shook a finger at him. "You'll have to do better than that," she taunted. It wasn't just her dark eyes that were oriental, her accent was as well.

One of Gregor's men foolishly took a chance and rushed the imposter. Moving with lightning speed, she whirled around in a tight circle and chopped the man's sword arm off. Screaming in agony, he clutched at his sluggishly spurting stump. Gregor uttered a wordless cry as the imposter almost casually spitted his man through the heart, ending his agony and his life.

Taking the flask I'd picked up off Gregor's floor out of my back pocket, I uncapped it. I'd had the vague idea that it might come in handy and was now glad I'd kept it. Lobbing it in a high arc, I yelled out a warning: "Fire in the hole!" I'd always wanted to say that, but had never imagined I'd use it in a scenario like this.

Startled, Luc, Igor and Gregor looked back at me over their shoulders. Luc saw the object spinning through the air and went into motion. Faster than I'd ever seen a vampire move before, he dove at Igor and Gregor and knocked them out of the way.

Turning in mid-air, liquid sloshed out of the flask and splashed on one of Gregor's men. Smoke rose, he shrieked and began stripping off his pants. The imposter whipped her gaze up to the flask, spear held ready. Finally realizing that death was flying at her and that her spear would be of no help, she turned to run. The flask of holy water hit her squarely in the back and it was her turn to scream. I expected her to disintegrate, but she defied my expectations. Crashing through a boarded over window, she disappeared outside.

"After her!" Igor roared. Geordie threw a panicked glance at me, then ran for the window. The others were still picking themselves up when Geordie jumped. Surprising myself, I was right behind him. We landed on the dewy grass three floors below with twin thumps. My legs didn't shatter on impact when I hit the ground as I'd half expected them to. I was constantly surprised by how much damage my body could take and keep on ticking.

Geordie brandished his sword, turning in a frantic circle as he searched for the imposter. I was ready to use the holy marks on her once she was within my reach. They were a far more effective weapon than a sword would be with my utter lack of training.

Spying footprints in the grass, Geordie pointed. "Quickly, she went this way!" The last thing I wanted to do was follow the crazy cow, but off I went anyway. We found her discarded leather suit, still steaming from the holy water, about fifty feet away. Her bare, delicate footprints led to a small woody area, then disappeared.

Luc and Igor caught up to us as we halted dejectedly. "She got away," I explained apologetically.

"How did she survive the holy water?" Geordie asked.

"The leather suit protected her well enough," Gregor answered as he ambled toward us. The suit, a ruined mess now, hung gingerly from his fingertips.

"So, she's running around out there naked?" I asked, then sniggered. Geordie shared my humour even if the others didn't. We sobered when Igor directed a frown at us and lifted his hand in warning to his protégé.

"She'll have backup clothing," Luc said, eyes searching the woods for our quarry. "We should hurry. She'll be heading for the Comtesse's estate next."

Gregor didn't look happy about possibly saving the Comtesse and I agreed with him wholeheartedly. The praying mantis had made me strip down in front of the whole Court the one and only time we'd met. I was planning on having words with that bitch once everyone knew who I really was. *She'll be grovelling at my feet then,* I gloated inwardly and mentally rubbed my hands together. I couldn't imagine anyone that arrogant actually grovelling, but in my fantasy she did a pretty good job of it.

"Are you coming, *chérie*?" Geordie called. I had been so wrapped up in thoughts of revenge that I hadn't noticed they had all left.

Running to catch up, I automatically checked that my cross was in its usual position nestled in my butt crack. It was fairly securely wedged in there and I hardly even knew it was there anymore. You could get used to almost anything over time.

Our small convoy of cars took off from Strovovsky's place. I assumed the man himself was dead because no one had introduced us. The few guards who had survived had fled upon our arrival.

We travelled along rough country roads with almost reckless speed. We'd left any major cities behind us long ago. The Comtesse must like her privacy when she left the Court. It made sense for undead nocturnal creatures to shun humans. Except when they needed food. I wouldn't be surprised if the praying mantis had a stable of 'volunteer' human cattle just like Vincent had. If so, I hoped they were housed in better conditions than in a cold dungeon cell.

The Comtesse's estate was a two hour drive away. We didn't see any cars ahead of us during the journey, but I could almost feel the imposter's presence. I really wouldn't mind it if she took down the Comtesse, but I felt a duty to at least try to stop her. It was *my* job to decimate vampirekind, not hers. *Yeah, if anyone gets to whack the living dead, it's going to be me,* I thought dryly.

Keeping his foot to the floor, Luc drove with grim determination. I drank in his profile, his straight nose, his pasty white skin, his inventive lips and was stricken with a sudden bout of grief. I'd never been in love as a human and didn't even know what the feeling was like. I felt *something* for Luc, but had no name for it. Infatuation would probably be the closest. He was handsome, foreign, enigmatic and for a brief time, he had been mine. But I sensed that was all about to change. I glanced away so he couldn't read my expression when he turned his head.

"We will be there soon," he said and I wasn't comforted by that knowledge. My destiny was rushing at me too fast. All I wanted to do was savour my existence for just a little while longer.

Luc pulled into a long driveway and I saw a dazzling white castle in the distance. Lights blazed from the lower levels. The upper levels, where the bedrooms were, would be shuttered. As we drew closer, we detected no signs of panic. A pair of guards stopped us halfway down the driveway. "Lord Lucentio," one said in amazement as he bent to look into the car. "May I ask why you have appeared unannounced?" He seemed nervous about questioning vampire royalty, but he had a job to do and was determined to do it right. The Comtesse would probably have his skin removed if he failed in his duties.

"Some dumb cow who thinks she is Mortis is on her way to cut you all to pieces," I replied pleasantly.

"We are here to try to stop her," Luc said with a frown in my direction at my choice of wording. *Whoops, I'm being uncouth again.*

Exchanging looks, the guards abandoned their posts and ran toward the castle. One was screaming like a superstitious peasant of old; "She has come! She has come to kill us all!"

The castle was beautiful, yet imposing and I had only a few moments to study it as we sped past the sprinting vampire guards. Four towers rose toward the cloudy night sky. A thin moon was revealed for moments at a time, then hidden again by thick clouds. The grounds were extensive and perfectly groomed. That was all the time I had for gawping before we lurched to a halt.

Chapter Thirty-Four

This time, I was right beside Luc as he dashed toward the castle with his sword in hand. Confused guards leapt out of our way as we entered. Dressed in ballroom finery, courtiers stared at us in momentary shock, then tittered behind their hands as we headed toward the back of the castle.

I saw the décor in flashes; opulent furniture, priceless rugs, even more priceless paintings. I was disturbed at the sight of white marble everywhere. It tickled my memory, but I couldn't remember what it was. Then we were standing on a red carpet and were heading for a throne.

I remembered where I'd seen this room before as my dream came back to me. I had an overwhelming feeling of déjà vu. It was the same white marble, red drapes, blood red carpet and gold throne as my dream from a couple of days ago. Unlike in my dream, the pretend Mortis wasn't standing defiantly before the delicate chair.

Clothed in another golden gown that showed off her tiny waist and voluptuous hips, the Comtesse sat on the throne. She wore a look of mild contempt for those around her that she probably wasn't even aware of. The other Councillors stood behind her. At the Court, they might be equals, but on her turf, she ruled. Making them stand had to be her not so subtle way of putting them in their places.

"What is the meaning of this, Lucentio?" she demanded when Luc strode forward. He dropped to a knee, but this time I just stood there. I admit the look I gave the Comtesse could be best described as insolent. This time I wasn't going to grovel on my face for her and I definitely wasn't going to take my clothes off. Her eyes narrowed at my lack of respect, but Luc drew her attention to him before she could order my death.

"Comtesse, the person who believes she is Mortis will be attacking your estate at any moment." I had to hand it to Luc, he didn't waste any time in getting to the point.

Flabbergasted, the Comtesse waved the information away with an arrogant toss of her small, white hand. "Nonsense! Who told you this drivel?" Beneath her annoyance were the first threads of fear. "We left the peasant behind in France. There is no reason to believe she is even in the country, let alone that she is about to attack my estate."

"She has recently attacked Gregor's, Isabella's and Strovovsky's estates," Luc informed her coolly. His gaze roamed the room, probing the faces and forms of the guests. Anyone dressed in black received his hard scrutiny before he moved on.

Startled murmurs spread through the room. Several vamps began making their discreet escapes. They were the smart ones. The rest of the Court seemed to think this was all just an entertaining diversion from their eternal boredom. The other Councillors huddled into a circle, whispering and throwing worried looks at the Comtesse.

Gregor entered the room and backed up Luc's claims. "I'm afraid Lord Lucentio is correct, my Lady." He gave the Comtesse a courtly bow, but he, too, searched the room warily. "Isabella and Strovovsky have been slain, as have their guards and servants."

"Guards!" the Comtesse screeched in a very unladylike manner. She had suddenly become a believer that she might be in danger after all. "Search the castle for the intruder. I want her found and executed immediately."

I rolled my eyes at the theatrics as Luc stood. He held his sword at the ready, but I didn't think he would need it. Instinct told me that the next fight would belong solely to me. Whether I was ready for it or not, it was my turn to shine. Or to be utterly humiliated first before hopefully then shining.

An itch started up between my shoulder blades. Someone was staring at me and I knew who it had to be. Craning my head back and pivoting slowly, I spied the imposter crouched in a window high above us. *What did she do, scale the building and somehow pry open the shutters?* Apparently, that was exactly what she'd done.

Her eyes were locked on me as if sensing I was the biggest threat in the room. Someone else spotted her, then pointed and let out a shrill scream. In ye olde times, half the women in the room would have swooned upon seeing the leather clad killing machine that was about to swoop down on us. Since they could no longer retreat into unconsciousness, many of the female vamps grabbed their male counterparts and used them as shields instead. I had no one to shield me even if I had been craven enough to use anyone in that fashion.

A quick thinking guard sent a crossbow bolt whistling toward the window. With grace that I was sure would make me look like a blundering hippopotamus, the imposter dove headfirst toward the ground. Falling thirty feet, she flipped in mid-air and landed on her feet like a cat. Court members cringed away from her and huddled closer together. The diversion was losing its appeal even if it did cut through the boredom.

Sauntering over to me, the pretend Mortis held her spear casually in her right hand. "You were the one who threw the holy water at me," she said in her clear, yet accented English.

"That's right," I agreed. Luc waved back the guards who rushed forward to surround us. They might be able to keep her busy for a few minutes, but why bother? I had to face her sooner or later and I might as well get the confrontation over with.

"Yet, you were not harmed," she said with a small frown, completely ignoring everyone else in the room. Her new suit was identical to the last. A mask covered most of her face, but I detected slowly healing burn marks on her forehead. Some of the holy water had splashed on her skin, but it hadn't been enough to kill her. Like the sunlight that had burned my finger to a crisp, it must take time to heal wounds made by holy water.

"Nope," I agreed.

"There is something…strange about you," the imposter said thoughtfully. She walked in a wide circle around me and I turned to keep her in view. I wasn't about to turn my back on her.

As I turned I saw Luc, Igor, Gregor and Geordie standing about fifteen feet away. Igor and Geordie looked confused about why I was the one standing ready to fight when I had no actual fighting skills. Luc and Gregor stood ready to take up the battle if I failed. They wore identical expressions of concern. The Comtesse still sat on her throne, but her fellow Councillors had drawn back against the walls. Their eyes darted, searching for an escape. Hemmed in by the courtiers, they would have to claw their way to freedom if they tried to leave.

The truth had to come out sooner or later and I was frankly sick of the wait. In the simplest, quickest way I could, I showed the entire room exactly who I was by holding my hands up, palms out. Noises of astonishment ran through the room and even the imposter's step faltered at the sight of the twin crosses. "Anyone could fake the holy marks," she spat. Sudden hate for me shone in her black eyes. In them I read the knowledge that, deep down, she knew she was nothing, but a sham. She was being used by the Japanese to put an end to the Court. I doubted her emperor even cared what happened to her after she had attained her goal.

"Like you did?" I asked pleasantly. "I know all about how the Japanese marked you before turning you. They might have trained you to be an assassin, but I am the true Mortis. You," I pointed out with a rare streak of cruelty that was unlike me, "are just a fake."

"We'll see about that," she huffed. Hefting her spear, she sent it whistling through the air in the blink of an eye. I had time to sidestep it, but why bother? It stabbed through my heart and the roomful of vampires went still. I bore the holy marks, but so did the imposter. Proving I was the one and only Mortis, I pulled the spear out and threw it to Luc. He caught it and passed it to Gregor.

"You'll have to try harder than that," I mocked her.

With a screech of rage, she launched herself at me. Vampires couldn't actually fly, but she did a good imitation of it. This time, I did move and wasn't where she expected me to be when she landed. Whirling, she pulled a knife from her belt and slashed me across the face with it. I retaliated by bitch slapping her. She shrieked and steam rose from her mask. Yanking it away, she dropped it to the ground. It lay on the immaculate white marble, still smoking from the contact with my holy mark.

"If you really are Mortis, you don't need knives," I taunted her. Her eyes went to my exposed palms and she touched her cheek in disbelief. A red, blistered mark in the shape of my cross marred her otherwise pretty face.

I read confusion, desolation and resolve in her expression before she renewed her attack. Her knife sliced me across my face, neck and arms before lodging in my chest. Just like I'd expected and dreaded, she was kicking my arse. As promised, Luc and Gregor didn't laugh. In the few glances I had of them, they were tight lipped and anxious. Gregor's advice came back to me, not much could hurt me now. Every cut I endured healed almost instantly. The imposter could stab me with a thousand knives until I looked like a vampire version of a pincushion and I would still be standing.

"What are you?" the imposter cried as she pulled another knife from her belt and slashed at me again.

"I'm what you're pretending to be, but the real thing," I replied and pulled the cross from its hiding spot down the back of my pants. Cries of dismay rang out through the throne room and most of the vampires cringed away. The cross went spinning out of my hand when the imposter did a fancy spinning kick. A Court member screamed and leaped to safety as the cross skittered across the floor in his direction.

Pummelled by feet and fists and being repeatedly sliced by her knife, I was beaten backwards until my back hit the wall. The second knife came to rest beside the first one, directly in my heart. I decided I'd had enough of the arse whooping and blocked her next punch. The imposter's eyes were wild and insane. I had a brief moment to wonder if she'd lost her mind before or after she'd been chosen for this fate. Then it was time for my epic comeback.

Grabbing the imposter's forearm, I held her tightly even as she stabbed me in the shoulder with yet another knife. Smoke began to rise from her leather clad arm. I grabbed her other arm before she could reach for a fourth knife. Smoke instantly started billowing from it as well. Our gazes locked in a silent staring match, neither of us would give an inch. The imposter's eyes widened when the leather burned away. She began to shriek when my holy marks touched her flesh.

In seconds, the leather was gone and her flesh had melted through to the bone. I had to fight back the urge to dry heave at the gooey feel of her flesh sliding through my fingers. Black gore spurted sluggishly from her vastly shortened arms. Staring at the useless stumps, she turned in a dazed circle. Cries of horror flew around the room when the Court saw what I had done to her. Staggering back to me, the imposter implored me for mercy with her eyes. "Finish it," she whispered.

The hand of destiny was on me now and even if it hadn't been, I still would have ended her life. I felt pity for her, but it was more than that. She had killed dozens, if not hundreds of our kind and she had to be put down. No one was going to do my job, but me.

Placing my hands on either side of her head, I winced a second before her skull disintegrated beneath my hands. "By the power invested in me as Mortis," I said quietly, "I pronounce you dead." Something metallic fell out of her hair and I clenched my right hand around it instinctively.

Giddy with relief that I had survived the ordeal, my brief moment of happiness was quickly replaced by unease. Every vampire in the room was staring at me as if I was a diseased dog. *Um, that's probably because you're fated to kill most of them,* I reminded myself. Of course they weren't going to celebrate my victory by cheering and carrying me around on their shoulders.

"What is this creature you have brought into my home, Lucentio?" the Comtesse whispered. Her gaze shifted from me to Luc. She pointed at him with one shaky finger. "Traitor! Seize him!" The guards hesitated, shifting their dismayed glances from me to Luc. At a glare from their ruler, they rushed forward.

"He has saved you!" Gregor shouted as Luc was surrounded by sword wielding guards. "If he hadn't found Natalie and brought her here, you would all be dead!"

Holding up a hand, the Comtesse put a halt to Luc's imminent death. "There is only one way you can prove to me that you are not a traitor and that you are not collaborating with this creature to end our existence." I knew what she was going to say even before the words came out of her mouth. "Cut off her head." A smile, small and vicious, flickered across her face and was gone.

The guards released Luc. He seemed even more dazed than I'd felt during the fight with my imposter. He shook his head in denial even as he dragged his steps towards me. The sword made metallic ringing noises each time the tip touched the marbled floor. Fighting against the compulsion, he closed the distance between us until he was standing only a yard away. Just like in my dream, the tip of his sword rested on the floor. His eyes implored me to run. I wanted to, but my feet were welded to the ground.

"I gave you an order, Lucentio!" the Comtesse thundered. Luc flinched and lifted his sword.

I'd known since I'd first read the prophet's journal that this was how I would die, but I hadn't expected it to be so soon. I hadn't had time to prepare for the idea that my short life as a vampire was about to end. *But I still have work to do,* I thought in dismay. How could the prophecy have been so wrong? I'd barely even started thinning down the vampire population. There were still so many of them left to kill.

"I am sorry, Natalie," Luc said in a voice low enough that only I could hear him. "But no one can disobey an order that their maker has given them." With that, my doom was sealed. He swung the sword up, then it flashed in a deadly arc and sliced through my neck.

Just like in my dream, my head flew through the air. It bounced a few times, rolled and came to rest at an angle where I could see my body. In slow motion, my headless corpse fell to its knees and stayed slumped over. At an order from the Comtesse, her guards ran forward and began hacking at my fallen body.

I felt every painful blow even though I should have been senseless by now. Luc was on his knees with his hands over his face so he wouldn't have to witness my final demise. I wished I didn't have to witness it either, but I was powerless to close my eyes against the massacre. My body was hewn into multiple pieces, then kicked into an unruly heap by the guards.

As my sight finally began to fade, I saw something that would have made perfect sense if I'd been alive enough to think about it. The Comtesse stood beside my dismembered body, nudging my unmoving torso with a golden shoe. Her shadow suddenly hunkered down, examining my hacked up body parts. As if sensing my scrutiny, the silhouette turned to view my severed head. I couldn't see its expression, but I knew it was smirking at me.

"Did you really think you were any match for us?" it whispered in my mind. "You have failed, Mortis and now we are free to return."

It all became clear then. I belatedly realized exactly what was going on with the shadows. I knew their goal and how close they were to success. With my death, no one would be able to stop them. Just as Alexander's book had prophesized, our ancient and long dead father's plan was coming to fruition.

I'd seen a sentient shadow possess its owner, but I knew that was just the beginning. When the demi-god's plan was fully realized, vampires would no longer be in control of themselves. Their shadows would be in charge and something told me their ultimate goal would be to take over the world.

Struggling futilely against my destiny, I was helpless to deny death as it beckoned me home into darkness.

27428580R00183

Printed in Great Britain
by Amazon